Laughton Osborn

The Last Mandeville

The heart's sacrifice, The monk, Matilda of Denmark - tragedies, being in

completion of the second volume of the dramatic series

Laughton Osborn

The Last Mandeville
*The heart's sacrifice, The monk, Matilda of Denmark - tragedies, being in completion of the
second volume of the dramatic series*

ISBN/EAN: 9783337343620

Printed in Europe, USA, Canada, Australia, Japan

Cover: Foto ©Andreas Hilbeck / pixelio.de

More available books at **www.hansebooks.com**

THE LAST MANDEVILLE

THE HEART'S SACRIFICE — THE MONK

MATILDA OF DENMARK

TRAGEDIES

BEING IN COMPLETION OF THE SECOND VOLUME OF THE
DRAMATIC SERIES

BY

LAUGHTON OSBORN

NEW YORK
THE AMERICAN NEWS COMPANY
117, 119, 121 NASSAU STREET
MDCCCLXX

THE LAST MANDEVILLE[1]

MDCCCXLVII

CHARACTERS, ETC.

JULIAN MANDEVILLE.

SIR RICHARD MANDEVILLE, Baronet, *his Uncle.*

ARTHUR, Viscount CAPEL, *Son of the Earl of Essex.*

HUBERT CARL, *Servant of Julian.*

FRANCES MANDEVILLE, *Julian's sister.*

ELINOR MORTON, *a girl in humble life.*

EUPHROSINE DE BEAUFFREMONT.

The Countess BEAUFFREMONT DE SENNECY, *Euphrosine's Mother.*

SERVANTS *of Sir Richard Mandeville.*

Madame de Beauffremont's SERVANT.

Swiss GUARD, &c.

———

SCENE. *Chiefly in London, and at Julian's villa in its vicinity. In Act II. in the Pays (Canton) de Vaud, in Switzerland.*

TIME OF ACTION. *With the license of the romantic drama, it includes a period of over a twelvemonth.*

EPOCH. *The reign of Charles II.*

THE LAST MANDEVILLE

ACT THE FIRST

SCENE I. *A room in the house of Julian's mother.*

JULIAN. FRANCES.

Jul. And now, sweet sister, that we be alone,
    Say on.
      Fran. But — I —— O, Julian, think! our mother ——
Jul. Timid, remember.
            Fran. But from love alone.
Jul. Yet thou too lov'st me?
              Fran. Brother!
                    Jul. And thy heart
  Is gentle like thy mother's, if more warm.
 [2] Then, when thou camest in, with cheeks all flush'd,
  And eyes that shone like flame, and trembling lips,
  Was it from fear, that cheek's augmented bloom,
  And thine eyes' brightness? And those innocent lips,

  Did the brief ague of a womanly dread
  Alone thus make them quiver ? —

      Fran. But, my brother, ——

Jul. Or was it not the glow of quicken'd blood,
  The fire of anger, the precipitate zeal
  That trembled in its haste to utter all,
  And crowded word on word, so fast, they fell
  Confus'd and broken, was 't not these, the signs
  Of a fond, generous, upright, candid spirit,
  Rous'd to unwonted action by the wrongs
  Of a lov'd brother, and an uncle's guile ;
  Frances, this, was it not, I saw ?

      Fran. Too well.
  But I am young, and took too little heed.
  And then — I fear — I do not ——

      Jul. Love Sir Richard ?

  Most wondrous fault ! a being so pure as thou ——
  Proceed ; the cause of thy emotion, all ;
  Quick, tell it, now our mother is away.
  This precious uncle ? —

     Fran. Is our father's brother.
  This did our mother, when she broke the tale,
  Bid us both ponder.

     Jul. And I have, too long.
  What power lurks in the name of Uncle then,
  Or kindred blood, that we, who are not debt-bound,
  Should brook oppression from the one, or fear
  To take in vain the other ? If Sir Richard
  Deceives me, let me know 't, that I may tell him.

[*]Say on, my sister. [*She hesitates.*

     Fy! thou silly child!
Dost judge so meanly of thy brother's brain,
To deem a slanderer's tooth could bite him mad?

Fran. But thou art hasty; and I fear —— O Julian,
If thou shouldst with our uncle come to strife! —

Jul. Why think'st thou that? Am I an idiot then
To war with every man who holds me vile,
Or speaks but slightingly of my desert?
I? If Sir Richard hath his kin in scorn,
Perhaps his kin doth quite as much by him;
And thus we are quits.

    Fran. But thou wilt tell him.

       Jul. Tell?

'Faith! and I will. If I do not! ——

     Fran. Oh Heaven!
For our dead father's sake! our living mother's!

Jul. Come, come, fair sister; let us hear this tale.

Fran. No, not for worlds! I do adjure thee ——

      Jul. Nay,
Showing these scruples, thou becloud'st my brain
With dark surmise. Yet, what hast thou to tell,
If not some trifle? Is 't not so, my sister?

   [*laying his hand on her head, and affecting to smile.*

Fran. It is but this, no more. Thou hast had, thou know'st,

       [*timidly.*

Some credit as a bard.

   Jul. Against my will;
Rank'd with the million whom half-sneering friends

And tender Saccharissas make divine,
The petty fires that sparkle in all skies;
While I would keep my orb unseen, unfelt,
Cloud-hid till at its zenith, then at once
Blaze on the world, enlightening and ador'd.

Fran. As, sure, thou wilt.   Might I but live to see
That brilliant hour, to know thy glorious beams
Shine on mankind as still they have shone on me,
I should die happy.

         Jul. Wouldst thou turn my brain?
Thou fond idolater! [*kissing her.*] —   What of the bard?

Fran. As thou hast heard, I have been at Essex' House,
And I had told thee, when our gentle mother,
Through tenderness for thee, broke off the tale,
I found there Uncle.⁴   "O," said Lady Ellen,
"Thou comest in time.   Here be some verses, given
By good Sir Richard to a friend of ours,
Written at her suggestion.   I pronounce,
They read like Julian's, and Sir Richard here
Would pass them for his own." —   "With pardon, no,"
Our uncle interpos'd. —   "Would have me then
Infer so much; for whose the parent brain
He will not tell.   Come, Frances, lend thine eyes
And more accustom'd sense, and sit our judge."

Jul. How were they nam'd?

         Fran. "A Vision of Queen Mab."

Jul. The folly that, a se'nnight since, I wrote
At his great instance!   Well?

         Fran. I said they read

A little like thy style, albeit the hand
Was certainly not thine. "There!" Ellen cried,
"The verdict hear, Sir Richard Mandeville!
The work is Julian's, but the transcript thine.
Besides, my good Sir Richard, know we not
Thou never wast warm'd by spark of poet's fire,
While thy hot nephew glows with it alone?"
"Tut!" quoth our uncle, seeming not to like
This raillery, "Julian yet is but a boy,
Scarce knows to tell the stamp and ring of verse,
Let alone coin it. Still, he showeth some parts,
And, when he shall have conn'd a little more,
And seen much more the world, will do right well.
But now, what sounds to you the throstle's song
Spirts from the chirp-pipe of a fledgeling sparrow,
And every thatch is dissonant with like music."

Jul. By Heaven! [*between his teeth.*

　　　　Fran. Soon after this he left. And Ellen,
Turning to me with that sarcastic look
She wears at times —— But, Julian, that strange smile!
　T were better not continue.

　　　　　　　Jul. Pray, go on.
A poet's vanity makes indeed his life:
Who stabs at that, strikes at his heart: and more, —
In the one other passion that divides
My spirit, O my sister! I have been
Of late so deeply wounded! —— But of this
Thou knowest nothing. Mind me not. Go on, —
I pray thee, Frances: I am not a child.

Fran. No, and thou art too gallant-soul'd and good
    To be so fraud-deluded, as thou hast been,
    Most frontlessly, my brother !

                         Jul. Ay ?   Go on.

Fran. "How odd," quoth Lady Ellen, "Sir Richard never
    Will listen aught in Julian's praise ! "   " 'T is like
    He was not in the mood to-day," I said :
    " He has I know for him much good will."   " Display'd
    After a quite new fashion," she rejoin'd ;
    " For, did I hold his portraiture well-drawn,
    When my own senses mark its lame design,
    Your brother must seem a schoolboy, overgrown,
    And self-conceited."

Enter SIR RICHARD MANDEVILLE.
He glances alternately from JULIAN *to his sister, and*
at last fixes his eyes upon the former, who looks
full at him, while FRANCES *holds her*
head down in confusion.

        Sir R. What has happen'd now ?
Jul. You had better dip for knowledge in its source,
    With Lady Ellen Capel.   Thence I draw
    The draught I have swallow'd.

                Sir R. Julian, thou art pert.
What 's to do, Frances ?   Thou, methinks, hast lost
Thy natural quiet ; and Julian has shot up
Six inches since I saw him.

             Fran. Uncle —   Julian —

Oh Heaven! dear Julian! —

         Jul. I will make reply.

Frances, release my arm: this arrogant man
Shall have from me his answer, as is fit.
This is to do, Sir Richard Mandeville: —
Why wear you here among us a saint's mask,
Warping my mother's over-pliant heart
By lip-praise of her son, that you may flout,
In your own visage, and gibe at him abroad?

Fran. Julian! my brother! Oh, what have I done!
Think of our mother. —

         Sir R. Stop not his brave breath.

I prithee, Fanny, let thy brother rant
Till the fit spend itself. I have not thriv'd
For eighteen thousand suns, to shake to pieces
At a mere cockerel's crowing, or be ruffled
By the swollen insolence of a braggart boy.

Jul. By Christ's death! Sister, pardon me. For you,
Sir Richard, have a care! the boy may prove
More than your match, for all your boasted years.

               [*Exit.*

Sir R. Indeed! [*smiling.*] — But lo, my sister!

    Fran. [*running to the side of the scene, as to meet her.*

             Oh, my mother!

    Scene closes.

12*

Scene II.

Julian's Study, or Library.

Enter JULIAN.
*He walks to and fro for some minutes in silence,
but in apparent agitation.*

Jul. Fool'd ! fool'd — past thought ! my open temper made
The dupe of —— But I did not trust him all !
How many covert sneers, how many taunts,
Veil'd in the semblance of a lying praise,
Rise naked now before me ! Yet, 't was wrong,
Wrong to give way to passion, if alone
For thy sake, Mother, — wrong, and most unwise.
But who that sudden had awoke, and seen
The death-fang'd adder coil'd beside his couch,
Would turn to sleep again ? Who durst ? Who could ?
I 'll not forgive him. — Yes, yes, well I know
My strong self-love alone it is that 's stung,
Hurt that I stand so low-plac'd in his eyes
Whose false thought-weighing I affect to scorn.
I have burrow'd in darkness, and my vision smarts
Turn'd to the daylight. Yet —— Why it is well !
I would not be at peace with one I hate,

Nor ever valued. I will not forgive him !

He sits down. A gentle tap is heard at the
room-door.

Is 't Frances ? Has she come to mourn to me
Her fond imprudence ? with her seraphs-voice,
To lay the billows of my storm-toss'd pride ?
And I too will console the gentle-spirit
I have griev'd, and, as I kiss away the tears
That rain for me, and on my heart make still
The throbbing of her bosom, lull to sleep
My vehement nature, and in a sister's love
Find the relief and reason moral lore
Knows not.

> *Aloud, but gently.*] Come in, if it is thou, my sister.

The door opens directly, and
Enter SIR RICHARD.

JULIAN *rises and stands upright.*

Sir Richard Mandeville ——
> *Sir R.* Soft, softly, Julian.
Not to renew a senseless strife I am come,
But to implore it be forgotten. Of thee
I ask no exculpation. For myself,
If I have done thee wrong, there, — I am sorry.
> *[offering his hand.*

Jul. [*drawing back.*]
I do not want your sorrow. Go back, and say,
To my mother who sent you hither, that for her care

I am duly grateful, but now am old enough
To act alone and choose myself my friends.

Sir R. This I had not believ'd from other lips,
Nor could have look'd for, Julian, in a heart
So generous as thine.

            Jul. Am I inept,
That you affect this style? Is 't not enough,
My youth to have deceiv'd and forward trust,
By feigning interest in my weal and feeding
My pride by praises that your heart disvouch'd?
Would you my senses mock, as nurses coax
Some peevish child? I would be left alone.

Sir R. Fy, fy! I see where thou art gall'd, but know
The hurt is nothing deeper than the skin.
What! shall thy father's son deny his brother
Impartial hearing? Come, come, set thee down,
And let us reason. [*Sits down and draws Jul. gently to a
    seat beside him.*] I have heard the tale
Brought by thy sister from Lord Essex'. Now,
The Lady Ellen, thou knowest, is a flippant ——

Jul. I know it not, sir. Lady Ellen Capel
Is a most excellent, right-thinking girl.

Sir R. Well, as thou wilt. But never story lost
By being told. What motive could I have
To play thee false? Ask of thyself; thou 'lt own
Thou wrong'st me. What advantage could I draw
By feigning interest, as thou sayst? And sure
Thou 'lt not pretend the Devil himself would feign
But for some purpose?

Jul. Ay, sir; and I do:
And many men are devils; and for no end
But being so.

  Sir R. Well, well; thou yet are young.
But say, is not thy father's and my blood
Sufficient cause of interest in thy weal?
Do be a man, and leave these phantasies,
Childish and mischief-fraught, to weaker minds.

Jul. Why there it is, sir! *Childish — weaker — man!*
Reminded well. I ask again, why here
Build you at home, to tumble down abroad?
Speak to the point, sir, — if you really would
Explain your doubleness.

  Sir R. Speak to the point!
How can I, when thy talk is but a riddle?

Jul. So solve it, then. Among our friends abroad,
Sir Richard Mandeville, you laugh to scorn
My *boyish* talents, whensoever made
The theme of idle converse, and take pains
To undervalue me where favor'd most.
I am asham'd, sir, this to say myself;
But you would force me to 't. And now, explain
Your conduct, if you can. [*Rising.*] Though I not ask it,
And rather would you 'd leave it as it stands.

Sir R. [*Rising, and after a brief pause in which he looks atten-
   tively at Jul.*
My words thou hast haply heard, but not their tone.
I say, as I said then, in the same mode
And with the selfsame feelings, kindling meaning

To be of use : thy talents, nephew mine,
Are more than common.   Thou wouldst make them steps
To thy aspiring.   It is well.   Not well,
That, in thy over-haste to climb, thou plantest
Thy ladder in the sand, and in thy tasks
Beginn'st where thou shouldst end.   Thou art too vain —
Forgive me — of thy genius, whose great strength
Thou feel'st, unconscious that its efforts rude
And ill-directed are the uncouth pranks
Of a young giant, liker far to harm,
Than profit, others or thyself.   Why, think,
Thou art not yet three-and-twenty !   Being so young,
Nor mixing in the world, what canst thou know
Of men ?   When yesterday thou didst return,
A twelvemonth gone, from France, thy wings then tried
For the first time, thou hadst thy primal course,
Thy first year's pupilage, gone barely through,
In the great study of mankind.   Till then,
Thy hours were spent in solitary thought,
Not even the poets handled that should be
Tutors at once and models : such thy pride.
Burst from thy monkish solitude ; one day,
One hour, with men who mingle in the world,
Will stead thee more than weeks of musing lone.
The princes of the line thou hast made thy walk,
Them study as thy masters.   And perhaps,
With perseverance, when thou hast attain'd
To perfect manhood, say some seven years hence,
Thou mayst aspire to lay the corner-stone

Of the great pile thou 'dst raise, and doubtless will
Do very well.

*During this harangue, which, especially towards the
close has been accompanied with sneers more or less covert,
JULIAN has appeared to be smothering a violent emotion.
He now speaks with studied calmness, and in a soft,
smooth voice : —*

  Jul. Sir Richard Mandeville,
Frances, I see, and Lady Ellen, both
Knew scarcely more of you, than you of me.
My father's brother has license ; but such prate,
Thrust on me by another, were held, as it is,
Impertinent and insulting.
  Sir R. [*with indifference.*] And no doubt,
With such occasion, thy fool-hardy humor,
Or wouldst thou christen it valor, Master Julian?
Had prick'd thee to defy him on the spot !
Jul. By Heaven, you have said it ! We will make at once
The occasion actual you have well conceiv'd.

  *Takes his sword from a couch, where it lies with his
  cloak and hat, and flings aside the sheath.*

Uncle and nephew now no longer, one
Alone of us shall leave this spot alive.
Draw ! draw, I tell you : ties are at an end :
We now stand, man to man.
     Sir R. Not quite, unless
Thou stand'st as madman ; which I am apt to think.

Jul. Liar and villain ! Draw, or like a dog
I 'll slay you.

      Sir R. Boy and fool ! thou dar'st not, lest
Thou hang as one. [*Sir R. as he speaks, strikes down suddenly, with his stick, the blade of Jul. and disarms him.*

Enter

FRANCES, *hurriedly.*

       Fran. For mercy ! stop ! oh stop ! —
No wound ? Nor thou ? Thank God ! — What — what
is this ?

Sir R. [*putting on his hat.*

      Thy brother, Frances, has been drinking deep
At Helicon. The sacred fount is strong,
More than I thought. [*Exit — Jul. springing at him. The
              door closes between them.*

      Fran. [*falling on Julian's neck.*

        O Julian ! oh my brother !
What hast thou done ?

      Jul. Hush ! sister — nothing.
And Mother — where is she ?

      Fran. In her own room.
She heard thee not.

      Jul. How happy ! Leave me now :
I have need of thought.

      Fran. But ——

      Jul. Fear me not : 't is past.

Fran. You did not fight ?

      Jul. No, no, thank Heaven ! but — I —

His lips — his eye — his cold insulting speech —
I could not brook it: I — I — would have fought.
There, [*kissing her on the eyelids.*

   dry those eyes; there, go. I 'll walk awhile;
The open air will help me to myself.

Fran. For God's sake! brother! No, no, no, thou canst,
Thou canst, not mean ——

     Jul. Mean what?

        Fran. O do not go!
Think, Julian, 't is thy uncle: O, for pity! —

Jul. Nay, on my word, which yet I never broke,
I have no thought, no wish to meet him. I will —
Avoid him. Let that satisfy thee: there.

Fran. But such a night! Thou wilt not go.

        Jul. Why not?

Fran. It is the dreariest gloom of black December.
The fog is dense, and through the unwholesome air
A cold fine rain is drizzling, and the walks
Are coated, in the uncomfortable streets,
With a thin, slimy mud.

      Jul. 'T will suit me well:
Darkness and rain and I are consorts meet.

Fran. Alas! — Thou 'lt come back to thy sister soon?

Jul. To her unmatchable love, her virtues, ay.

        [*Exit Fran.*
Pure being! who hast thy mother's tender soul,
Without its weakness. Would, would I had lov'd but
 thee! —
O Elinor! — That woman should have writ

Her faith with water ! Twelve, but twelve brief months !
And so complete a change ! Her heart alone,
Why that were monstrous ! but, to give up all !
All ! all ! and in twelve —— Death and Hell ! the work
Is searce the half that old. Six months ! And I —
For three whole years —— But I — derision ! I —
I lov'd her purely, lov'd her with my soul :
I would not wrong her, and — O fool ! for this,
Left home, and country, tore my heart away,
That some less scrupulous lover ——° Madness ! Down,
Thou swelling heart ! why should —— But no ! rage on :
I fled the house, and left the door ajar,
That thieves might in and strip the unguarded wealth ;
I set a trap and left it, that, when sprung,
They who had neither plann'd, nor watch'd, might stop
And laughing snatch its spoil ; abhorr'd delict !
I brought the tree to bearing, nay, shook down
Its mellow'd fruit, and let it strew the ground,
For chance to gather. Cursed be the fears
Of heart-pale righteousness, the stumbling virtue
That turn'd me from the field of my long tilth,
That one who had not toil'd —— No, Julian, no !
Parley not thus with conscience ; let thy heart
Swell with disdain or sorrow, not the throbs
Of frustrate passion ; be not so deprav'd
To thirst for the polluted stream, whose draught,
When bubbling free to thy parch'd lips, and tempting
With sparkling freshness, thou didst timely shrink,
Shrink honestly, from tasting. Oh ! polluted ? —

Elinor! Elinor!   And it was I,
I, with my friendship, that was love scarce mask'd,
And treacherous caresses, who arous'd
The sleeping passion in thy innocent breast,
And in thy unus'd veins the venom pour'd
Whose prurience no medicine, alas!
Of reason will allay; I, that broke down
The rampire of thy chastity, and laid
The city open to the spoiler; I!
What! do I weep? 'T is well. But, wo is me!
Oh Elinor! the tears Remorse distils
Fall like the rain upon the rivel'd flowers,
When a long drought has wither'd leaf and stem
And burn'd into the roots that gave them life!

He buckles on his sword, wraps himself slowly in his
mantle, and takes his hat.

At this — this hour, — how often! —— I 'll not think
    on 't.
What 's Elinor to me? I now to Elinor? '
                                    [*Exit.*

Scene III.

A retired street in the better part of London.
A dark and misty night.

Enter Julian, *muffled in his cloak and walking slowly.*

Enter, directly after him, Elinor.
She grasps his mantle timidly.

Elin. [*softly and tremblingly.*
Julian!

    Jul. [*drawing his mantle closer round his face.*
    Ah!

        Elin. [*imploringly and grasping his cloak more*
      boldly.] Julian! Wilt thou leave me then
To [*voice choked with sobs.*] — die in the streets?

        Jul. [*shuddering, and to himself.*

                Can it be Elinor,
That touches me, and speaks such words as these?
aloud.] Elinor!

      Elin. Yes: dost — do you not then know me,
Jul — Master Mandeville, I mean. Has then
A twelvemonth so much chang'd you?

             Jul. No, — not me;
I am the same; but, oh God! Elinor!

How has it changed thee !

> [*She smites her hands together and hides her face.*
>
> Unhappy girl !

How is it we meet here ?   Why art thou out
Alone, and at this hour, on such a night ?
What, what have *I* to do with thee ?   What *now ?*

Elin. Have I no claim to your compassion then ?
None ?   No — no I I have none.   Good night, sir ; God
Forgive you ; I can die like other creatures
Wretched like me ; I — I can live like them.

Jul. Stay, Elinor I   What means this ?   Speak to me I

Elin. Mean ?   Julian I   Oh I   I am a poor, unhappy ——
Why didst thou leave me ?   Why refuse my prayer
To follow thee ? [*Bursting into tears.   She clings to him,
> and hides her face in the folds of his
> mantle.*

> *Jul.* Poor girl I [*He puts his arm, covered as it
> is with the cloak, about her, and draws
> her like a child to his bosom.*

> Speak, Elinor.

What is 't distresses thee?   Why hast thou come
To seek me such a night, when all the day
Is open to thee ?

> *Elin.* Let me hide my shame

In — in thy mantle, — and — and I will tell thee. —
My mother died this morning.   The last friend
I had on earth lies cold there [*pointing behind her, but with-
> out raising her head.*

> — in the house

Where I no more can dwell.　I kill'd her; my —
Dishonor broke her heart.　She has left nothing.
Our little all must go to pay our debts.
To-morrow — oh, oh, oh! — to-morrow, Julian,
Elinor is without a roof to shelter her,
A bed to lie on, or a crust to eat.
Believe, believe her, she would not appeal
To thy compassion, were it less than this:
But — but — I cannot live the life of shame!
Indeed I cannot, Julian! [*sobbing.*

     Jul. Lift thy head.
Thou hast a right to my compassion, Elinor:
And it is thine.　Thou need'st not quit thy home, —
Save for a better.　I will see, to-morrow,
That all thy wants are answer'd.

 ELINOR *raises her head, looks up into his face for a*
  moment, then turns and walks away.

 JULIAN *stands a moment as confounded, then*
follows her quickly.　She breaks into sobbing, and
before he touches her, sits down at the door of a
house, on the opposite side of the scene.

       What means this?
       [*trying to raise her.*
Didst thou not hear me?
    Elin. [*motioning him away.*
    Go — go! Leave me, sir.
I will not tax your charity's forc'd aid.

I 'd starve and rot first; and I will, I will.

Go away, Master Mandeville; go, go!

Leave me alone; I may as well begin
            [*with a frightful levity, and wringing her hands.*

My trade now as a month hence.

                    Jul. Elinor!

Elin. Leave me, I say, directly; go, sir, go!

Unless [*with same unnatural levity.*

            you 'd buy the first fruits of my shame?

You do not wish to purchase, do you? *you?*

                    [*attempts to laugh, but bursts into tears.*

Jul. [*endeavoring to raise her.*

    Elinor! Elinor!

                Elin. [*with angry vehemence.*

                    Leave, leave me, sir!

Jul. Never! —   Dear Elinor!

                Elin. [*looking up.*

                    Indeed! And tears?

Tears, scalding tears, from *your* eyes, on *my* cheeks?

My wicked cheeks!   Oh Julian!

            [*burying her face in his lap, as he leans over her.*

                    Jul. [*raising her.   She hides her*
            head on his breast.] Elinor,

We both are wicked.   But for me, oh God!

The villain, that has wrong'd and left thee thus,

Haply had ne'er assail'd thy virgin heart,

Or left it whole, thy mother were alive,

And thou still happy, for thou wert content.

Alas!   But come; the night is deadly damp,

And the chill rains will pierce thee to the bone.

       [puts her arm through his.

Poor orphan, we will seek thy desolate home,
The home my crime has darken'd of its sunshine,
And vacant left of all things but despair.

         [Exeunt.

SCENE IV.

A naked and poor chamber in Elinor's lodging.
A farthing-rushlight burning in the
empty hearth.

Enter JULIAN *and* ELINOR.

Jul. [looking round him with horror.
Good God !

   Elin. Speak lower : my poor mother lies
In the next room.

     Jul. No chair ? no table ? not
A spark of fire ?

      Elin. Nothing : seiz'd on all, —
Save the straw pallet where I us'd to lie ;
And that — *she* lies on, now : they tore her bed
From under her, — although, upon my knees,
I pray'd them leave it for a single night.

I could not bear, though well I knew that she
Could feel no more, to let her body lie
On the bare floor, — she too, who was — who was —
So good, so —— Oh! oh! oh! oh! oh!

> *Jul.* Hush, Elinor:
Give not this way to sorrow. So. Poor child! —
This is too horrible : and all alone.
I 'll send, straightway, some persons of thy sex,
And all that will be needful for the time.
And there; [*putting his purse on the chimney-piece.*
          thou wilt have want of it. Hush, hush!
Thou wouldst not grieve me further? So. To-morrow,
When thy poor mother —— Do not weep again —
When all is over, — thou shalt lodge elsewhere.

Elin. Thou — thou 'rt too good for me! What shall I say ?

Jul. No, no! Say nothing: 't is thy due from me.
Thou shalt be shelter'd elsewhere, where strange eyes
Alone can scan thee. Thou shalt want for nought.
But — let me plainly speak — not while the mark
Of thy mishap deforms thee wilt thou oft
Behold me : 't were a sorrow to thyself,
And a sore trial unto me. Perhaps —
I cannot say — perhaps dislike might come. —

> ELINOR *bows down her head and crosses her*
> *hands upon her bosom in resignation*
> *and submission.*

> *After a brief pause,* JULIAN *resumes :*

And thou 'lt not tell me who thy wronger was ?
VOL. II.—13

Elin. Tell *thee?* THEE? Never!

       Jul. Well —— It is as well.
Yet thou couldst take this serpent to thy breast?
Methinks, the heart, that was for Julian gone
Sick even to death, recover'd wondrous-well,
To learn a new love in six little months.

Elin. Speak not so bitterly! Indeed, indeed,
I am not light of faith. My heart has never,
Even in my ruin, for one moment swerv'd
From its first, its sole love.

      Jul. And this to me?
To me? [*looking on her fixedly and scornfully.*
   while on thy ——

     Elin. [*with great vehemence.*
   By the corpse
Of my poor murder'd mother! her whose heart
I broke by my dishonor! [*falling on her knees.*
    By the abus'd
And wounded spirit, that even now is kneeling
To Heaven for vengeance on my guilty head! ——
Rising abruptly.] But thou wilt not believe me:
        't is no matter.

  Appearing to weep silently, she hides her face
    against the mantlepiece.

Jul. I will forgive thee, Elinor. [*taking her hand.*] That is much.
Take courage. I will send, as I have said.
We meet, to-morrow. Until then. [*Exit.*
     Elin.] 'T is just.

My God! my God!   I have deserv'd it all;
Much more from him, much more.   Yet comes it hard.
Ah, did he know! ——   Oh horror! that were death:
I then indeed ——   'T is agony to think on 't.

> [*pressing both hands on her heart, and gasping.*

He never will suspect him — him: no, no!
The traitor, hypocrite! —   What wiles, what lies,
To make me his! while Julian — Julian ——   Oh,
How could I be so blind!   Alas, dear Julian!
Why didst thou leave me, when I begg'd and pray'd? ——
Ah, hadst thou yielded! ——   But thy heart was pure,
Was noble, was too loving: thou didst not
Dream the poor Elinor could prove so frail.
Thus didst thou say —   'T will do me good once more
To read his feelings: it will spare, the while,
The agony of thoughts I dread to meet
Alone with thee, O mother! —   'T is still here:

> [*taking two letters from her bosom.*

Poor Elinor has no place to keep it else. —
Reading.] " I have been the fool of fancy and a dream."
So have we both.   But 't is not that. [*refolding the letter.*

> That — that, —

The first, — *that* warn'd me of our danger, bade
The adieu, which ruin'd me.   Why did my words,
The passionate words I wrote him in return,
Not move his nature?   But, he answer'd thus. —

> [*opening the second letter and kissing it.*
> *Endeavoring ineffectually to read it over, weeping.*

I cannot read it now: I have no eyes.

But oh! the words are ever on my brain,
Where he so passionately bade farewell,
Yet spoke of change, of change for both of us,
Which time should make, and he would know to reckon.
Yes, thou didst say so.   Then thou wouldst come back.
A change?   'T is come: but how unlike to that
Thou thought'st to calculate!   And thou art back;
And thou — thou art unchang'd — unchang'd, thank God!
No, no! it is my hopes speak: would he else
Have quit me thus? so lone? so —— O, my mother!

Looking in terror toward the room where
the body is supposed to lie.

Heavens! what was that? The dead — they hear not! No!
Else were the silent grave no place of rest.
There! — *[starting again.*

          — 'T is the people Julian sends.   Dear Julian!
Ah, let my hopes speak still!   He must, he shall,
Shall love me, or I 'm wretched — past all thought!

Knocking at the door.   ELINOR *puts up the*
letter, first kissing it passionately. —   As she
moves to the door, taking the rushlight
with her,

the Drop falls.

ACT THE SECOND

SCENE I. *The foreground represents a footpath on the declivity of a mountain (in the Pays de Vaud, in Switzerland.) On the far side of the path, a rough rail supported by rough posts — both appearing to be of the limbs of trees with the bark still on. The Lake of Geneva seen behind. To the back of that, the menacing mountain of Meillerie. On the Right, the Dent du Midi, crested with snow ; on the Left, the Jorat and the Jura ; the lake spreading off in the distance, between its mountain-banks, which soften, as they recede.*

JULIAN

is seen, leaning over the rail. After a time, he comes slowly down.

Jul. Beautiful Nature ! — *Nature,* only thou ;
Man is but art, — sophistication vile. —
Here, goddess, is thy most magnificent seat :
Thy throne is on the never-lessen'd mountains ;
Thy voice resounds in thunder 'mid their caves :
The sempiternal snows thy coronet ;
The purple forests, thy imperial robe ;
The broken cataracts, the ceaseless base
That, with thy multitudinous other sounds,

Of wood, and flood, and, in their season, birds,
Makes up the music that attends thy state.
Though awful, yet thou smilest; and the tints
That deck at times thy coronal; the vine,
Whose tendrils, round thy throne's unshakable base,
And clustering fruit present a contrast sweet,
Fragility with firmness, grace with power;
The mirroring water that reflects thy charms,
Nor less thy majesty and seat divine;
All these are lovely, soft, seducing, bright.
Gladly am I thy worshiper: for man,
With man disgusted, weary, heartsick, spent,
Finds solace in thy silent intercourse,
Thy tongueless eloquence. Thou, unkind Elinor,
Thy wayward fancies, and reproachful frowns,
Are here forgotten. Nature nought to thee,
Thou hast no portion in these wondrous scenes,
And Switzerland is to thee but change of place.
Ah well! I 'll look once more on Meillerie,[8]
And on thy waters, Leman: then, for home;
To love — ay, but exacting — and to gloom.

He retires up the stage, and leans over the rail.

Enter, on the path,
MADAME *and* EUPHROSINE DE BEAUFFREMONT,
in conversation, — followed by a footman.

JULIAN *starts, turns, bows, and makes way for them, by pressing
closer to the rail, when they pass him singly, —* EUPHRO-
SINE *acknowledging his courtesy by a slight inclination,*

but showing confusion at his evident admiration. JULIAN
*follows her off the scene with his eyes, and continues gazing
long after they have passed.   He·then turns, with a sigh,
and Exit in the opposite direction, but still in the path.*

SCENE II.

The Souterrain of Chillon Castle.

Enter JULIAN,
followed by HUBERT, *who bears a campstool
and a portfolio.   At Julian's beck, he places the stool,
and handing the portfolio to his master,
the latter sits down and begins to
sketch the scene.*

Enter
the COUNTESS *and* EUPHROSINE, *attended
as in the Scene preceding, and a Soldier of the Castle
as their guide.* JULIAN *and* EUPHROSINE's *eyes encounter.* She
evinces slight embarrassment. JULIAN *looks pleased, but
bends his head and affects to resume his task, watching however, from time to time, the figure of
Euphrosine, while the ladies examine
the place.*

Euph. °And this is where St. Victor's aged Prior,
For Freedom and for Truth, his limbs resign'd

To fetters. And the heroic martyr's tread
Has worn the vault's rock pavement, as they tell.

Coun. Ay, so the poets, guides, and travelers say.
And so this Swiss would teach, but not our eyes.
Yet, in this column gray, lo where the ring
That kept the good man to his weary round
(If chain'd he was indeed) for six long years !
Hideous monotony ! Yet, oh my child !
How many, that conceive themselves at large,
Live worse confin'd, and in worse cells than this !

Euph. But that conception, Mother, makes them free :
The fetters, that are self-impos'd, fret not
Into the spirit: as we think, we are.
But is 't not strange, that in this castle old,
Where crown'd Savoy once aw'd his little realm,
This only is to see ?

        Coun. Strange, were it so.
It is the keeper's secret, who, his ease
Consults in showing the least may earn his fee.

Jul. [*coming forward.*
Pardon the freedom: will you condescend
To look these sketches over, where I have taken
All the old Castle boasts of any mark,
You will at a glance be able to pronounce.
This, [*pointing, while the ladies hold the book between them
    and turn over the leaves.*
    this, I think, is the sole part that may
Repay a visit; a saloon of old,
For banquets haply, or the council us'd.

Its marble columns, ceiling quaintly carv'd,
And antique windows well may claim regard.

Coun. What say'st thou, Eu'phrosine?

       Euph. O, by all means!

JULIAN speaks to the guard, slipping privily into his hand a piece of money. Exit GUARD. JULIAN consigns his portfolio and pencil to HUBERT, who folds up the camp-stool, and falls with the other servant into the rear, and the whole party Exeunt.

SCENE III.

[The middle court of the Castle.
In the foreground, the inhabitable part of the Château, with a narrow entrance in an angle facing the right of the scene. On the_left, a large arched opening in a rude wall, leading from the interior to the outer court, drawbridge, etc. ,

   , JULIAN, COUNTESS, EUPHROSINE,
       conversing ;
   HUBERT and the other servant behind.

Jul. [*to Coun.*] 'T is, as you say, a rude and ugly place.
But who can tell? perhaps, in after time,'
Some mighty bard may visit where we have been,
  13*

Lend fiction's hue to color these blank walls,
Through the old dungeon pour a deeper gloom,
And make its thrall immortal as the skies.
But lo, the guard.

Enter
through the Arch, the Soldier with the keys.

          I 'll bid him, with your leave,
Show you the chapel, cemetery, all
That may amuse you, then no more intrude.
Coun. O sir, we thank you warmly : in a stranger,
  This gentle courtesy ——
        Jul. [*looking at Euph., whom he has not failed*
    to regard from time to time, while addressing the Coun.
               Repays itself.
My deepest recollections of this place
Will not be of its vault nor moated walls.
    Bowing profoundly, while the ladies acknowledge the
      civility. — He turns and gives directions to the
      Guard in dumbshow, then Exit on the right with
      HUBERT, *while the rest proceed up the stage through*
      the Arch, and Exeunt at the left.

SCENE IV.

The exterior of Chillon Castle.

Enter
from the bridge of the Castle, JULIAN,
followed by HUBERT *with the draw-*
ing-implements, &c.

Jul. Go on: I 'll follow slowly. [*Exit Hub.*
                        — Euphrosine!
Sweet name! And what? Hark, Hubert! Stay!

Re-enter HUBERT.

How is that lady nam'd? thou hast doubtless learn'd.
Hub. Madame de Beauffremont, so please you, sir.
Jul. The younger lady?
                Hub. Her sole daughter, sir.
Jul. Not married?|
                Hub. No, sir.
                        Jul. English, as 't would seem.
Hub. The elder: but the Count de Beauffremont
    Was French.
            Jul. Was?

Hub. Yes, sir ; he is some years dead.
'T was so, at least, I understood their man.
Jul. Thank thee. Thou need'st not wait. [*Exit Hub.*

Pensively.] De Beauffremont?
Methought there was an accent, slightly foreign,
That seem'd to sweeten more her honied speech. —
Euphrosine de Beauf —— I could have sworn
Her name was Euphrosine! 'T was made to suit her. —
What grace! what gentleness! — I never saw,
I think, a form so perfect, yet so slight. —
Her very motions seem'd to woo support;
Yet unaffected — wholly.   O, to shelter
So fair, and seeming delicate a creature,
And guard her, with one's own broad breast, against
The rains, the frost, the driving pitiless winds,
Of this so wintry and ungenial world! —
Ah! I had quite forgotten, — there is one
That needs all my protection.   Shame, O shame!
Let me shake off this daydream; 't is dishonor. —
" *The fetters — that are self-impos'd — fret not —*
Into the spirit " *:* what a birdlike voice! —
Why this is madness! I am not in love!
No, no; nor shall be. —   But I must see more
Of this bewitching sylph. —   And then, her soul!
What purity! what gentle, winning grace! —
" *The fetters, that are self-impos'd* " —— By Heaven!
'T is a false sentiment: I feel that well:
What know I of her *soul?* —   Poor Elinor!
" *But is 't not strange that in this Castle old?* " ——

Vexation! — Euphrosine. [*Moving on, musingly.*

- " By all means." —

Repeating the name with increased soft-

ness, and still musingly.] Euphrosine.

[*Exit.*

SCENE V.

A mountain-path, leading up to the
Village of Montreux, which is
seen upon the right.

Enter JULIAN.

The pastor of Montreux should know these dames.
In his position, persons of their rank
Must —— I will ask him. Stay! what do I do!
Since Elinor is with me, were it well? ——
No; and, as yet, I have acted on that plea,
And shunn'd to visit him, that good old man.
So let me still: 't were vile; 't were —— Ah, by Heaven!

The COUNTESS *and* EUPHROSINE *are seen to*
enter the Village from the left at the top of the path
and turn toward one of the houses.

And toward the very house! They knock! They enter

Is it fatality that sends her thither ?
I know not.   *Her* I *must* know.   Euphrosine.
          [*pronouncing the name softly and tenderly.*

He ascends rapidly, yet with apparent
labor, the mountain-path,
and Scene closes.

SCENE VI.

A room in a Swiss Cottage.

ELINOR *is seen seated at a window, with her eyes fixed*
vacantly on the glass, over which her fingers
wander as if she was unconscious
of her occupation.

Enter,
with an air of happy animation and of triumph,
JULIAN.
He observes Elinor's gloomy abstraction and changes countenance.

Jul. My fault ! my fault !   How could I so forget ?
    Poor orphan ! [*He approaches her softly and kisses her cheek.*
          Elinor, art thou not well ?
    What ails thee ?
          Elin. [*turning from him and answering with asperity.*
              Nothing ; nothing that is strange :

Thou hast us'd me to neglect. [*She rises haughtily and Exit.*

     Jul. How! Is 't for her

To show resentment? her, who my affection

First slighted, then dishonor'd? her, to whom

No tie unites me that I may not sever?

Whom, at this very moment, I could —— No!

No, no; I must not think so: I am bound

Still to protect her. Yet, it is unwise,

This peevish humor; ay, if not ingrate. —

Haughty, dull Elinor! I will fly to Euphrosine:

She has no eye of fire, to kindle rage,

No frown of ice to chill me to neglect. —

Ah, let me pause! why should I visit Euphrosine!

This day I have seen my danger; and I thrill, —

But not with terror. O, delicious day!

The lake before me, and herself beside,

The sky all beauty, and the air all balm,

How could I but be eloquent! Love breath'd

Upon my lips, and Rapture shap'd my words.

She listen'd, Euphrosine, — in silence deep,

And knew it was her presence mov'd to all.

   Voices heard within, in violent altercation.

What now?

   The door is suddenly thrown open, and
      Enter ELINOR,
 in a transport of resentment, followed by HUBERT,
   who is earnestly imploring her.

   Hub. But, madam! ——

Elin. Villain ! —

They see JULIAN. ELINOR *retains her look of passion, but
with more of dignity :* HUBERT *looks confounded and terrified.*

> *Jul.* [*after looking from one to another for a
> moment in silence.*] Hubert Carl,
Thou art no more my servant. On the morrow,
Come to my chamber for thy due, with means
To take thee back to England. Go, sir. [*Exeunt, Elin. and
> Hub., — Elin. by the door, Hub. at the side scene.*
> — So.

I do conceive this villany much more
Than marvel at it. She has lost, poor girl,
Her right to be thought pure ev'n toward the base.
Yet, for my menial ! [*lapsing into musing.*
> thus on Euphrosine ! —
Fy, this is dotage ! Be it ; 't is relief.
And why not think on her ? Delicious day !
I saw the blush upon her virgin cheek,
When our eyes met, and my heart fill'd responsive.
She 'll love me, Euphrosine ! for I shall make her :
I see it now. And I will love her more.
But then, I 'll not avow it : my fate is fix'd ;
Body and soul I am tied for life to Elinor.
But I will have a holiday and dance
Till my chains rattle — will their weight permit,
Why not ? What harm can come thereof ? Once parted,
I shall be swept from Euphrosine's young mind
By newer conquest, while for me this beam

Of summer beauty and joy, forgotten never,
Will help to make life's winter seem less drear.

Re-enter ELINOR.

Elin. Julian, I would — a favor ask.
                     Jul. I, grant.
What is it, Elinor ?
                 Elin. Thou 'lt pardon Carl ?
Jul. What ! Is it thou that ask'st it ? and of me ?
Elin. But only in his words he gave offence.
Jul. Enough. What wouldst thou have ? The same respect
   I myself claim, I have bid him show to thee.
Elin. But I am hasty, and 't was his first grave fault,
   And verbal, as I have said ; and then, poor wretch,
   He is so repentant, and pray'd me, as for life,
   To intercede. I know thou 'lt not refuse,
   Thou, who art generous, and kind, and just,
   To Elinor this act of mercy and grace.
Jul. Not when she smiles, and pleads without a frown.
   As thou wilt, Elinor. I hope, one day
   I have no cause to wish thou hadst not prevail'd.
   For never yet my head obey'd my heart,
   Or my will follow'd those it should have led,
   That I not rued it. 'Faith ! 't is strange ; but —
   Could I be superstitious, I should deem
   This now were some presentiment of ill
   Whose shadow darks my vision. Let it pass :
   My word is given. Only, this observe :
   Thou hast not blinded me ; and Hubert's fault

Is more presumptuous than thou dar'st admit.

         [Exit.

Elin. Thou art wiser than thou think'st. But wast thou more,

        [Rings a handbell.

Thou shouldst not blind my jealousy. Come in.

    Re-enter HUBERT.

I have bought thy pardon with an aching heart.

There, go. No words. Our compact bear in mind.

         [Exit Hub.

O Julian, Julian! and can this be true?

Inconstant? — But, oh me! what, what am I?

Yet, this detested — woman! —— Mercy, God! *[gasping.*

O, that these Alps would fall together now,

And crush us both! — De Beauffre —— Noble! —

  Death!   *[Rings bell again, violently.*

   Again Re-enter HUBERT.

And is this —— Is she — Is she then so beautiful?

Hub. Not as some others I have seen. *[bowing significantly.*

   Elin. [*passionately.*] Don't trifle.

Is this a time, or am I in a mood? — Speak: answer me.

Hub. [*maliciously.*] Beautiful as an angel; with a voice! ——

Elin. Go, go!

  Hub. My master's gone there now.

      Elin. Begone! [*passionately.*

        [Exit Hub.

Insolent villain! — Cursed Switzerland!

What brought us to this execrable place!

Beautiful?   It is false!   I 'll not believe it :
The wretch beheld my agony, and spoke
To torture me.   I 'll see her : I 'll — I 'll see her :
I 'll ——   Beautiful!   Eu — Euph ——   My heart! my
    heart!   [*Exit.*

----

¹⁰ SCENE VII.

The mountain-path, with the background, &c.
as in the first Scene of the Act.

Enter,
from the right, JULIAN *and* EUPHROSINE.

Euph. [*looking back.*] My mother and the Dean are far behind.
    Let us await them here.
                Jul. As you shall please. —
'T was here — on this same spot — by yon rude rail, —
My eyes first saw — your mother and yourself.
I never shall forget it. [*with deep expression.*
        Euph. [*after a pause of embarrassment.*
            Yet there be
Scenes near us, of much greater charm than this.
What is the one you pictur'd to my mother ?
Jul. Ah, 't is a toil to reach it few would like. —

Behind the sunny village of Veytaux,
There winds a footpath, broken, steep, and scant,
Up to the summit of the Jaman peak,
Where peeps the cheese-hut dimly through the mist,
And the strong herd their glistening pasture crop
Through snows whose thin drifts never wholly melt.
Surpassing is the view, to him who climbs
That path at early dawn! The minish'd lake,
From horn to horn of its crescentic course;
Towns, villages, and hamlets; ridge on ridge
Of mountains, — tufted here, even to the peaks,
With giant firs, — there, rearing their bald heads,
Stern and unblenching, in the face of heaven;
All seen below his feet — before his breast —
Softly remote — sublime in vastness near!
Lo! scuds the vapor 'twixt it and his eye;
Ascends the mist, from vale and mountain's side,
And wraps him like a mantle; he sees nought, —
Nought but the spot whereon he stands, — the while
The driving shower wets him to the skin.
Sudden, forth bursts the sun! before it rolls
The gray and billowy haze, and, like a veil
Rais'd slowly from the face of beauty, shows
In dazzling brightness all the landscape wide.

Euph. You fill me with great longing. Could I see? ——
    Should I be able to ascend so far?

Jul. 'T were cruel to permit you: 't is a toil
    Even for a man; but you! — so softly made —
                  [*looking at her admiringly.*

So —— Pardon me. A brief way, it is like,
You might go up. —
   Euph. No, no, I will fix here.
It is my mother's scene ; and — it is mine.

   They look over the rail, for a brief while
      in silence.

Jul. [*suddenly pointing with his left hand forward, and to the*
  right of the stage.
 See, see, how beautif'lly the setting sun
 Tinges the white top of the Southern Peak !
Euph. Most beautiful ! the very tenderest tint
 That decks the petals of the new-born rose, —
 The inner side o' the leaf !
     Jul. You soon return
 To England, I am told ?
    Euph. [*turning as with surprise at his abruptness.*
      Yes; for some time
 We have waited a relation from the south.
 His coming is now look'd for, every day.
Jul. And, as the rose-tints we but now admired,
 So will your recollections be of me,
 If at all pleasing.   Mark, even while I speak,
 They are vanish'd; and the scene is left all cold,
 And hueless as before. —   But I [*looking to the right, where*
     the Countess is expected, and speaking
     quickly.] — but I,
 If I may dare to say it, I am like
 The sun which gives those evanescent tints :

In a brief moment, he will disappear ;
But 't is to bear with him, to other climes,
The aspect which he show'd in this.

                 Euph. [*confused —*
                     turning to the right.] Our friends :
They are nigh us, now : let us go back, and meet them.

                             [*Exeunt, to the right.*

Scene VIII.

The sandy shore of the Lake, near Villeneuve.
The water is partly bounded by the mountain Meillerie. The
moon in full splendor, just above
the mountain.

Enter Julian *and* Elinor —
walking slowly.

Jul. It is a lovely evening.
         Elin. Yes.
              Jul. The sky
How beautifully tranquil, and the lake !

Elin. Very.

  Jul. The atmosphere, though still, most sweet.

   They walk to and fro awhile, in silence.

Observe, my Elinor, that sheet of light

Within the mountain's shadow.   How much less

Of beauty would it have, if narrow'd not,

And clear-defin'd, by that black shadow broad,

And blacker Meillerie himself, who looms

Grandly obscure behind its brightness !

   Elin. [*stopping short, and facing Jul., while she lays*

    her hand upon his arm in an impressive manner.

             Yes.

And such, such even as that sheet of light,

Art thou to Elinor, — the brighter, ay,

More precious, because single and defin'd

Amid the darkness of her gloomy fate.

Thou hast made me what I am : to thee I owe

What little of refinement I possess,

The excited talents and acquired tastes

That fit me to participate thy joys,

And comprehend thy feelings.   But to thee

I owe it, likewise, that I am alone.

And when the moon shall set behind those peaks

(It threatens now,) what, what will then be left

To the dark, desolate mountain ?   Not its own

Dark shadow even.   Such will be my fate.

'T is even so near.

   Jul. Thou art poetic, Elinor.

Elin. Do not deride me, Master Mandeville.

'T is more than I can bear — or I deserve —
When my heart 's breaking; 't is indeed.

       Jul. [*putting his arm soothingly*
                 about her waist.] Dear Elinor !

Look on this lake. Thou hast taken from it an image:
Let me draw one for thee. See, how it lies
In beautifully even surface, catching
Not less the pale stars in its water, than
The brightness of the moon. Say, is it not
More wooing-soft, more lovely, thus compos'd,
Than broken up by storms, as last we view'd it,
Lurid and swollen, its angry waves breast-high,
Chafing and roaring, on this narrow sand,
Like Ocean on his beaches?

                Elin. Would not I
Be as yon lake, but for thy ruffling moods?
Thou, Julian, thy caprices, are the storm
That works me into passion. Mark me now.
Think me not ignorant of what is passing,
Of what has late seduc'd thee from thyself,
If not from me. Thou lov'st another: thou
Art swearing unto her the faith that 's mine.
Julian, beware; beware, I say! I am
Dependent on you; but I will not be
A slave to an unkind master. I can go,
Go from you; I — I will — go from you — go —
Go anywhere, from ——

          Jul. Weeping, Elinor?
              [*compassionately and tenderly.*

Elin. Weeping, sir.   You have left me nothing else
But tears.   [*Then with fierceness, raising her head boldly
and haughtily :*
Were I a man, I — would not weep.

She makes a step from him, as if to walk alone,

and the Drop falls.

VOL. II.—14

ACT THE THIRD

Scene I. *As in Act I. Sc. I. — A room in the house of Julian's mother — in London.*
A writing-table in one corner, with a folded letter on it.

FRANCES. SIR RICHARD.

Fran. Uncle, I must not, and I will not hear
  These wicked tales of Julian. If you must,
  Poison my mother's ear; but leave mine pure.
Sir R. Thou 'rt marvellously constant, and, methinks,
  Of late infected with thy brother's gall:
  Thy speech smacks of its bitterness.
                                  Fran. 'T is time,
  When not my maiden state, nor the dear tie
  That binds me to an only brother, nor
  My fatherless condition is remember'd,
  To vindicate my rights myself.
                          Sir R. Thy rights?
  And, prithee, what be *they?*
                          Fran. To be respected,
  As a young maiden, sister, and half-orphan,
  Should be respected by the man that claims
  To be her father's brother.
                    Sir R. Quite his style:

High, pithy, enigmatic.   Thou improvest.

Pray, Mistress Frances, is it of thy rights,

Thy virgin, sisterly, half-orphan rights,

To quote these wicked stories to thy brother,

     [pointing with his stick to the letter.

And lay the sin of malice on thy uncle,

Thy natural guardian ?

    Fran. I am no tale-bearer.

Sir R. And darest thou then to let me see that scrawl ?

   FRANCES *hands it to him.*

Quite spirited.   And, treating thee in kind,

I should return the tender sheet unread.

Fran. No, since you doubt me, read it, I entreat.

Sir R. [*reading.*

 " Dear brother, it may be very bold in me,

 " A woman, and so young, to dare advise thee."

How modest !

   Fran. [*extending her hand for the letter.*

   If you mock me ——

     Sir R. On my soul ! —

Ah, this is goodly stuff about his " honor "

And " fame " — Oho ! — " in peril ! " — and say'st thou

 here —

Reading].

 " Forgive me, if I err ; it is well meant."

The cozening plea of all your mischief-makers.

Reading.]

 " Strange stories, Julian, reach us " — [*Reads to himself.*

     What is this ?

"A maiden should not understand, I know,
Such things " ——   The Devil took early care of that,
And maidens are as wise now as their dams.
But [*reading.*] thou confessest — let me see what 's here –
— " Am so far ignorant, I better see
The extent of evil, than conceive its kind."
A well-push'd argument of virgin shame.
Thou shar'st thy brother's genius, with his gall.

Fran. Again, Sir Richard!   Give me back the sheet.
I lent it to your jealousy, not scorn.

Sir R. O, thou shalt pardon me.   I 'll mock no more.
In sooth, fair niece, I 'm wondrously inclin'd
To know if thou hast spread in brain as limb :
When last thou wrot'st to me, thou wast a child.
Reading.] " Can it be possible ? " —— [*Reads to himself.*
                                        Ahem, ahem !
" Unprincipled woman " ——
                                " Noble-hearted brother " ——
And — " When in earlier days my little arms
" I flung about thy neck " ——   How very fine !
There, take the letter.   Thou art still a child.

Fran. And yet —— [*checks herself.*

        Sir R. What wouldst thou say ?

                                Fran. I am old enough,
To know my duty, and to say no more. [*Going.*

Sir R. And dost thou dream to lead thy brother back
To the straight path, by such a clue as that ?

            [*pointing scornfully to the letter, which Frances
            takes with her.*

The labyrinth of vice is more perplex'd.

FRANCES *colors and appears about to speak, but represses
her feelings, and turning her eyes again from her
uncle, whom she had faced, Exit.*

Sir R. It is the accursed spirit of our race:
A Mandeville, for all her woman's heart.
I should not hate her for it; yet I do:
For I do doubt she reads into my soul.
Let her: it is a valiant one at least,
Albeit what fools and boys would christen base.

[Exit.

SCENE II.

In a villa in the vicinity of London — a parlor.

JULIAN,
reading a letter with an appearance of deep emotion.

Jul. O Frances, Frances! what remorse and shame
Thou wakest here. *[pressing his hand heavily on his heart.*
Thou gentlest, best of sisters! *[Folds
the letter and presses it to his lips and forehead.*

'T is worse, yet better than thou think'st.   And thou,
Thou, Euphrosine, [*pronouncing the name with great softness.*
            whom I love desperately !
The thought of thee too is a mortal pang,
Although I bless it, — thee, whom, but for this ! —
Yet, hopeless, I have follow'd thee : thou gone,
What were the mountains and the lake to me !
I have follow'd thee, — to see thee, hear thee, breathe
The air thou breathest, and to feed my heart,
In secret, with a joy I dare not own, —
A joy that wastes me even while it feeds.
Why should I, for a ——   But I 'll not abuse her.
Yet to give all, for one who gave up me !
One whom my pity, not my love protects !
Ha ! this needs more reflection.

                Enter HUBERT.

                            What, sir, now ?

Hub. A letter by express.   [*Exit Hub.*
            Jul. [*examining the seal, as he breaks it open and
                undoes the silk that ties it.*
                These arms I know not.
He reads it to himself, with an appearance of great trouble.
Distraction !   Do I dream ?   Decline my visits ?
And then, the enclos'd ! —   But let me read again.
Reading.] " In sending Master Mandeville the enclos'd,
" Madame de Beauffremont the occasion gives him
" To evidence its falsehood, if he can.
" His word shall be sufficient.   Until then,

" The honor of his visits is declin'd."

Patience! I shall go mad. This billet. [*unfolding and*
      glancing at the enclosure.] Death!

Here branded as a libertine and known

Seducer! [*reading apparently with great difficulty and sev-
      eral bursts of passion.*

     Living with a ruin'd girl

In Switzerland, while! —— Horror! [*again reading in
      the enclosed note.*] And-my love,

My pure, though passionate, my religious love,

For Euphrosine, made what I dare not name!

Liar! Infamous liar! [*crumpling the enclosure together.*

      And — who? who?

Elinor? Ha! To compass their revenge,

Women will stoop to anything: she knew

My love for Euphrosine! she told me so!

Resented it! —

     Enter ELINOR.

    Didst *thou* write this? Didst THOU?
      [*forcing the billet into her hand.*

Elin. [*Reading it to herself, and coloring.*

   I did not, sir.

     Jul. But thou didst know of it?

Of this rich villany? Speak!

      Elin. When Elinor deals

In such work, Master Mandeville, rest sure

You shall not be the last to hear thereof.

I could have wish'd you, sir, more nice of mind

Than to disclose me what I have notic'd thero.

[Exit — indignantly·

Jul. To read the allusion to herself might call
That blood-spot up; and her denial was firm.
Her anger?   That I reckon nought: for rage,
Like the dark fluid of the ink-fish, hides
The evading conscience, chas'd by just reproach,
And haughty carriage oftener is the strut
And swell of empty show than the demean
Of innocence wrong'd, too proud for self-defeuce.
But then the writing. [*Considering it.*

In it is no trace

Of Elinor.   My uncle's hand — disguis'd?
*He presses his hand to his forehead, and goes up the
stage to fling himself upon a couch, but starts
back and picks up something from the
cushion.*

How came this here?   His signet!   His! [*Examining it.*

His crest!

Deep as the Devil himself had graven it there!
*Stands motionless for a moment, as if perfectly
overcome — then rings a bell
violently.*

Enter ELINOR.
She starts at his expression and changes countenance.

Elin. [*timidly.*

Hubert just now is out.   Is there aught, Julian,

That I can for thee?

    Jul. Yes; 't is thou I want.

 He shuts the door behind her, and, seizing her arm,
  holds the ring directly before her face.

What is this? Look at it! Is it known to thee?

  ELINOR *stands as if turned to stone.*

Ha! Is my suspicion just? Was — was it he? ——

How came it here? How came HE here? Dost thou

Know him? Is he thy friend? Was 't he that — that? ——

 He gasps, but still holds Elinor's arm grasped tightly,
  while he gazes on and in her face.

Elin. [*falling at his feet and clasping his knees.*

 Mercy! Forgive me! Oh, forgive me, Julian!

Jul. [*struggling for breath.*

 'T was *he* then — HE — that wrote this — this damn'd

  billet? [*tearing from his pocket Mad. de B.'s letter with*
            the enclosure.

Speak — if thou wouldst not kill us both. Speak —

 woman —

Devil — was it *he?*

    Elin. It was. My God! my God!

Have mercy on me! oh!

    Jul. And here — here — *here* —

Here in my house — he plann'd this devilish wile,

That was to ruin me? with thee to abet him!

'T was he too that — was 't not? Out with it, woman!

Confess it all — all! or — my heart will break —

And thine to gaze upon me.

    Elin. Julian — I —

 14*

I know not what you mean.

      Jul. 'T is false ! thou dost.
Wouldst thou then have me to repeat my sense,
And blast thee with the echo of thy shame ?
He 't was that did debauch thee — in my absence —
This precious uncle ! Was it not ? Speak — speak !
Elin. My God ! forgive me !

     Jul. Why, that 's true — thou need'st it. —
Ha, ha ! 't was playing the devil with a will,
And to some purpose, to befool my mistress,
When I was gone, lest I should do it myself;
Dost thou not think it was ? to gather in ,
My harvest, lest 't should rot for want of harvesters.
O, curse him ! curses on him ! Though he were
Ten times my father's brother, curses on him !
And thou — thou ——

     Elin. Do not kill me ! Mercy ! mercy !
Jul. Kill *thee !* What should I kill thee *now* for ? If
I had done 't some eighteen months ago indeed,
It had been well for both of us. — But for thee, —
Thee, Elinor — whom I lov'd — and would not harm
Because I lov'd thee, — oh ! for thee — to — to ——
Elin. You weep ! You 'll not then hurt me ?

       Jul. Do I weep ?
True ! I forgot it was my uncle, then —
My uncle, dost thou hear me ! I forgot
It was my flesh-and-blood own uncle thou
Didst wanton with. Oh ! oh ! oh ! — A last word :
That child ! — was 't his ? [*Elin. cowers.*

Thou 'rt worse even than my thought !

Off! off from me! wretch! harlot! let me go.

He flings her off. ELINOR *falls on the floor; and the*
Scene instantly closes, — JULIAN *being seen to*
go off without regarding her.

SCENE III.

Another room in the villa.
A table furnished with writing-materials and a lighted taper.

Enter, hastily, JULIAN.
He sits down at the table, and appears to write,
with agitation and rapidly, a letter, which folding, he drops
therein his uncle's signet, then ties the letter
with a silken thread and seals it, in
the fashion of the times.
He comes down with the letter in his hand.

Jul. If aught will bring thee to the point, 't is this.

Thou art a Mandeville, — no dastard then:

And here is what would fire a heart of ice.

The world will term a parricide's my act.

That shall not move me: let it judge my wrongs.

The woman that I lov'd debauch'd, as 't were

Even in my arms, is injury itself
The deepest possible.   What, when the injurer
Is one whose previous malice I have known,
But not forgot; whose gibe, and sneer, and smile
Still rankle in the heart!   O this, for that
He is my father's blood, I might forgive.
But when this secret enemy has crept,
Like a foul toad, unto the naked root
Of my most delicate and dearest hopes,
And blasted them, it may be, for all time,
Exuding the cold poison of his malice
Where e'er my name is cherish'd most, — conspiring,
In a refined deviltry, with her
He had robb'd me of, to ruin me in the eyes
Of one still dearer, make me vile before
The simple mother that lov'd me with such trust,
The sister that ador'd me, and the friends
That honor'd me ! —   No !   Heaven alone, or Hell,
May shake my steadfast purpose ; man shall not.

[Rings bell.

Enter
HUBERT, *with a letter in his hand.*

Saddle the bay, the one Lord Capel gave ;
And seek Sir Richard Mandeville with this.
Bear back his answer with all speed.   That done,
Let my effects be pack'd without delay ;
But mine alone.

Hub. Sir, Mistress Morton 's gone.

Jul. Gone ?   Whither ?   When ?

                     Hub. But shortly since, sir ; where
We know not.

             Jul. Why not tell me this before ?

Hub. I knock'd, sir, often at your chamber door ;
You did not speak : and, sir, we were not bid
To stop her. She has left this letter.

                Jul. [*to himself.*] Gone ? —
Thou need'st not pack to-day. Go, where I bade thee.

                        [*Exit Hub.*

Gone ?   Gone ?   Unfortunate, misguided girl !
I would have left thee with a home at least,
And means to save thee from resort to crime.
Crime !   But what poverty constrain'd her first ?
What now, to this prodigious sin, whose die
Makes wantonness beside it look snow-white ?
And with my uncle too !   O cursed fact !

        Tears open the letter violently.

With his eyes on the page.] Keep me in sight ? —

                  I never shall espouse ? ——

        Pausing.

'T may be even so. [*sadly.*] — [*Reads.*

           " Farewell. I 'd say, God bless you ;
But you have planted in my heart a sting
Which will not let me pray for good on either."
And that is true, poor wretch ! and thou in mine:
My fault was weakness ; thine, to me —— God grant,
Its bloody fruits may not weigh on thy soul !

        Takes his hat and Exit as Scene closes.

Scene IV.

A wooded lane, near Julian's villa.

Julian, *with a paper folded as a note, in his hand.*
Hubert, *booted and spurred, and dusty, — his right hand
armed with a riding-whip.*

Jul. [*to himself, but aloud, and looking on the note.*
    Writ with a crayon ? No seal ? Not even a thread ?
Hub. Sir Richard was about to mount, to ride :
    His foot was in the stirrup, and one hand
    Lay on his horse's mane, when I drew near.
    Soon as he op'd your missive, sir, he hah'd,
    And dropp'd the ring it cover'd in his glove,
    Then ran the writing o'er with troubled brow,
    And, crying, " Very fine ! " tore off the back,
    Laid it upon his saddle, and, thus, wrote ;
    Then, handing me the billet folded, said :
    " There is thy master's answer. Take 't, good Hubert:
    " And take good care of him ; he has it here " —
    Touching his forehead, sir, in this wise.
                 Jul. [*sternly.*] Sirrah !
Hub. Pardon ; I thought 't would please you, sir, to know
    All that he said, and did.

Jul. But with such zest

To make the repetition, is —— What then?

Hub. He sprang into his saddle, and rode off.

Jul. Alone?

  Hub. Yes, sir.

    Jul. Which way?

      Hub. The same, 't would seem,

I came myself; I pass'd him on the road.

Jul. Bring me Black Rupert, and take back the bay.

     [*Drawing tight the buckle of his sword*

Be quick. [*Exit* Hub.

   — And to my servant, too! O rage!

[*Reading the note.*

" If thou be mad, I have my senses still.

" Live sparingly, good nephew, and thy prayers

" Say oftener, or thou wilt oblige thy friends

" Take care of thee. 'T is Bedlam gives repose

" To witless bards and disappointed swains."

Malignant fiend! But I will have thee yet.

O, on one hand, a palace of delights,

And Euphrosine to share them; on the other,

A desert, and that man — that man and I

Alone in 't! Would I not choose *this?*

      — Great God! [*looking*

 to the left, whence a sound is heard as of a horse coming

   from a distance at full speed.

Am I distracted? 't is himself! This way?

His horse is past control, — will throw him: ha!

      [*Sound as of a fall.*

God! he will drag him to his death! I 'll save him.
          [*Running out to the left.*

Re-enter JULIAN
supporting, with an air of great reluctance, and
even loathing, SIR RICHARD, *who is*
without his hat, and his dress
in great disorder.

Jul. There; lean against that tree: ere long, will come
One that may help you with more will than I.
          SIR RICHARD *supporting himself against the tree,*
JULIAN *retires a step or two.* SIR RICHARD *passes his*
left hand over his brow, and seems for a moment or two to be
gathering his thoughts, then extends his right hand
to Julian with an appearance of some
warmth and frankness. JULIAN
draws back, coldly and
haughtily.

Sir R. Why then, at peril of your own limbs, save me?
One minute more, my death had taken place
Without your agency.
                    Jul. And my revenge
Unsatisfied.   Perhaps for that I thought
'T were malice perfected, to make thy life
Thy enemy's charity.
               Sir R. [*impressively, after looking at him, for*
                         a full minute, from head to foot.
               Well, thou shalt have
The amend thou seekest, — if thou 'll take it now:

Thou hast left me without power to refuse.

Jul. [*calling to the right.*

Fasten the horses there, and come this way.

Re-enter HUBERT.

Assist Sir Richard : help him to his steed ;
Thou 'lt find the creature tied to yon dwarf beech.
Wait on Sir Richard home.   If thou should find
The beast unruly, mount him in his stead,
And lend thine own.

      Sir R. [*to Jul.*] Thanks.   Prithee, first, good Huber⁊,
See my girths tighten'd.

      HUBERT, *who has looked from one to the other*
with an air of inquisitive surprise, Exit.   SIR RICHARD
    takes Julian by the sleeve, comes forward,
      and in an under tone, but deeply,
        while he smiles :

              Thou shalt have thy wish,
Though thou wast twenty times my brother's son.

Jul. [*pressing Sir R.'s hand passionately.*

    And I — I will exact it, though my sire
Himself stood 'twixt you and my wrath.   Look to it.

            [SIR R. *smiles again.*

Sir Richard !   Sir !   Sir Richard Mandeville :
Do not look so.   We now know one another.

Sir R. Even so — and *hate.*

Again re-enter HUBERT.

Hub. All is secure, sir, now.

I 'll bring him to you?
>Sir R.< No, go on, my friend;
I am better now: I 'll follow to the spot.
                              [*Exit Hub.*

SIR RICHARD, *as he moves slowly after him,*
turns half-way round, smiles again, and touches the hilt
of his sword significantly. JULIAN *half-raises his, sheathed, with*
his left hand, and makes a step forward, as if to
rush on him, but, by a seemingly violent
effort, restrains himself. — Exit
                    SIR RICHARD.

Jul. [*clasping his hands passionately together.*
He hates me too at last! O blessed chance,
That I should save, at peril of my own,
The life he had rather lose than feel my gift!

SCENE V.

An open space in a grove, near Julian's villa, —
the front of which is seen through the
intervals of the trees.

HUBERT. ELINOR.

Elin. Thou dost with my impatience trifle, Hubert.
I came to ask thee of thy master.

Hub. Well,

And I to tell thee.

    Elin. *Thee?* Dost thou forget? —

Hub. That treachery makes us equal? No, not I !

Besides, if I must speak so plain ——

      Elin. What! — No !

Thou darest not so insult me ! But, go on ;

Go on: I mind our compact.

     Hub. It is well :

I thought, by Jude ! you had forgot it quite.

After the note Sir Richard sent, (that scrawl,

I show'd you ere it reach'd my master's hand,)

They had a meeting.

    Elin. Who? Not? — Speak !

       Hub. I mean,

Sir Richard and his nephew.

    Elin. Fought?

      Hub. I know not.

I found them in the lane. Sir Richard's horse,

It seems, had thrown him ; and, 't is like, his life

My master sav'd. If so, his thanks were odd :

For, as they parted gravely — on the spot,

I saw Sir Richard give a devilish grin,

And touch his sword-hilt.

    Elin. And? —— What then ? what then ?

Hub. Last night, there came a billet for my master.

I never saw him yet so fill'd with joy.

His eyes flam'd like two coals ——

    Elin. Stop !

Hub. Hear me out.

He shook his clench'd fist high above his head —
Holding in 's other hand the note. —

  Elin. [*with a gasp of relief.*] I breathe.

Hub. 'T was all that then I saw ; he bade me go :
But, pausing at the door, I heard him shout,
" *At last !* " and then the clash and ringing sound
Of metal thrown upon a table.   Soon,
He left his chamber.   I embrac'd the chance.
There on his table lay a heap of swords,
A string, and — guess.

    Elin. The letter ?   And thou hast it ?

Hub. Ay, in my head : how should I dare to take it ?

Elin. On, on !   It was ? —

   Hub. A challenge from Sir Richard.

Elin. Sir Richard ? and to — him ?

    Hub. From him to him.

Elin. O God !   Say on.

   Hub. 'T was more the acceptance than
The offer of a fight.   It simply said,
The baronet would pass the house this day,
Soon after daybreak, and alone, his sword
His only weapon, and about him borne
A note, to certify, in case of death,
He fell in duel fairly ; and he pray'd,
His nephew would the same grace do to him.
The cord was measure of his blade.

   Elin. Well, well ?

Hub. This morn, at daybreak, for an hour or more,

My master pac'd the lawn, (I rose to watch him.)
Each minute (as it seem'd,) he gaz'd the east,
Or look'd upon his watch.   At length, he bade
The groom his blood-bay saddle, cursing him
For being slow : the first time that his mood
Was ever, to his servants, less than mild.

Elin. But whither did he ride ?

       Hub. To town, be sure,
To meet Sir Richard.

    Elin. And ? —

       Hub. To fight, I think.

Elin. Thou canst not think so !

      Hub. Humph !

        Elin. His father's blood ?

Hub. They are both Mandevilles.   At Naseby fight,
When Noll had lopp'd off, at the shoulder-joint,
Sir Julian (that 's Sir Richard's sire) 's right arm,
The tough old baronet, with his left arm, strove
To put his poniard through the usurper's throat,
And would, but Cromwell seiz'd him by the wrist,
And cleft him to the chine.   His son, sole brother,
And junior of Sir Richard by a year,
Smote, with his glove, his enemy in the face,
In a church-porch, and died in duel for 't.
My master is his mother's child, 't is true,
But not the less his father's.

     Elin. O my God !
And they will fight !   We must prevent it, Hubert.

Hub. I see not how.   Besides, it is too late :

My master has by this time reach'd the town.

Elin. And he may perish! Stop them! save him, Hubert!

Hub. Sir Richard?

        Elin. No, no! Julian — him — thy master.

Hub. What 's he to you?

        Elin. No matter. O! enough,

That 't is my fault. Hast thou no feeling? none?

He never wrong'd thee: and he did forgive thee

The wrong thou wouldst have done to him. Think too,

'T is partly thy fault ——

        Hub. And who tempted me?

Elin. Not I! Don't say 't was I!

        Hub. Thy beauty, then.

Elin. Curs'd be its fatal influence! To this,

My ruin and —— But save him, save him, Hubert!

Repair thy fault!

        Hub. It is too late, I say.

Nor could I, were it not, or if I would.

Is it not Master Mandeville you speak of?

My master? Are you mad? What could *I* do, —

His servant? Do not wring your hands. Reflect;

He ruin'd thee; and thou but payest him back.

Elin. Cold-blooded, dastard villain! it is false.

Hub. Oh! very well. [*Going off.*

        In future, Mistress Morton,

Plot by yourself. My master may survive;

And the French lady ——

        Elin. Ah! — Stay, Hubert! stay!

Come back: I did but jest: I —— Wretched me!

Hub. [*coming back slowly.*

But, mistress, to receive, for pay, bad words ——

Elin. Thou shalt not any more.   Thou must not mind me.

Hub. No, but it seems my service is for nought.

The recompence you promis'd was not this,

Nor will I longer work without my hire.

Elin. But yet the work 's not done; nor canst thou claim

Thy guerdon, till it be.

      Hub. I know not that.

I know not why I should not pay myself,

         [*advancing rather quickly*

While it is in my power.

      Elin. Traitor !   Ah !

Thou dar'st not ! [*Putting her hand into her bosom.*

     And I am not in thy power.

Advance a step, and I will strike thee dead.

         [*He retreats.*

Why so.   What canst thou say, thou foolish man ?

Have I yet broke our compact ?

      Hub. But, 't is hard ——

Elin. To wait for thy reward until 't is due ?

No, I will keep my word : when Hubert does

All I demand, then Hubert shall receive

All he deserveth ; when my great revenge

Has taught to —— Ah, my God ! yet save him, save !

I 'd not destroy him ; not by —— Still there 's time.

Is there no help ?   Oh ! wilt thou not take pity ?

Hub. And the French lady ?

      Elin. Ah !

Hub. Young, noble, rich,
And beautiful.

  Elin. No more! thou 'lt drive me mad.
Let — let him, her, me perish, all the world!

      [*Exit. Hubert follows, smiling.*

Scene VI.

*The house of Sir Richard Mandeville.
An antechamber. Several servants in livery whispering
together. Their manner indicates some extra-
ordinary and horrible event, of
recent occurrence.*

*Enter
Another Servant, in different livery.*

New Servt. Where is the master?

    1st Servt. [*exchanging looks with his fellows.*

      Oh!

    New Servt. Sir Richard Mandeville?

1st Servt. Sir Richard? [*The servts. again exchange looks.*

    New Servt. Yes; my lady is a-dying:
I cannot stop; I must away, post-haste,

To Master Julian: wilt thou ——

    2d Servt. Hush! he comes.

    Enter JULIAN.

See! he has heard of it: how wild he looks!
I never saw an heir so sore-distress'd.
Jul. [*to himself.*] What terrible event does this imply?
These solemn and affrighted looks! ——

    [*Passes on, — Servant leading solemnly the way
    towards a door.*
1st Servt. [*holding back the new comer who is about
    to address Julian.*] Not now:
I 'll tell thee why.   A moment, he 'll be back.

    *As Julian's conductor is about to open
    the door, Scene changes.*

Scene VII.

*A room.   Several persons, servants and others, standing
in a group.   A couch with what, from the form, &c.,
appears to be a dead body, covered
with a white cloth.*

Enter
JULIAN, *with the* SERVANT.

Jul. Ha!   What is this?

    Servt. The body of my master.

VOL. II.—15

Julian stands as if petrified.
The servant falls back in dismay at his
expression, and the various other spectators use
various gestures of affright and wonder-
ment, as they gaze upon him.

Jul. Speak! How? By? —— Dead?

He turns his head over his shoulder, and gazes thus,
fixedly, on the body the whole time while the
Servant answers.

Servt. We thought you knew it, sir.
This morning, we were waken'd by a fall
That shook the house, when, coming down, we saw
Sir Richard prostrate on the lowest floor,
Expiring.   As his hat beside him lay,
And by the door the groom stood with his horse, —
Waiting there by his orders, as he said, —
'T is thought the baronet, for some rencounter,
Descending when the lamps were burning dim,
Had miss'd his step, and o'er the balustrade
Of the great spiral stair, two stories' height,
Pitch'd headlong.

Jul. [*now turning his face from the body, to the servant.*
Spake he aught?

Servt. One word :
" Aveng'd ! "

Jul. Oh ! [*covers his face with his hand, and averts it.*

Servt. And, that said, his head fell back,
The eyes roll'd horribly, and life was gone.

Aside, to the rest.] His grief is sore; 't is fit we should retire.

[*Exit, with the rest.*

Jul. [*removing his hands as the door shuts.*

 I came to shed thy blood ; and there thou liest
Cold, lifeless, mangled, all incapable
Of thought or feeling. I have pray'd to be
Alone with thee ten minutes ; and alone
I am with thee at last, — may be for hours,
If so it please me, and with none to hinder :
Where is my satisfaction ? I have vow'd
Avengement on thee : Fate has ta'en it for me,
And wreak'd it to the utmost. Lifeless, cold,
Mangled, incapable of thought or feeling ;
I might upbraid thee now, thou wouldst not hear me ;
I might make mock of thee, thou wouldst not see me ;
I might thy body wound, thou wouldst not feel me.
" Aveng'd " ? Thou felt'st it so : but I am not.
No : Elinor — seduc'd from me — defil'd —
Made to conspire against my joy and peace —
Elinor has left me ; Euphrosine
I have no more the right to visit now,
And could not, if I had, for very shame.
I am alone, alone now, — disappointed,
Dejected, wretched, — while, foul cause of all,
Thou liest at rest, on that oblivion pillow'd
Which thou hast robb'd me of, perchance for ever,
Till I shall join thee. Oh ! 't will harrow me,
This thought, this thought ; 't will cling around me still,
Press on my brain, and eat into my vitals.

Dead — dead — dead : but not within thy coffin
Will my revenge be buried : it will tread
The earth with me, move wheresoe'er I move,
Dwell in my heart, and there, there, at all times,
In every place, cry, ceaseless, to be sated.
Dead ! I will look on thee. [*He lifts the cloth, and looks
upon the face.*] Ha ! dost thou smile ?
Dar'st thou ? [*He raises his hand as if to strike, but drops
it, and retreats.*
· 'T is the mockery of fancy.
Thou dost ! [*looking again.*] Vile thing ! [*raising his hand
again, but dropping it.*
Oh God ! the lips are curl'd
And rigid with past agony.   Shame ! shame !
[*covering his face with both hands.*
This demon passion ! to have sunk me thus·!
*He is about to leave the room, but, when he
reaches the door, stops, as with a
sudden thought, and turns.*
That note he was to bear on his person : ah !
'T were worse than death to leave it — to be seen,
Talk'd of, perhaps, among the fools of court !
*He goes to the body, gazes in its face, turns down the
cloth, lays one hand upon its breast, and
thrusts the other into the pockets.*
Ope not thy sightless orbs, to blast me now ;
Let not thy blue lips curl, to drive me mad !
It is the dreadfulest act I e'er have done.
Oh God ! I feel, even through his habit's fold,

The solid flesh, all cold and stark.   There — there.

[*drawing forth the note and replacing the cloth.*

Reads.] " In fair, though secret, duel fallen, fought,

" On my own challenge, with my loving nephew.

" Let none pursue him therefore.   If he live,

" The madhouse will save justice all that pain."

Crushing the note together, in his hands.]

O villain ! villain ! scornful to the last !

Malignant fiend ! if that I deem'd thy soul

Hung o'er thy body and would feel the blow,

I —— Wretched me ! while yet I am myself,

Let me go hence ; and pardon me, high Heaven !

[*Exit, looking once more back, as*

the Drop falls.

ACT THE FOURTH

SCENE I.   *A room at Sir Julian's residence in London.*

SIR JULIAN, *in deep mourning.   He appears*
sad and abstracted.   LORD CAPEL
endeavoring to arouse him.

Lord C. Why, worse and worse, thou sullen eremite !
   Where shall this end ?   Wilt thou wear sackcloth, man,
   Adore the Saints instead of maidens' eyes,
   Set amorous strains no more to Waller's lute,
" Or force even Dryden own thy satire's nerve,
   But tag King David's psalms with monkish rhyme ?
   'T will stead thee much when Charles's wit is cold,
   And his dull Grace of York 's our master : now,
   Be more of the day, and, if thou must be sage,
   Wear lace above thy camlet.   But, ah me !
   I did forget ; forgive my heedless vein :
   These weeds are for thy mother ; and this grief ——
Sir Jul. Broods not above her sepulchre, my lord.
Lord C. Not then thy uncle's ? —
                    Sir Jul. 'S death ! [*walking from him, in*
                                    great agitation.
                    Lord C. I did not know
   There was such love between you ; though indeed

A fate so awful ——

   Sir Jul. Good my lord, have done.

      [Lord C. looks surprised and hurt.

Pardon me, Capel, this abruptness; more,

My seeming coldness. True, as only, friend,

If mortal could assuage my sorrow, thou

Wert call'd to minister. Ask now no more.

Lord C. How chang'd I in one brief year. Yet, why complain,

 Who have my own griefs which I may not tell?

Sir Jul. Well have I mark'd it. We, who heretofore

 Kept our hearts like an open book, for each

 To read at will and comment-on uncheck'd,

 Have double-clasp'd them now, like friends at court,

 Where envy teaches cunning, and dissembling

 Is rivalry's sole armor and chief weapon.

Lord C. Yet such wear smiling faces; we do not.

 And one of us, — which, Julian, is not I, —

 Has kept aloof, and each day grows more strange.

Sir Jul. A melancholy, Capel, deep as mine,

 Would come like mildew on the social hall,

 Bespotting all things with unsightly mold.

Lord C. Not where all things are humid as itself.

 If my mood be not sad enough, my lady's

 Is of a temperature to match thine own, —

      [Sir Jul. abruptly walks apart.

At least is grown so now, since my return.

Being so congenial, old acquaintance too,

Enamor'd both of Switzerland's romance,

Its lakes and mountains never-tiring theme

For spirits such as thine and Euphrosine's ——

     SIR JULIAN, *whose step has grown more and more*
        rapid and agitated, now turns abruptly, and,
          in a voice broken by emotion :

Sir Jul. My lord — you know ——

            Lord C. Thou art the strangest man !
That silly slander of a low amour
(Monstrous delict for Charles's saintly reign !)
Is no more listen'd now than Cromwell's psalms.

Sir Jul. Thanks to thee, Capel.

            Lord C. To thy sister, say ;
Who loves thee, Mandeville, as men love life. [*sighs.*
And I do love thee more, that she does so.
When I was wed, thou wast again away,
Wandering, men said, in Wales, but none knew where.

Sir Jul. Flying from thoughts that chas'd, and chase me still,
Eternal hunt ! that, dreaming or awake,
Will never slacken, till the harass'd brain
, Sleep — like my uncle's. — Pardon. And my sister ?
Thy wedding —— What was 't, Capel, thou wouldst say ?

Lord C. [*who has been observing him with anxious surprise.*
     Madam de Beauffremont being then with us,
Her prejudice against thee (Euphrosine's
Never I think had any vital warmth)
Vanish'd, like mist, before the steady day
Of truth and love — thy sister's love, I mean.
She honor'd at the time my father's roof.

Sir Jul. Which, since the desolation of our own,
Has spread its shelter o'er the orphan maid,

Shelter no other noble house can give
In these degenerate times.

> *Lord C.* Thank then her love,
Not mine ; or, if thou owest my friendship aught,
Be oftener near my hearthstone.

> *Sir Jul.* What to do ?
To deeper grave my sorrows, and to carve
Like lines of wo in hearts that yet are free —
Free from such shapes at least as furrow mine ?

> [*He has walk'd up the scene again, and, turning
back, adds solemnly :*

My lord, there 's danger in my contact ; shun it ;
Or from one common blight God keep us all !

Lord C. Indeed ? [*looking at him with increasing wonder.*

> *Sir Jul.* I say it, and Amen !

> *Lord C.* Then should
The plague-spot of thy grief be well-defin'd.
But yet I see it not.   Well, Julian, be 't
Even as thou wilt.   Come seldom ; only come.
Or, shall I rather visit here ?

> *Sir Jul.* [*eagerly.*] Yes, here.
Here, often as thou canst ; come every day,
Each hour, so thou have heart for 't ; for mine
Can never have enough of thee.   But there,
There in thy home — where — where ——

> *Lord C.* I understand :
And though the shame or pride is overcharg'd,
'T is noble : more so, that the age is gross.

> [*Sir Jul. shows great uneasiness.*

15*

Be that for time to lessen and efface,
[12] That equally will scar thy sorrow's wound,
Deep though it be and hidden.   Yet some time,
If rarely, let my lady see thee.   Even now
I left her in a mood that sorts with thine.
Go and console her while I am away.
Thou startest.   Thou 'rt the oddest man!   Here I
Urge thee myself to visit mine own wife,
And clear the way for thee; and one would think
I 'd bid thee court my grandmother!   I would
Thou hadst a wife, Sir Julian; thou shouldst see,
I would not be so churlish, didst thou ask me.

Sir Jul. Thou 'rt like to other preachers, my dear lord;
Thy practice and thy doctrine differ wide.

Lord C. Thou dost me right: albeit a cavalier,
'T is not in morals.   'T was a false mirth, wasted
To seek to dissipate thy heavy gloom.
Adieu awhile.   Thank Arthur's honest love, —
Or fellow-misery, wouldst thou judge more near, —
Mad Villiers [13] makes thee not, for this sour mood,
The palace-jest. [*Exit.*

                    Sir Jul. [*looking after him with sadness.*
                    'T would be at thy expense.
Yes, I will call to see thy ——— [*choking.*

                              Oh! not mine!
Not mine, not mine! though still to me but Euphrosine.
I 'll see thy wife, Lord Capel, — tell her all, —
Then fly forever from this fatal scene,
Where I die daily, lest a living death

Fall on far worthier hearts.

Going, stops, and turns, as hearing something.

What have we here?

Frances? And Capel, blushing like a girl,
Steps eager after. Oh! another knot
In this entangled skein. But one at least
I go to sever. 'T is my dear heart-strings
That twine it; and, may God grant, mine alone!

[Exit, at one side, while

Enter, from the opposite,
FRANCES, *followed timidly, yet eagerly, by* LORD CAPEL.

Fran. [looking after Sir Jul.

What, not one word? Unkind!

Lord C. Nay, Mistress Frances,

Seest not he waves his hand? pray, stop him not.
Alas, our Julian is not in that mood
Thy converse would give joy to. *[joining her.*

Fran. Oh my lord,

What is there wrong? Time was, even from his friend
I needed not to ask what ail'd my brother.
His heart was open then; but now, so chang'd ——
Pardon, my lord, I cannot help but weep;
Though vainly do I search my conscience through
To find the cause in me.

Lord C. The cause in thee!

Then were my friend, thy brother, chang'd indeed.
Why even the idle court thy love's devotion
Have learn'd to reverence, and who come more near,

To know thee, and to —— warmer hearts, I mean,
Find him worth envy even for this alone.

Fran. 'T is envy then which follows true desert.
     ¹⁴ When other brothers merit half the love
That Julian does, they will not lack their due.
This better than Lord Capel who should know ?

Lord C. If to be good and loving were but one,
     Then none indeed.   But were your brother's friend
All that your very fondness for that brother
Bids you assume, yet could not Ellen be
That brother's sister, worthy though the while, ʼ
Most excellent maid, to be that sister's friend.

Fran. Lord Capel does forget it is his blessing
His sister cannot love him with that love
I bear to Julian, orphan and alone.

Lord C. No, not alone, God knoweth ; for there be hearts
     That love, adore thee, more than any kin — [*eagerly, in a
                    transport of admiration, taking her hand ;
                    then embarrassed.*

     I mean ——
          Fran. [*gently disengaging her hand, and shrinking from
                    him, but timidly and with emotion.*
          Yet are not kin for all.   Whereas
Ellen has both her parents and yourself:
And you, have you not parents, sister, — Euphrosine ?

     Lord Capel, *visibly moved, in turn shrinks from* Frances,
          who, without looking at him, hastens to add :
But do not mock me by this courtly parle.
My brother's gloom, his wild and absent look,

His thin, wan cheeks, his voice, and oh, my lord,
His harsh impatience, his, who to my love
Was wont to be as gentle as a child,
This makes me restless.   Fill'd with fancies vague
Yet terrible, I came to try, once more,
The power that was my glory once and joy :
But, oh my lord, you saw !

     Lord C. Foresaw.   And 't was
That I foresaw [16] this shock to thy sweet spirit,
And would avert it, or abate its force,
That I presum'd to follow thee unbid.
O gentle lady ! even now thy brother
Repell'd my friendly urgence.   In this mood,
Impracticable and averse, think'st thou,
Though thou art dear as ever to his heart,
Thy solace would be timely, thy love's quest
Meet ready answer ?   Let me tend thee home.
Trust me, there is no reason for alarm,
Though much for sorrow, seeing him thus chang'd.

Fran. I will indeed withdraw ; but you, my lord,
 [16] Think not of me : I would beseech you wait
 Till Julian come ; and let the anxious hearts
 That yearn for him beneath your father's roof
 Be gladden'd through your instance.   Take him else
 To your own home, or —— But, alas, I see
 You have no hope to move him.   O my lord,
 You will not leave him wholly to himself?

Lord C. Sweet lady, no.[17]   I comprehend thy wish.
 And is there wish of thine that Capel's spirit

Bounds not to meet, though 't were of lighter kind
Than now exalts, and makes thee in the eyes
Of God in Heaven an angel like his own ?
Go to the roof that, honor'd as thy home,
Gives me the right to feel myself thy brother ;
I will not quit this place till Julian c me.
What o'er his mood I may, though little hoping,
I will essay for thine, for all our sakes.
Rest tranquil : and now let me lead thee forth.

                                        [*Exeunt.*

SCENE II.

Twilight.

Charing- Cross.   The Statue of Charles I.

ELINOR *standing in its shadow.*
To her
Enter HUBERT.

Elin. Thou 'rt faithful ; but thou 'st kept me over long.
Hub. Faithful !   Hold thou thy truth as I shall mine,
    And, pretty Mistress Morton, Hubert's place
    Is better than his lord's.
                        Elin. Wilt thou have done ?

Speak but once more in that insulting cant,
Our compact 's broken, and thy master learns
What viper he is warming in his kitchen.

Hub. Oh, if you come to vipers, what was she
My master warm'd so lately in his bosom ?
Pardon ! you stung me.

　　　　　　Elin. With a broken fang.
Go on, sir : what news bring'st thou ?

　　　　　　　　Hub. Precious.　Hear.
All things are order'd for a prompt departure.

Elin. I trust that thou dost lie.　I —— Mercy, Heaven !
Go, and unpunish'd !

　　　　　　Hub. Nay, I said not that.
If what he longs for most, and you pretend
You long for with him, is to be the whip,
He is like to feel it.

　　　　　　Elin. Ah !

　　　　　　Hub. Guess whence I come.

Elin. From — not from — From ? ——

　　　　　　Hub. Lord Capel's, be you sure.
I track'd him thither, driven as he were mad.
Why do you smite your hands?　I thought 't would
　　please ye.

Elin. Her ruin would : their love — it drives me wild.

Hub. That 's passing strange, when, as my dull eyes see,
You hope that ruin only of that love.

Elin. And yet it makes me heartsick, mad, I tell thee.
But what hast thou, thou sneering, bantering devil,
To do with that ? —　So, all is over.

Hub. No.

Elin. Was it a lie then?   Does he not then go?

Hub. In one hour hence, Sir Julian leaves the kingdom.

Elin. Then all is over, villain.

Hub. [*with mocking emphasis.*] Lady, no!

Elin. Didst thou not dog him, furious with his lust,
  To the adulteress?

                    Hub. To his lady love,
The honorable wife, whom even the Duke
Dares not asperse, nor Rochester lampoon,
Of the lord Capel, to that lady's house —

Elin. Stop, or I strike thee!

                    Hub. Soft; the statue hears. —
To that fair lady's dwelling did the hound,
Call'd Hubert, track his master's step, to please
His master's —

            Elin. Cast-off mistress.   *I* will say it:
Thou shalt not dare it.   Even in this place ——
                    [*putting her hand into her bosom with a
                            threatening gesture.*

Hub. [*mockingly.*
  What! where his martyr'd Majesty looks down,
Commit a murder? —   But a truce.   I see
You want me not; and, if these eyes are stone,
            [*carelessly indicating, with his head, the statue.*
Others are round us, and quick ears besides.
I'll see you where 't is safer.

                    Elin. Stay: 't was wrong
And very foolish to be angry.   Yet

To see one's plans of womanly revenge,
So painfully upbuilded, all o'erblown ! —
Hub. And once more, I say, " No ! "

      Elin. Yet is he gone
To bid adieu !

    Hub. Do people always do
What they go bent on doing ?

      Elin. Fellow, yes,
Thy master does. His honorable soul —
Don't sneer, sir ! — his romantic love of right
Are urging him — I see it all as plain
As if he told me (have I not good cause ?) —
To break off this connection. And he 'll do it.
Hub. To put the broken parts again together,
As he did once in Switzerland, and here.
Elin. Thou growest refin'd.

     Hub. I see you now and then. —
But men in love are much like men in drink;
They know they stagger, yet they walk not straight.
And my romantic, honorable, master
May fall the sooner, striving to keep up.
Hush ! by St. Jude, see where his carriage comes,
Hot driving ! as he went. 'T is well for us,
The blinds are down. Look, Mistress Morton, look !
The coachman has his head bent o'er his shoulder :
Are they pursued ? Or does he fear —— See there !
He laughs now with the footboy, and makes signs.
All 's safe : but something 's inside, I would swear.
Elin. Dost think —— [*vehemently, but in a suppressed tone.*

Hub. 'T is time that I were gone.   Farewell.
Elin. If it be done! ——

       [with restrained, but convulsive emotion.

    Hub. Don't keep me.   Nor forget
How I have labor'd. *[moves off hastily.*

     Elin. Thou shalt have thy wage.

Take now my thanks — *[Exit Hub. —   Elin. looks after
       him with vindictive expression.*

   and hatred, and deep scorn.

         [Exit Elin.

Scene III.

Same as Scene I. of the Act.

Lord Capel

*alone, seated in a musing and melancholy attitude.
After some minutes :*

Lord C. O foolish, foolish visions!   Worse than mad,
 To let these shadows of fantastic joy
 Steal o'er my spirit!   What to me should be
 Her spotless beauty and her stainless soul?
 What could be, were I libertine as loose
 As Wilmot [18]?   Fatal bond! too rashly tied!
 And she, poor Euphrosine! though not her heart,

More than my own, went with her wedded hand,
Yet must the indifference I cannot hide
Deepen her sadness.   Noble that she is,

                    [*He comes down.*[19]

Her pale cheek sinks, like Julian's, yet no murmur ——
Ah! can it be?   It flashes through my brain
Like lightning in deep darkness!   Do they love?
He will not see her — they were friends abroad —
He shudders at her name, she thrills at his ——
Death!   I 'll not think it!   it were madness round —
Julian, and Frances, Arthur, Euphrosine,
All wretched, yet all honest.   Be this true,
It makes my dreams more deadly-wicked still.
Yet, O voluptuous twilight of the soul!
Down from the glowing heaven where Love reposes
Thy rosy atmosphere pours all around me,
And the hush'd sense is happy but to feel!
Frances! [*with softness.*] —   Why am I here? [*with sud-
    den animation, or starting, as if rousing himself with
        an effort.*] To wait for Julian!
To keep him from himself.   Who shall keep me? [*sadly.*
If he knew! —— if! ——   It is his footstep! —   Yet
'T is strangely heavy, dull, as though some weight ——
Julian! my friend! —   Ah!

Enter Sir Julian

with Euphrosine *lying, apparently senseless, in his arms. Her
hair, all disheveled, drops over them and over her dress,
and her head unsupported hangs down.*

JULIAN *lays her on a couch, then, looking wildly on* CAPEL, *who stands motionless, as with horror and amazement, bursts into a frantic laugh.*

Sir Jul. Ha, ha, ha! 'T is she;
It is thy wife, I say; and I have robb'd her
Of all right to that name. Why dost thou stare?
Hast thou no weapon? I have kill'd thy wife,
And bring a life to thee. Where are thine arms?
Is thy sword rusted in its scabbard? Look.
                              [*pointing to Euphrosine.*
Lord C. [*rushing on him with fury.*
      Villain! — Or [*slowly, in a deep and mournful tone.*
            art thou mad?
            Sir Jul. Both — both, I tell thee —
Mad and a villain. Ere thou cam'st, I lov'd her —
Lov'd her! O how I lov'd her! I had given
My soul för one kiss of her virgin lip,
Which then no man had tasted! but to strain her
Once in these longing arms before I died,
I would have borne all woes that ever fell
Upon the wretchedest of mankind! — And now ——
            [*He turns slowly round to the body, but without moving from his place.*
O Euphrosine! [*bursts into tears.*

Suddenly breaking into fury, and advancing two steps towards Capel.
      What! hast thou eyes? or ears?

I tell thee I have foully wrong'd thy wife,
The lady of Lord Capel. There she lies.
Thou wouldst have me to see her; thou wouldst trust her
To me, her lover — and her lov'd, as that

> [*pointing to her body.*

Should tell thee, wittol! coward!

> Lord C. [*drawing and rushing on him.*
>
> Ah, come on.

Sir Jul. Yes, yes!

> Lord C. [*noticing his strange delight, drops the point*
> *of his sword, with a look of mingled*
> *pity and horror.*

No, not by my hand. Capel's sword
Can do no murder.

> *Sir Jul.* 'T is a woman's sword. Take that,
>
> [*striking him with the flat of his blade.*

For thy wife's sake.

> Lord C. [*attacking him instantly.*
>
> Let her bewail the victim.

SIR JULIAN, *after a few passes, lunges purposely aside, and flings*
himself with great force on the point of Capel's weapon.
It passes through his dress, under the arm.

Sir Jul. Unlucky chance! I trusted to have perish'd
By thy lov'd hand. Why wouldst thou spare me?
Lord C. [*solemnly, in a voice deep in tone,*
slow of movement, and mournful.

> Julian,

Thy punishment rests not with me. If 't please thee

To have set a thorn for ever in the breast
Of a true friend — of one who lov'd thee — as —

                              [*his voice breaks.*

He lov'd no other man — be pleas'd. Be kind —
To — her. 'T is all that thou canst do for her,
For the brief while that will be left : her shame
She will not long survive, to be a curse
In thy chang'd eyes.

                 [*He looks at Euph. a moment, stifles a groan,
                   and bursts from the apartment.*

       Sir Jul. Gone. Left her all to me.
Well — we must live together. It will be
A sad life, Euphrosine : but we must set
Our shoulders to the task, and bear the load
Between us. 'T will not be for long.
He said well. Fragile as thou art, poor girl,
Thou canst not long sustain the iron weight
Of the charg'd conscience. Pity 't were thou shouldst.
How still! She looks as though —— Perhaps! ——

                    [*He kneels beside her.*
                         No breath!

He puts his hand to her cheek.]
Cold! — Can it be ? — Dead ? — No, no.

                       Yet, unhelp'd,
She may die. Let her : 't is a mercy thus.

       He rises, and walks gloomily from the couch.
Let her die thus. Mine only now forever,
Would God she were the grave's! —   [*Starting, he turns
                              eagerly round.*

Hush! is 't? —— She stirs!

She! —— [*Darting to her in a seeming ecstasy of delight.*

Euphrosine! my love! my life! my soul!

He throws himself beside her — raises her from the
cushion, fans her lips, chafes her hands, &c. &c. She revives
with a deep sigh, opens her eyes, and recloses them. He
renews his efforts, repeating what follows raptur-
ously, yet with deep tenderness, (kissing
her passionately, from time to time) :

O open yet again those mournful eyes!
Speak to me, Euphrosine! 'T is I that call thee.
I only am beside thee, no one else.
These are my kisses; let thy still pale lips
Return them — only once! O, do but waken:
I am thy Julian, and my sun, my heaven,
My breath of life is in thee, only thee!
Thou wouldst not frighten me? O ope those lids!
Speak to me but one word! I am thy Julian:
Dost thou not know me then?

Euph. Alas! too well.

He clasps his arms about her rapturously, still kneeling
at her feet. She throws her arms around him,
and her head, enshrouded in its tresses,
rests on his bosom.

Yes, hide me; let me creep into thy heart;
I am not fit to see the light again.

Drop falls.

ACT THE FIFTH

SCENE I.   *The same as in Scenes I. and III. of Act IV.*

SIR JULIAN

seated, in a riding-dress, disordered and travel-stained, —
his neckcloth off, the collar of his shirt open, his face
pale, emaciated, and haggard, and his hair
and beard undressed.   On the floor,
his hat and riding-switch, and
the neckcloth.

Enter HUBERT.

Sir Jul. Did Mistress Frances say that she should come?
Hub. Sir, on the instant.

       Sir Jul. Go. [*Exit Hub.*] — Until she come,
I 'll con this cursed billet o'er again.

       [*drawing a letter from the pocket of his coat.*
It burns into my vitals like hot iron.
But, not to read it, horrid phantasies
And memories adder-fang'd would hiss me mad.
Devilish Elinor! [*tearing the billet open.*]   So far away.
How knew she too my hermitage?   I deem'd
There I and sorrow might be safe at least.

Hubert ? — My mind misgives me.

                    Reads :] " You have known
" The misery greater than of seeing frustrate
" The heart's desire. — Your *lady*-leman 's dead." —
Viper! how sharp the first bite of thy teeth!
" Now for the finishing stroke. Watch well your sister.
" 'T is sweet revenge for him you have grossly wrong'd,
" To pay you home in your own coin. No doubt,
" Before this reaches you, your mother's daughter
" Has given him a receipt in full." — 'T was I,
Who made her cunning in discourse. My hands
Have given its temper to the steel that slays me. —
" 'T is of no good I mean you, that I write.
" Yet may you credit me. The very Devil
" May tell truth when it suits his purpose." — Ay ;
But 't will need searching, for the brimstone source
It comes from. [*Tears the letter into fragments.* —

             'T is the carriage. [*listening.*] On the stairs
Her foot springs light and joyous. Surely guilt
Bounds not to meet the accuser!

                Enter FRANCES.

                  Fran. Brother! [*with eager joy.*
                  Sir Jul. Frances!
        [*sternly and coldly, yet with strong expression.*
FRANCES *stands arrested, gazing as if speechless, with an air of*
  mingled grief, astonishment and terror. Suddenly, she
    stretches her arms to him, and would spring to his
      embrace, exclaiming, with deep feeling :
VOL. II.—16

Fran. O my brother!

        Sir Jul. [*grasping her arm.*

           Stay! So. Let me look on thee.

  Art thou still pure? Speak. Art thou still my sister?

He unties the ribbons of her hat, and, removing it, flings it on a
   chair. Her hair, loosened by the rudeness of the action,
      falls about her head. He puts it back from
        her forehead, and gazes into her eyes.

Fran. My brother?

   With melancholy joy, he throws his arms about her.
        She leans upon his breast.

      Sir Jul. There is comfort yet for me.

O Frances! thou 'rt the only good Heaven leaves me;

Precious, more precious even now than when,

A happy boy, I taught thee lisp my name,

Thy innocent prattle sweeter to my ear

Than schoolmates' call to play. Ah! did thy heart

Now throb with guilty trembling, had the flush

Of shame that white brow crimson'd when I touch'd it ——

Fran. [*drawing from his embrace, and throwing back her hair*
     that she may look on him, while her eyes wander un-
     easily over his disordered dress and haggard features.

What mean'st thou, Julian? Art thou wild, indeed?

Sir Jul. Arthur. [*slowly, but simply. — Fran. blushes, she casts*
        down her eyes, she trembles.

      Is 't true then? [*with rekindled passion.*

           Is there only left

    Revenge? [*He drops her arm, and adds mournfully:*

    Have I indeed no sister?

Fran. Oh !

What have I done ?   I know not what thou meanest.

Sir Jul. [*with renewed violence.*

   Thou dost not ? dost not ?   Know'st thou not what 's said
Of thee and Capel ?   *Capel,* dost thou hear me ?
There ! there !   Ha, ha !   Thy face speaks out ! it does !
O why, why cannot I destroy with curses !

Fran. My face is burning, but 't is not with shame.
So help me Heaven, I am innocent of all wrong !
    She gathers her hair in her hands, and holds it
       like a veil to her face and weeps.

Sir Jul. [*laying his hand gently on her shoulder, and speaking*
        with less harshness, yet solemnly and sadly.

   Frances, on her death bed our mother bade me
Watch over thee, and be to thee a brother, parent,
All in thy present state that I should be.
We stand alone together in the world,
Last of our father's race that bear his name.
What should I feel then, were —— I will not shame
Thy purity, repeating that dark thought.
Yet, Frances, the lord Capel —— Thy flesh creeps
Under my fingers !   Essex' heir, I say ——
How thou dost shudder !   Hear !   That man I lov'd
Better than e'er I shall love man again.
Now, my heart loathes his image.   What appals thee ?
He is thy brother's foe : 'twixt him and thee
Can be no commerce not to thy dishonor.

Fran. O, thou mistak'st him !   Thou art so deceiv'd !
   Arthur ! ——   [*She catches herself and stops abruptly.*

Sir Jul. Indeed! Is 't come to that? So close
Already? Has he dar'd? — No matter. Frances,
Hear me, and once for all. I 'd rather see thee
In the churchyard than wed to Arthur Capel.
Fran. Then God have mercy on me!

> *She staggers — he catches her in his arms. With a*
> *sudden effort, she rises from his support, and*
> *dropping on her knees, twines her*
> *arms about his limbs.*

Do not be
So violent, dear brother! Deep and awful,
Thy voice affrights me, and thy eager looks
Pierce through me that I have no breath to speak.
But be more gentle, as in other days,
And I will tell thee all.

> SIR JULIAN *seems embarrassed, and ashamed of*
> *his violence. He raises her.*

Sir Jul. I ask it not.
What I have said is said. Forget Lord Capel.
So beautiful, so good, accomplish'd, rich,
Thou canst not want for suitors; and thy portion
Myself will double; wealth is now to me
No more of any use: but for Lord Capel —
Think not of him.

Fran. Yet — hear me. Be not so —
Impatient, Julian! I — I could not deem ——
I thought —— Thou knowest ——

Sir Jul. I know what thou wouldst say.
I know Lord Capel loves thee — or did love;

I think thou couldst have once return'd his love:
But now —— No more of it! While I am living,
Never shall Capel's blood commix with ours!
Never his head be pillow'd on the breast
Of Frances Mandeville!

With a faint scream,
FRANCES *seizes the skirt of his habit.*
SIR JULIAN, *escaping from her grasp, falls back upon a*
couch, seemingly exhausted. At the sight of this distress,
FRANCES *appears to forget herself, her brother's tyranny,*
and, throwing herself before him on her knees,
and taking his hands in hers, she exclaims :

Fran. Alas! dear brother,
Where hast thou been ? what suffer'd ? Thou art wan,
And thin, and sore-dejected. O forgive,
Forgive me, Julian! I was very selfish,
Not to see thy distress; I was indeed!
Thou hast travel'd far and fast no doubt, and art
Weary and worn.

SIR JULIAN, *as touched to the soul, leans his head*
on his sister's neck, as she kneels before
him, and appears to weep.

Sir Jul. Yes, I am worn and weary ;
I have travel'd far and fast to come to thee,
I am sick with abstinence and want of sleep;
But 't is not that — not that! I am alone —
Lonely and sorrow-shaken: I want some heart
To feel for me, some hand to press my forehead,
Unhired to the task. Wilt thou not come,

And stay by me, my sister, till I am better,
Until I am able to endure my self?

Fran. Forever, wilt thou let me! O my brother!
Would we had never, never parted!

       Sir Jul. Would,
We never had!

    Fran. But thou wilt still be happy,
Dear Julian. Thou 'lt be better, and so soon!
When thy own sister is near thee. 'T is a life
So wretched-lone thou lead'st, with none around
But creatures mercenary! — O my brother,
This gentle sufferance makes me truly blest!
Forthwith, I 'll write to Lady Essex ——

       Sir Jul. No.
To-day, I must not part thee from thy friends;
Thus sudden, 't were uncivil. But to-morrow,
So they will spare thee ——

    Fran. Let it be to-day.
Now I have seen thee, could I else have rest?
Think of the long, long twelvemonth, since away ——

Sir Jul. [*covering his eyes with an expression of pain.*
  Spare me!

    Fran. Alas! I had no thought to grieve thee!
Yet therefore beg I only more to stay.

Sir Jul. Be it, blessed creature, even as thou wilt.
Hubert shall wait thy orders. Now —— [*offering to lead
         her out.*

     Fran. My brother?
     [*Spreading her arms towards him.*

Sir Jul. True ; we have not embrac'd. [*For a moment, he holds his sister strained to his breast, in silence.*

O, if e'er Heaven
Looks down with favor on its creatures here,
May its choice blessings on thy virgin head ——

[*Fran. bursts into tears, and struggles to free herself.*
What ails thee ? Tender heart !

Fran. O let me speak !
Brother, I — I am —— [*sobbing convulsively.*

Sir Jul. — Best of mortal angels.
And being such, what hast thou to confess ?
Not now at least; and therefore will I quit thee.
This night, I have made thee over all my soul :
To-morrow, thou shalt let me share in thine.

[*Exit.*

Fran. Julian ! — [*calling after him with broken utterance.*
This is not right. Good cannot come
Of any such concealment : and from him ! —
Yet, it is terrible to face his rage. —
And I am guiltless ! — O'er my troubled spirit
Spread chilly shadows of a vague foreboding,
And night, all starless, suddenly come down,
Seems to shut out the lingering rays of hope. —
Would he had listen'd ! This suspense affrights me.
And yet, I know not why. — I needs must weep.

[*Exit.*

SCENE II.

Sir Julian's Study.
On the right of the scene a window, and in the embra-
sure a seat.   In face, a painting of a landscape.
In the centre, a table with books. —   In other
respects, the usual furniture of such a
locality, — with busts, statues,
and other articles of
taste and virtù.

Enter
HUBERT, *a-tiptoe,*
and shuts the door behind him softly, his finger
on his lip, as if afraid to be heard.

Hub. By Jude ! my web was nearly brush'd away !
Were not my master a most vehement fool,
He would have listen'd.   What could he have done ?
Blown his rage out — then pardon'd her.   But now —
What if it end in bloodshed ! If I thought ! ——
I would not harm her ; she has still been kind. —
Why should it end so ?   When he bursts upon them,
Certes, she ll own the marriage.   It is time
I had my due or Elinor : to-morrow

The vixen would require fresh space, to hatch
New plans of vengeance; the old is well enough.
But of the marriage, Hubert, not a word!
Fierce as she is, the jade might scruple. Eh!
Is it so wicked? —— What is that to me?
If the bride keeps the secret, so should I;
If 't work her mischief, I am not to blame. —
I 'll trust to Providence. — Once mine, dame Elinor,
I 'll put a bridle on thee, saucy jade!
Thou shalt not fling me, as thou didst my master.
He fed thy mettle: I 'll starve it. — [*Handbell sounds
within.*] 'T is his bell. [*Exit,
by another door, while,
from the one at which he had entered,
Enter* ELINOR,
*with hat on &c. — She moves
cautiously, as if apprehensive of discovery. Yet
there is nothing mean in her manner, as
was the case with Hubert.*

Elin. Was not that Hubert? — But I dare not call.
*She examines the room with
attention and emotion, mixed with slight surprise.*
This must be Julian's room — the poet's room —
The scholar's room — the —— Sneers are wasted: see!
[*drops her tone of bitterness and speaks softly.*
There is the window — opposite my own,
On the other side the street. 'T was thence he gaz'd,
And won, without a word, my virgin heart.
What dreamy hours I pass'd! He was my sun,
16*

And here as to the eastern sky I turn'd
For light and warmth. How my heart open'd then,
Sending up fragrance to requite its warmth!
And now — O now! —— [*she covers her face with her
hands and sobs low.*

     Why am I here? Small cause
Have I, who —— I am choking! — 'T is this room:
The air is stifling: dust is on the books.
I see, I see! It brings me to myself.
   [*recovering all her energy and determination of tone.*
For *her* these rooms are desolate so long.
O that the dust were thick upon my heart,
As it is now on hers! — Thou comest in time.

    Re-enter HUBERT.

    He looks surprised.

Hub. How got you here? [*with animation, yet in a suppressed
tone — in which the whole of the conversa-
tion is held, whatever its spirit.*

    Elin. I ask'd for thee. The fool,
That keeps your portal, left me in the hall.
'T was not the place. So I am here.
      Hub. 'T is well.
But better, that you need not come again.
Elin. Well? Know'st thou then this room? My better angel
Guided me hither, to dissolve my purpose.
But the same door let in the Devil. My eyes
Beheld this dust, [*sweeping her fingers passionately over the
books.*] and put dumb question to it;

And the mute witness told a tale ——

               Hub. Another

Had told much better.   Let your beadle-devil
Call into court yon picture.   Question that.
See you the rail in front and on your right,
Guarding a mountain foot-path?   Look sheer down :
That water is Lake Leman — and those walls
Are Chillon [20] Castle — and, behind the walls,
Yon menacing mountains ——

       Elin. [*putting her hand on his arm, and speak-*
             ing passionately, but still low.

      Stop ! I have seen enough.

Hub. Not heard, though.   Over the rail that figure leaning,
As if his neck were nothing, is my master —
Or leans as he did, when the Countess pass'd
With the young lady ——

       Elin. [*vehemently — yet in under tone.*
       Scoundrel !

          Hub. Have a care. —

My master painted it, and when Lord Capel,
Praising it, said he had surpass'd himself,
Sir Julian, smiling — with so sad a smile !
Gravely replied, " I painted it *with love.*"

Elin. Lord Capel understood him not.   I do.

            [*with clenched hands.*

Hub. [*smiles with satisfaction, and pursues maliciously, watching*
     her with keen expression.

There is another picture, lovelier still.
It seems to me to match our three *Vandykes*

Sir Peter [21] dotes on and King Charles would buy.
This too he painted ; but he never shows it.
It is the Lady Capel at half-length.

Elin. I 'll stab him to the heart !

        [*Moving passionately to the door.   But her voice is*
               not raised, though the tone is intenser.

          Hub. Pray find him first.

Doubtless this moment he is on his knees
Before that picture, praying as to a saint.
She never sat for it, yet 't is life itself.

Elin. Thou art a villain : but thou whett'st my purpose.
Hast made all sure ? [*firmly.*

        Hub. I have been sending now,
By my young lady's order, for her maid —
Who is her confidant, you know, — for pay —
As I am hers — for love —

         Elin. Both knavish parts,
Fitting the actors.

       Hub. And enjoy'd by you,
Sole audience. — But we will not quarrel, here,
For rank in villany. [*Elin. motions him impatiently to go on.*
               I sent a note,
Feigning the lady's wish to see her lord —
hastily.] I mean, the girl's lord — on the instant —

         Elin. [*contemptuously.*] Who
May be from home, or may not choose to come.

Hub. Who is at home, and who will fly to come.
Lovers, I thought that Mistress Morton knew,
Ere they grow tired, are very birds to move ;

And these be fresh ones.   Pardon me, again.

Elin. Thou art a devil! [*through her teeth.*

     Hub. I have practis'd much of late,
Under a mistress might keep school in Hell,
And hope one day to honor my instructress.
My life on 't, while we waste this precious time,
Lord Capel is but a stone's throw from the door.

Elin. And on this chance! —— [*scornfully and angrily.*
      Couldst thou not then have waited?
That message will betray thee, and mar all.

Hub. Content you; I had reasons.

     Elin. Reasons?   Thou hadst?
Why what art thou?

     Hub. Your workman, not your tool,
And creditor for wages, due too long.
Sir Julian's eyes are open'd nearly wide:
This night I saw it.   To-morrow, I must pack,
In any case.   Wouldst *thou* have waited?   Look!
      [*pointing to the picture.*

Elin. Reach me some paper — ink.
    [*He sets the paper before her, and examines
    the standish.*

     Hub. The ink is dry.
My master has been very long away.
But here be crayons — plenty.   They were pointed
A twelvemonth back.   He has not drawn since then. —
    [*Comes down the stage, while Elin. writes.*
She has got the devil in her now again:
Those thrusts went home.   To-morrow thou art mine,

By thy own compact.   When I wear thee ! —
>   [*Elin. rises.*

>   What !

Done already ? [*taking up the paper.*
>   *Elin.* Insolent wretch ! [*to herself, as he proceeds*
>   *to read.*

>   *Hub.* " Who trusts

" Unboundedly must often be deceiv'd.

" Women see no dishonor in deceit.

" Learn from a woman that.   Some hour this night,

" Your sister's rooms will lodge more guests than her." —

Pithy enough !   Sir Julian taught you that.

Elin. Lay 't where thou wilt.   Now lead me forth, at once.

Hub. And in good time.   By Heaven, I hear his step

Along the corridor !   *This* way.
>   [*drawing Elin. in a contrary direction*
>   *to what she was going.*

>   Still as death !

>   [*Exeunt.*

> *After an interval*
> *Enter*
> *from the opposite side,* SIR JULIAN.
> *His air is still profoundly melancholy ; but his dress,*
> *which has been changed for one of deep mourning,*
> *is no longer disordered, nor his person*
> *neglected.   He wears no sword.*

Sir Jul. Long unaccustom'd haunt, once more I greet thee !

Thy wholesome aspect is but little chang'd,
And doth reproach me for the much I am.
Yet, when I last beheld it —— O, no more,
That dreadful retrospect ! — And yet, how fit
That here it should awaken ! in this spot,
Deem'd consecrate to study and the muse,
But by love's folly desecrated.   Ah me !
The seeds are oft in gladness sown, whose fruits
Are sorrow-gather'd, and the holiday gait
Of thoughtless vanity leads the dance to crime !
Let spirits akin to mine mark that, and learn
The heart's most natural passion may become
Unlawful, and the indulgence that o'erlooks
The sacrosanctity of duty ever
Engenders, and is, sin.   Thou conscious window !
How well might Paradise be painted there,
But that its futile joys have cost me Eden !—
And the avenging angel's sword of fire
Gleams on me still.

*As he walks by the table pensively, his eye
is attracted by the paper.*

A paper ?   What, again ?
Wretched malignity ! — Who laid it there ?
Dares she invade my very house ?   Methought,
Even as I enter'd, some one quit the room. —
I 'll read once more. [*Peruses silently the writing.*
O falsehood's blackest filth ! —
Yet is the charge specific.   Frances' self
Shall brand it infamous.   No clearer way

To end all doubt, and put the mind at ease.

He rushes out, with a paper open in his hand, and
the scene, instantly shifting, reveals a corridor,
with doors opening into it in front, and
one at the end of the corridor on
the right of the scene,

as

SCENE III.

SIR JULIAN *comes forward from the left side,*
moving rapidly, as if toward the door at the other
end, behind which Voices are now heard. He stops short, and
seems as if riveted to the spot with dismay and hor-
ror (pressing his right hand to his forehead
with an expression of intense anguish,
while his left hand violently
crushes the paper it is
holding.)

Sir Jul. God keep me sane !

Voice of Capel (behind the scene, at the door indi-
cated) [elevated as in resentment.

Yes, Frances, go I will, —
But 't is to *him* / [*Interval of confused sound ; then the*
voice rises again with still more
vehemence.

Usurp'd authority ——

[*Again the interval.*

Tyrannical brother ——

Again a confused sound, as of a female voice expostuluting, and
of sobbing. SIR JULIAN, *starting from his stupor, springs*
forward as to cross the scene, and, when half-way, stops
again, as the voice of Capel is again heard.

What hast thou to fear ? —

No ! No ! — dear, dearest Frances, no !

SIR JULIAN *flings down the paper,*
and turning short round hurries from the
scene by the side he had entered. The next
instant he Re-enters with a naked sword, and rushes,
seemingly frantic with rage, across the scene. As he
reaches the door, it opens : CAPEL *comes forth, and receives*
the extended blade in his bosom. He scarcely moves.
Holding with one hand the door, which he was in
the act of closing when they encountered, he
presses the other on his wound, and look-
ing sorrowfully on Julian says
slowly :

Lord C. Thy hand
Is heavy on me, Julian. My first wife
Thou took'st from me : my second thou hast robb'd
Now of a husband.

SIR JULIAN *holding the sword, with the point a little dropped,*
stands, staring with dilated eyes on his victim, nor offers to
support him. LORD CAPEL *staggers in the midst of his*
reproach, and as he utters with difficulty the last
words, FRANCES, *from within, runs forward to*
the door, which slips from Capel's hand as she appears.

Fran. [as she approaches.

         Arthur! —   [*Coming out.*] Ah! —

           [*Capel sinks on the floor.*] O God!

             [*falling senseless over him.*

Sir Julian *stands in the same posture, with the same*
look, motionless as a statue, with eyes fixed like
stone ; and — after a brief interval, the
scene closes, slowly, on the group.

Scene IV.

AND THE LAST.

A room hung completely with black cloth.
Directly in front, far up the stage, a coffin raised on a scaffold
breasthigh, in the manner of a catafalque, and covered with
a violet-velvet pall, as the platform is with black cloth.
Wax-lights burning at the head and foot ; and on the top,
lying diagonally across the coffin, a naked sword. —
Over the catafalque a picture, covered with a black curtain,
with a long cord pendent to it, as if to draw aside the
curtain on occasion. The left side of the scene represents
a long casement-window ; the right, a door.

SIR JULIAN *is seen*

*seated in a chair with his back to the coffin. His long hair
is matted, and hangs in disorder over his forehead; the
collar of his shirt is open; his dress (deep mourning, as
in preceding Scene) otherwise disordered. His hands hang
down beside him helplessly, his head droops on his shoulders. He is motionless, as in a stupor, and in all respects
showing the most absolute and desperate moral and physical prostration, or paralysis from moral grief, the horror
of past scenes, and long sleeplessness, that the power of the
Actor can delineate.*

*Saving the light necessary to relieve the full misery of his state,
the stage is in darkness, except where lighted behind him
by the candles of the catafalque.*

*After some minutes, the
door opens, and
Enter,
as prepared for a journey, and veiled,*
ELINOR.

*She comes slowly before Sir Julian. She throws
back her veil. He covers his face with
both hands, and groans.*

Elin. [*answering to his manner.*

Yes, I am Elinor — Elinor Morton — Elinor
Whom you once lov'd, and who now loves you still,
Even while she hates. I am come, Sir Julian Mandeville,

To ask you where is that elysium now,
You promis'd.   Are you happy, sir ?   Am I ?
Groan on ; the fruit you gather is of your planting :
I hope it suits you.   Full indeed has been

SIR JULIAN *drops his arms, and resumes in all*
respects his previous attitude and air.

Your cup of bitterness ; more full and bitter
Than I intended ; and I see 't is drain'd
Even to the dregs.   If I could pity you,
Now would I.   Not a word ? [*her voice losing its depth and*
solemnity and growing more sharp and
womanly in tone.

Not even a look ?

Too bitterly resentful to reproach me ?
You need not be.   Sir Julian Mandeville,
You are the wronger, You.   Your precious wisdom, —
Which, moonstruck dreamer, you would teach a girl,
Who better lov'd your eyes than all the stars,
Your knowledge, sir, — you sit there like a stone !
Your wisdom, I say, and knowledge should exalt you
Above such littleness ; but what to women
Hath Heaven given, to defend their rights,
But pride, and envy, and *revenge ?*   Good night —
As when you had dragg'd me to the brink of ruin,
Then flung me back, lest you should fall yourself,
You said to me — good night ; good night, forever.

As she has her hand on the lock of the door,
it is pushed open softly, and

Enter HUBERT
cloaked and girt, as for a journey, with hat on &c.
He takes her by the sleeve with a signal of
impatience. Withdrawing violently
her arm, ELINOR *dashes him*
backward.

Stand back ! fool ! dog ! Hired servant of my lover,
Dar'st thou to put a finger on his mistress,
Except to touch her shoes ? Mean, treacherous villain !
Think'st thou I 'd stoop to such a thing as thou ?
Thou be my master ? Learn, to serve her ends
When Elinor plots with wretches like thyself,
She pays their services in other coin :
Such as that ! [*flinging a seemingly heavy purse in his*
face.
There ; spend it like to Judas
As thou hast earn'd it. [*Hub., with a threatening gesture of*
rage and determined revenge, Exit.

SIR JULIAN, *during the preceding brief*
passage, has looked steadily at Elinor. — She now
turns again her face to him, and her whole manner at once
changes, from the violence of scornful resentment
and irritated passion to tender emotion.
She moves slowly, and even timidly,
towards him, — her eyes moist,
her lips quivering, her step
unsteady.

Her voice is sweet, low, and mournful.

Julian.

He moves not, nor takes his eyes off her.   She ap-
proaches him, still slowly, — touches him.   He does not stir.

You are much chang'd.

[*she speaks tremulously,*
while, passing her hands over his forehead, she puts back
his hair, holds it thus a minute, and gazes on his face.

You are much chang'd — very much. —   Could I have
thought —

By the motion of her eyelids, she seems to
shed tears, slowly and silently.

But 't is no matter — we have both — both suffer'd. —
She bends down her head — she touches his
forehead with her lips.

It is the last. [*to herself and muttered.*
She turns from him to leave him.
But Sir Julian, *with a shiver over all his*
frame, rises suddenly.   She pauses, and watches him,
fearfully. —   Sound without as of a violent wind, which,
during the rest of the scene increases to a storm,
accompanied at intervals by the rushing
sound of a shower.

Sir Jul. Stay. —   Hark !   Was that the wind ?
'T is a sad night.   The winter days and I
Are going out with rough music.   Ending meet
For both of us ! — for me 't is.   How the wind
Roars in the chimney and sweeps along the casement !
I like its tune — now rising, and now falling —

And the rain's hiss betwixt.   Hear 't there!   Who
knoweth?
There may be spirits that ride the unseen blast:
'T is a brave night to gallop in!   Howl on:
I am coming soon, if 't is for me ye cry.

> *He goes to the casement and opens it.* ELINOR
> *moves hastily, but still timidly, towards*
> *him, and seems to fear his motive.*

Elin. [*imploringly and sobbing.*

Julian!

Sir Jul. My brain is burning.   I would lean
Out at the window.   I want the cold night wind
And the strong rain to beat upon my head.

He leans out for a few moments, while ELINOR, *with her*
> *hands before her face, endeavors to stifle her sobs.*

'T is not a breath of air nor drop of water
Cools the mind's fever. [*He speaks musingly again, his head*
> *bent down, — Elinor continuing all the*
> *time to watch him anxiously.*

We must sleep for that —
Sleep sound and long — close-cover'd, where the rain
Soaks through but wets not, and the wind's deep base
Roars all unheeded.

> *Elin.* [*in an imploring tone, and with an ex-*
> *pression of terror mixed with affec-*
> *tion and remorse.*

Julian!

Sir Jul. [*listening at the open casement.*

Revelers!   Hist!

*Voices are heard singing without, below the window,
and at a little distance.   The air is solemn and
mournful, and the movement slow.*

*Voices. They lie below, asleep beneath the snow,
And the morning-drum shall waken them no more.*[22]

Sir Jul. Strange! with my solemn purpose how accordant!
The sentiment they sing they-feel not; yet
They do it well: their voices on the blast
Rise grandly, heard by fits.

                  Voices. *They lie below* ——

Sir Jul. Practice — practice.   Soon from playhouse-tears [23]
We gather that sad moral of the heart.

Voices. The morning-drum shall waken them no more.

Sir Jul. Thanks: and farewell, my last of human sounds.

                        [closes the casement.

The morning-drum shall waken me no more.

                    [Moves towards the catafalque.

Elin. [*throwing herself on her knees and speaking with deep
anguish.*

    Julian! —   O God! O God!

    *He moves on without regarding her. — 'She
grasps his dress.*

                  Do you not know me?

Sir Jul. Woman! Know thee? Too well. Think'st thou
indeed
That I am mad? or have forgotten? Look!

                  [pointing to the coffin.

Where is Lord Capel? where my sister? where ——

                  [his voice falls.

I cannot ask thee where is Euphrosine.²⁴

Elin. [bows her head on his hand — sobbing.

    Oh! oh!

      Sir Jul. [shaking her off.

           Tears? murd'ress! on my hand? from thee?
Will they wash out the blood that has been spill'd?
The blood upon that blade? the innocent blood
That mix'd with it, and made a double murder
For thee, as me? Last night —— Last night, my sister —
My only sister — my first-lov'd — my last —
My beautiful, and good —— I must not weep —
Not before thee; 't would wake the immaculate dead
Thy presence outrages. Look on that coffin.
What had the angelic being so silent there
Done wrong to thee?

        Elin. [groveling on the floor.

        O spare me!

         Sir Jul. Didst thou spare?

Elin. I knew not — I call God to witness! ——

          Sir Jul. Peace!

Last night — she died. Her crimeless heart had broke
Over her husband's body, slain by me,
Her brother. From her mouth I saw the blood
Gush out a torrent, and mix with that I shed.
She died — and bless'd me — murmuring my name.

    He stops a moment — as overcome. ELINOR *con-
tinues to sob — but low.*

I will not desecrate her ashes further

By thy most wicked presence. This remains

    VOL. II.—17

To crown thy work; the last blood-offering,
As he speaks, he takes solemnly and reverently the
sword from the coffin, and kisses the blade.

But not atoning sacrifice.   The altar —
Behold it deck'd [*indicating the coffin.*

        — the priest prepar'd — the victim —
Elin. [*throwing open her arms.*

    O ready!   Let thy blade drink deep — and bless thee!
Sir Jul. [*shortening the sword in his grasp.*

    Drink deep it shall — but of a purer stream. [*Buries*
                      the sword in his breast.

ELINOR, as in unutterable anguish, draws her breath
    through her teeth, like one in sharp agony. —
        SIR JULIAN *draws the sword out, and*
        speaks painfully, looking on the blade.

'T is the last Mandeville — thou gallant Arthur —
Wets with his life thy stiffen'd gore. —
    Supporting himself by the chair, he turns his
        face to the coffin.

                      My sister!   [*sinks*
                      into the chair.

Life ebbs apace —   O that some hand — would — draw —
That curtain! [*Elinor moves to do it.*

        — Not — not thine!   Dare not —
With thy — impure — thy hand! —   I will essay.
    Rising with difficulty, he staggers towards
        the picture.

Where is the cord? [*groping.*

        — My eyes grow dim — I die —

And cannot see thee [25] ! — Frances ! Euphrosine !
Uttering these names suddenly with a loud,
eager, and alarmed cry, SIR JULIAN
falls dead.

ELINOR, who has moved upward with him, with
her arms spread, as if to sustain him, yet
without daring to touch him, buries
her face in her hands, and sinks
on her knees, beside his
body.   And the

Curtain slowly falls.

THE LAST MANDEVILLE

1.—P. 271. THE LAST MANDEVILLE] An adaptation to the stage of the author's novel, *Confessions of a Poet.*

A copy of this play was entrusted in London, in 1851–52, to Mr. Benjamin Webster, Sr., of the Haymarket Theatre ; and I never could get it out of his possession. Remembering what the late Mrs. Shaw once said to me, — that a playwright could so use, and often did, another author's composition, that he would not be able to identify his own property, — I have thought it well to make this memorandum, lest at some future day I may be charged with having borrowed what in fact had been stolen from myself.

2.—P. 273. *Then, when* etc.] The Stage may omit from this point to " Proceed " on p. 274, — eighteen verses.

3.—P. 275. *Say on,* etc.] Omit to " *Fran.* No, not for worlds ! " fourteen verses.

4.—P. 276. *I found there Uncle.*] Make the remaining hemistich to read, " After he was gone " ; and then, omit to " How odd, etc." on p. 278.

5.—P. 280. *I'll not forgive him.*] Omit here eight verses; then convert the ten next into one, reading it:

    "Is 't Frances? Enter, if 't is thou, my sister."

6.—P. 288. *That some less scrupulous lover —*] After this break, omit to "Oh! polluted?" nineteen verses. Or, exscind the entire soliloquy.

7.—P. 289. *What's Elinor to me? I now to Elinor?*] There is a resemblance here to a well-known verse of Shakspeare's. I point it out, lest somebody should do it for me.

    "What's Hecuba to him or he to Hecuba,
      That he should weep for her?" (*Hamlet*. II. 2.)

Again, previously:

    O Elinor! — That woman should have writ
    Her faith with water! Twelve, but twelve brief months!
    And so complete a change! Her heart alone,
    Why that were monstrous! but, to give up all!
    All! all! and in twelve —— Death and Hell! the work
    Is scarce the half that old. Six months! And I —

      "That it should come to this!
    But two months dead! — Nay, not so much; not two.
    So excellent a king; that was, to this,
        etc. etc.
    .   .   . And yet, within a month —
    Let me not think on't. Frailty, thy name is woman." (*Ib.* I. 2.)

These resemblances are purely accidental, arising out of the character and situation. None but a fool would, designedly or undesignedly, make such an imitation, or, in the latter case, would leave it uncorrected. I am not conscious of having done either; and both passages are in idea and in construction as truly my own, as if *Hamlet* had never been written, or Shakspeare, for the glory, and at the same time the injury, of English dramatic literature, had never been born.

8.—P. 300. — *Meillerie* —] The double *l est mouillée*, as the French say. Therefore, pronounce: *Mail'yer-ie.*

9 —P. 301. *And this is where,* etc. etc.] For the Stage, read, — as more directly intelligible:

> And this is where the heroic Bonnevard,
> For Freedom's sake and Truth, his limbs resign'd
> To fetters ? And the aged martyr's steps
> Have worn the vault's rock pavement, as they tell.

But, for the Stage, the entire Scene, together with the two next following, may, and perhaps had better be, omitted, and Sc. V. be made a direct continuation of Sc. I., by omitting, at the close of V., the name "Euphrosine". — All these Scenes however, as likewise Sc. VIII. (which is marked for omission,) have that attractiveness for the eye which has become a main requisite in theatrical pieces and is at all times, whatever the character of the drama, an advantage in representation.

I may add for the critical of my readers, that there is not sufficient time between the first and second scenes of this Act, to allow even in imagination the change of movement and place on the part of *Julian.* It is one of those faults of construction to which the laxness of the romantic drama tempts imperceptibly, and which, in that drama, are rarely detected and never condemned. I am only now, while the play is going through the press, aware of an oversight which discovered sooner I should have endeavored to correct, if indeed, but for the desire of reproducing the Novel as nearly as possible (an ill-considered vanity, but excusable under the circumstances which attended the publication of that work,) the Act itself had been written at all in the form in which it now appears.

10.—P. 313. SCENE VII.] This and the following Scene are to be omitted altogether in the representation. They are unimportant to the action, and lengthen the Act too much for the Stage. The Drop therefore falls on the *Exit* of Elinor at the close of Scene VI.

11.—P. 348. *Or force even Dryden,* etc.] Omit this verse; also, below, "forgive my heedless vein."

12.—P. 352. *That,* etc.] Omit from here to the period.

13.- P. 352. —*Villiers* —] The profligate Duke of Buckingham.

14.—P. 354. *When other,* etc.] Omit, from here to "But do not mock me" — seventeen verses.

15.—P. 355. — *foresaw* —] After this word, omit to "That I" — Then, in the same part, the verse "Though thou art, *etc*", and "thy love's quest Meet ready answer."

16.—P. 355. *Think not of me.*] Omit. Then, in the same part, all after the semicolon to "my lord," (inclusive.)

17.—P. 355. *Sweet lady, no.*] After this, omit to the interrogation-mark. Then, the two verses before the last.

18.—P. 360. — *Wilmot* —] Earl of Rochester.

19.—P. 361. He comes down.] Or, starting up, at the 2d line after, — "Ah! can it be? etc.," — as more natural; or, at the middle of the 3d line after, — "deep darkness"; or even at the 4th, — "He will not see her." But the Actor will not much regard the direction, but adopt the movement at his pleasure. And, in fact, it is a matter of convenience and of effect.

20.—P. 377. — *Chillon* —] Here again the double "l" is softened and made fluent, as in "Meillerie." Pron. *Shil'yon.*

21.—P. 378. *Sir Peter —*] Lely.

22.—P. 390. They lie below, *etc.*] From a French song : —
> " Ils sont là-bas, qui dorment sous la neige,
> Et le tambour ne les reveillera plus."

23.—P. 390. *Practice — practice.* Etc.] The long pauses and the double trochee make the rythm full, though, to count, it wants a syllable. It is a matter of choice with the writer and not necessity

> *Practice — mere practice. Soon from playhouse-tears*

would satisfy all the requisitions; but it is not so natural. *Sir Jul.* still talks musingly, without paying the least regard to Elinor:—

> Practice — [*pausing thoughtfully.*] — practice. [*pause.*] Soon, *etc.*

24.—P. 391. *I cannot ask thee where is Euphrosine.*] As it is the final accent alone which marks the length of the verse, all such verses as this, though in constant use by the best writers, are really defective. But, to give it due length, as thus:

> *I cannot ask of thee, where, where is Euphrosine.*

would give a different sentiment from that I intended.

25.—P. 393. *— thee !*] Revising for the press, I find this pronoun equivocal. It applies, not to Elinor, but to Euphrosine, who is supposed to be the subject of the curtained picture.

17*

THE HEART'S SACRIFICE

MDCCCLXIX

CHARACTERS

MELVILLE, *Edith's accepted lover.*

HAMPTON, *another of her suitors.*

SAVILLE, *Melville's friend, and wooer of Athlia.*

ATH'LIA, *Melville's cousin.*

EDITH, *her younger sister.*

BERTHA, *their widowed aunt.*

———

SCENE. *A castle in England, and its grounds, — the life-estate of Bertha, and joint residence of herself, her nephew and nieces.*

EPOCH. *The beginning of the 17th century.*

THE HEART'S SACRIFICE

ACT THE FIRST

SCENE I. *The platform in the rear of the Castle.*

MELVILLE. EDITH.

Mel. For this consent, lov'd Edith, take my thanks:
My thanks? that is too cold: the passionate vow
Of my heart's deepest gratitude, and love
Which will not cease, I think, to live and glow
While life has left one heart-beat.
                              Ed. So, I read,
Thinks every untry'd lover; but the heart .
Throbs not the less with divers passions, whereof
The weakest grows to be, in time, that love
Which was to out-pulsate all the rest.
                              Mel. A love
Unsolid and sensuous, not like mine for thee,

Bas'd on unperishing worth, nor built alone
Of animal longing and the fragile sense
Of outward beauty, albeit thereof thy store
Is vast, if not exhaustless.

Ed. It is well
Thou hast not overlook'd it. I had taken else
To my mirror, and ask'd there, was the altar gone,
Evanish'd like its images, whereat
Thou mad'st diurnal worship and sent up prayer
As of a soul in anguish.

Mel. Both sincere.
Hence my deep gratitude and o'er-welling joy,
That thou didst list me unworthy, and, goddess-like,
Gave to long homage and the ceaseless fume
Of love's sweet incense what were not vouchsaf'd
To personal merit.

Ed. Am I then so vain ?
Or thou so humble ? That thou art preferr'd
Should satisfy thee. To be so preferr'd
Implieth large worth that puts thee to the fore
Of those thou wast preferr'd to.

Mel. But in vain
It had pleaded, had not Athlia's generous self
Lent sisterly persuasion and the force
Of her great self-denial. What a soul
Is hers, O cousin Edith !

Ed. It is good,
And little selfish. Yet I fail to see
Much generous abnegation in an act

Self might have prompted.   That she lent her aid
To incline me to thy suit, was that her heart
Is given to Saville.

     Mel. But her fortune then ?
Ed. She must have lost it by our uncle's will.
Mel. No ; for that bids, if Athlia and I
 Should not agree to marry, then the one
 With whom the fault lay should unto the other
 Abandon all.   She only had to wait
 Till I had won thee ; yet she gave up all,
 That I might win thee.

     Ed. Since thou seest it thus,
 I wonder that thou didst not woo and win
 My sister.   Interest then and love perhaps
 Were hand in hand, and Athlia had been spar'd
 The sacrifice that lifts her in thine eyes.
Mel. Canst thou be jealous, Edith ? thou, so bright
 In beauty and the grace of subtle wit ?
 Leave to sad Athlia, thou who too art good,
 The homage due her goodness.   Unalloy'd
 It is, I am sure ; and Saville has no place
 Nearer her heart than I have.

     Ed. Which perhaps
 Is in the core.   But list Aunt Bertha.

    Enter BERTHA.

       Aunt,
How tenders Athlia Saville ?   Melville here
Thinks her still heart-whole, and of love alone

For himself and me, half stoic and half nun,
Turning her back on fortune.

      Ber. Not the part
Worst-favor'd in her.

      Mel. O aunt, though sad and wan
With illness, (if it is ill-health indeed
Gives her those mournful and appealing eyes
And pales her once red cheek,) her features still
Are comely, if not handsome. Saville finds,
Nor do I wonder, a soul-look in her face
More winning than mere beauty.

      Ber. As in his,
With its coarse outlines, Athlia seems to see
But manly boldness and the marks of that
She fancies great in herself. They are close friends
Thou knowest, and I know are something more.

Mel. I am glad of it, aunt; although it lessens not
  My debt to her goodness. But I see not why,
  If she loves him, as he I believe has love,
  More than a friend's, for her, she should so pine.

Ber. 'T is of her gloomy temper and grim pride
  Of righteousness.

      Mel. No, no; she has no pride,
And least of all in what is most her own:
Nor call that gloom which is so touching-sad
And knows not sourness.

      Ed. Melville finds enough
The hand he has won, and yearns now for a heart
Before mispriz'd.

Mel. O Edith!

          Ber. Melville knows

That Athlia from her childhood has been grave,
While thou wast alway cheerful, and he chose
The sunshine to disport in. Let him bask
In its warmth and brightness still, nor be thou vex'd
His eyes at times should turn to the shade, whose gloom
Attracts by contrast, and may be relief
To wholesome sunlight, though he loves it not.

Mel. It is nor light nor shadow, aunt, though each
    Without the other would lose effect. I love
    My cousin none the less that I revere
    Her sister. But that shadow! it grows black
    As death. I sometimes think it is of death,
    And shiver in its chillness.

          Ber. Athlia's health

Perhaps was never good, even when, a child,
She appear'd most round and rosy. It is like,
Her body's weakness adds a deeper hue
To her mind's fix'd gloom. — But to the sunshine now.
Is the day nam'd, my children?

          Mel. Edith, speak.

Ed. Thou hast not ask'd me, Melville, all this time.

Mel. First, in my joy; then —— Ah, that beaming smile!
    Yes, this *is* sunshine. When shall be the day?
    To-morrow? No? Next week? The next? Nor that?

Ed. 'T is the first quarter of the moon now with us.
    When the next moon shall show the selfsame phase,
    Then ask, and thou shalt have.

     Mel. Till then — in pledge
Of our betrothal.
     Ed. [*as he puts the ring on her finger.*
   It is pretty. Go
Now with Aunt Bertha, and make Athlia know
Of our near marriage. Thou must be prepar'd
To see her startled.
     Ber. But with joy.
       Ed. Even joy
May prove a shock to the broken.
      Mel. In this case,
I think not. But I shall be wary and slow.
Wilt thou not iu with us, Edith ?
      Ed. No, awhile
I will walk here in the stillness, and grow calm.
    [*Exeunt, into the Castle, Mel. and Ber.*
How blind he is! Aunt too. But she, in hate
Of Athlia, whose great soul she envies, or fears
Looks down upon her own, has fail'd to see
What breaks too often on my jealous sense. Thus some
Come to this world fools made, while others grow
To be such by prejudice, peering with dim eyes
Through passion's haze or the two-sided glass
Of interest which dwarfs or swells at will.
I too hate Athlia ; but 't is that I feel
I have wrong'd and wrong her. Yet, is that then sure ?
Left to himself, must Melville still have chosen
Beauty and grace, and left plain-hooded sense,
And virtue ungainly, unador'd. That she

Is suffering, may it not be from disease
Now first develop'd? And am I then to blame? ·

Enter, from the left,
HAMPTON.

Here comes the best, as boldest, of my slaves.[1]
Hamp. Fair Edith! To my wish; and all alone.
Ed. Is that too to thy wish? 'T is not for long.
Wilt thou come in?
    Hamp. No. But a moment, pray.
It is so pleasant here! so still and sweet!
And thou, in the midst of all this natural pomp
Of lawn, and forest sparkling in the sun,
And waving in the breeze its many heads
And arms toward thee in homage and in joy,
And short-liv'd flowers with their amorous breath
Wooing thy kisses, seem'st to be of all
Creative goddess. Let me worship too.
Ed. What! with thy breath? or arms? or head?
      Hamp. With all,
If thou wilt; but most with the heart, as I have done
Since first I knew thee.
    Ed. But must do no more.
Hamp. No more?
    Ed. What pity, that like the trees and flowers
Thou canst not woo and worship without heart!
Hamp. What should that say?
    Ed. Even this: I am betroth'd.
Hamp. It cannot be! Thou couldst not do such wrong.

Ed. There is my troth-ring.

     Hamp. Let me take it off,
  And give thee another.

       Ed. It is now too late.
Why wast thou backward ?   Melville got before.

Hamp. I was deceiv'd : I thought thy uncle's will
  Had tied him to thy sister.

        Ed. She refus'd.

Hamp. Refus'd him ?   And the fortune ?

         Ed. 'T was to save
The fortune for my sake, lest Melville should,
In love for me, resign it, Athlia came
To woo me on his part, annulling thus,
And elsewhere openly, her claim for aye
To share that great bequest.

      Hamp. Stupendous deed !
So vast a fortune !

     Ed. But she lov'd him not,
And knew his love for me.

      Hamp. 'T was not the less,
Nay, it was more, high-soul'd.   What woman else
But had taken with him the fortune, or, without,
Had kept both shares for herself ?

       Ed. Why none.   And thus,
Melville and I are partners.   Let us in.

Hamp. Edith !   Forgive.   But what have I to do ?

Ed. Not shoot thyself, nor drown, nor make a noose
  Of thy sword-belt, but, a man, accept as fate
  What cannot be averted.   Talk no more

In the strain thou hast indulg'd in.   It nor suits
Me nor thyself, and jeopards fame with both.

Hamp. But what shall bind the thoughts ?   These still will act,
And build thy altars in the heart, where prayer
Shall be more fervent unspoken.

                      Ed. But, unheard,
The worshiper flags, then tires, till by and by
The altars are thrown down, or yield their place
To those of some new goddess.

                Hamp. Not with me.
I am thy adorer ever.

            Ed. Lightly said,
As with all promises.

          Hamp. Shall I prove it ?

                   Ed. How ?

Hamp. Fly from these walls with me to-night.   Ere morn,
Thou shalt be lady of all I own : not worth
The double wealth of Melville, but enough
To keep thee in ease and honor in that state
Whereto thou wast born.

               Ed. That thou wast heard uncheck'd
Impute to my surprise, which kept me dumb.
Hast thou consider'd, Hampton?   In these walls
Thou art a guest.   Wouldst thou break trust, and faith
Imply'd, or strip me in thy passion of that
Thou never couldst replace — my truth ?   Thy love
Is shallow, or but self-deep.

            Hamp. No, Edith, no ;
I prize both truth and honor.   Said I not,

I worship ?   Is thy soul then nought to me ?
But love is not deliberate : it is thou
Wast hasty and didst do my passion wrong.

Ed. No, thou who wast slow and lukewarm.   Let us in.
Speak never again of this.   Come.   No ! stay thou.
We should look guilty, seen together thus.   [*Exit above.*

Hamp. Ah, dread'st thou that ?   To fear suspect of guilt
Comes of the conscience.   I may hope withal.

[*Exit to the left.*

SCENE II.

A   room   in   the   Castle.

ATHLIA. MELVILLE.

Mel. Sing me the songs I love ; one, only one !
Thy voice is sweeter, Athlia, when thou sing'st,
Than any sound I know.   See ! I have brought
Life's roses to thy cheeks.   Thou art not so ill
To-day, then, cousin ?
                    Ath. Yet too feeble quite
To sing as I would : and then, my soul is sad.
I could not sing a sad song with a heart

Deject already.

    Mel. Why is it deject?
Would I could heal thee, cousin ! Now again
I have call'd the flush to thy cheek. Thou art not well:
Something disturbs thee, Athlia. But I have news
I know will cheer thee.

          Ath. 'T is then to thy good.

Mel. O greatly, cousin. Canst thou not then guess,
Thou who hast done so much to bring to pass
What tends most to my good?

          Ath. 'T is of thyself
And Edith thou wouldst tell. She has ——

          Mel. Consented.
Athlia ! what ails thee?

          Ath. I am faint.

          Mel. Sit down.
I was very selfish. Edith warn'd me too
'T would startle thee : thou art so quick to feel,
With those poor nerves.

          Ath. It is over now. Mind not.
I will stand up. I am well again. Dost see?

Mel. I see thou smilest : but oh ! so sad a smile
It brings tears to my eyes.

          Ath. Thou foolish boy !

Mel. I sometimes think indeed I have been foolish,
To love thee not far better, cousin Athlia,
Than Edith, — thou who art so good. —

          Ath. Hush, hush !

Mel. And I do love thee, Athlia ; not indeed

As I love Edith; but as one might love
An angel that watch'd over him, in blood
Immortal, but with human smiles and tears
For his joys and sorrows. —

Ath. When will be the day?

Mel. A·month from to-morrow, Edith says.

Ath. A month —

From — to-morrow? It is — it is — soon.

Mel. My God! thou art ——— . Help there!

Ath. No, no, hush.

My heart — a little faintness ——— I shall — soon ———
Let me lean on thee. Tell nobody, Melville.
I shall — soon be — better. I — I ——— [*swoons.*

Mel. Athlia!

Drop falls.

ACT THE SECOND

SCENE I. *A room in the apartment of Bertha.*

BERTHA,
*at a writing-desk, looking over
some written instrument.*

Enter EDITH.
Whereupon, BERTHA *hurriedly returns the parchment
to the desk, and shuts and locks the latter, taking out the key.*

Ber. Ah, my bright child!   Thou com'st in time ; in time,
I mean for my instant thought, and what thereon
I would devise and counsel.   Should thy sister
Wed Saville ——

   Ed. That she will not.

       Ber. That she will.

He loves her. —

   Ed. Admires her.

       Ber. Well.   And she in turn
May love him. —

   Ed. No, I am sure not.

       Ber. Be that so :
She may withal accept him.

     Ed. And refus'd

Melville !
 VOL. II.—18

Ber. Why not?   This loving is caprice
Of fancy often, oft a mere return
Of grateful vanity.   Saville, Melville swears,
Is noble of mind as blood; both subtle points
Of cogency with a maid who apes, like her,
Scorn of things vulgar and affects to soar
To acts magnanimous.

          Ed. Well, conceive that so.
Saville is here to-day.   Suppose he press
His suit to Athlia, which, with her plain face,
Pallid and seeming wo-worn, is the last
Of fancies probable; say that she accept, —
Which I maintain she will not, — what comes then?

Ber. The loss belike of thy fortune, of that part
At least thy mope-ey'd sister flung away.

Ed. Aunt!

   Ber. Would her lord submit, think'st thou, to waive
His right to reclaim it?   It may be reclaim'd.
Thou look'st aghast, my love.   Well mayst thou be.
There is, in thy uncle's hand ——

          Ed. Another will?

Ber. Some later day, I may tell thee.   Now, enough
Thou art warn'd of thy danger.   With thy charms and arts,
Thou mayst avert from Athlia the mishap
Of finding her bounty futile.   I must go.

   She has been playing with the key of the
desk all this while, and now, while concluding, shuts it up
   in a press, the key of which, though turning it,
       she leaves in the door.

My secret, for thy own sake, will be safe.
Let the grave bury it with thee. [*Exit.*

       Ed. That is sure.
But first I must have it. Was it not that leaf
She held as I came in ? She put it by
In seeming hurry, but hath left the key
As if to tempt me, or perhaps in trust
Of my honor. It may be so ; but nature's stress
Is more imperious than the law of right,
And self-defence rules paramount. [*Takes out the parchment*

        What is here ?
A codicil — dated just before his death.
Ah, and he says : because of his esteem,
Growing day by day, for Athlia, whom he deems
Noblest of women, and well-assur'd her choice
Will be most wise and right, he here revokes
The will's conditions as regards her only,
Making absolute his gift in her behalf,
With his last love and blessing beyond death. —
So Uncle had his senses at the last.
I shall have mine. Why had not Aunt too hers ;
The codicil is witness'd by none else ?
Perhaps she felt a superstitious dread
To burn the good man's writing. Means she then
That I should ? I too dread ; but solely her :
She must not know I have seen it. But I can :
So mar both signatures, they shall in law
Be held as forgeries, while they seem unchang'd.
She sits down at the desk, and takes up a pen, but pauses.

'T is a sad work, and makes me almost thrill
With horror.   But I have no choice.   And then,
Is 't worse than Aunt herself did?   And what wrong
Can it do to Athlia, who cares not? —   It is over.
   Restores the parchment, and locking the desk returns
        the key to the press.
So far, 't is well.   But, to make doubly sure,
The courtly Saville shall from Eros' eyes
Strip off his blind, that he may shoot more straight.
I might, whate'er betid, have try'd my charms.
But now, [*gazing on a mirror.*

      — look, eyes, thy sweetest coyest gaze,
Take, lips, the lure of thy most amorous smiles:
Thou want'st not Saville, Athlia, nor shalt have.
                      [*Exit.*

Scene II.

The same as Scene II. in Act I.

Athlia.   Saville.

Ath. How canst thou urge affection?   Seest thou not
   I am unworthy to return thy love,
   So feeble and care-worn?
                Sav. Even that thou art so
Gives tenderness to a feeling which is fed,

Not by thy outward graces, but the charms
That spring of the soul alone.

     Ath. To earn this praise
From Melville's friend is pleasant. Let my thanks,
Esteem, my friendship if thou wilt, requite it.
'T is all I can give, and more thou shouldst not ask.

Sav. O Athlia,— let me, without being judg'd
Bold and familiar, as thy cousin's friend
So call thee when alone ——

    Ath. At all times so,
Or by what name thou wilt; the modest lips
Of Master Saville never can use speech
That is presumptuous, nor his courtly modes
Appear familiar : and to be address'd,
By Melville's friend, as if I was a cousin,
Is grateful compliment.

    Sav. Since thou hold'st me so,
O gentle lady, it makes what I would ask
Less difficult. Let thy friendship, thy esteem,
As thou say'st, be mine, until a warmer feeling
Requite my passion; if not love itself,
Yet something nearer what a loving man
Asks in the woman he would woo and wed.

Ath. That hope not. There be reasons ——

     Sav. Thou art ill !
Let me bring water.

   Ath. No, 't is often so. —
Thou seest how poor a wife I should make. Speak not:
I know what thou wouldst say. There are other maids.

A man like thee, so fitted every way
To win the loveliest, noblest in the land,
Cannot be long heart-vacant.   Here, with me,
'T is a vain quest.

    Sav. Yet haply ——

      Ath. In no time
Canst thou prevail.   Thou mayst increase indeed
The honor in which I hold thee and stand next,
If thou dost not now, to Melville in my love;
(Thou hear'st; it is a strong phrase :) but beyond
Can never be.

    Sav. Thou griev'st and gladd'st me both.
Second to Melville, for whose sake thou hast done ——
Ath. What I would double, as I would die to-morrow
To make him blest.

    Sav. Indeed?

      Ath. What else ?   Thou hast heard
We were brought up together, 'neath this roof.
Ah happy days, when I was all in all
To Melville, and when he ——   Though he is chang'd,
As natural, in his manhood, loving now
Another with not now a brother's love,
Yet I am still the sister that I was
In those glad days of childhood when my cheek
Was red with health and my fresh heart so light.
Sav. How well the tears that stand i' those eyes become thee!
Let me dare say it, who praise therein thy soul,
Which is my deity.   Wilt thou in one time
Call for more worship, yet refuse to fill

The shrine I have built thee ?

     Ath. Keep it for a form

Of some true goddess, and let me at her feet

Sit as thy sister. Thou mayst be to me

Indeed a brother, all that Melville was

In earlier days, perhaps is now, if so

Thou wilt be to him a brother.

      Sav. Am I not ? What then

Wilt thou have me do to prove it ?

      Ath. Thou shalt know ;

But not to-day. My cousin is, I fear,

In peril of losing —— No, no ! not to-day.

And perhaps I am wrong too. Heaven grant it so !

When I can doubt no more, then shalt thou learn

What thou must do for Melville. But meanwhile

Say nothing to him — even of what thou hast heard

That not concerns him. I am now quite spent.

Thou wilt pardon me. [*Giving him her hand. He raises*

      it to his lips.

    Is that a brother's kiss ?

      [*with a melancholy smile.*

Sav. No, that should be on the forehead.

      Ath. When thy shrine

Receives its goddess, thou mayst place it there.

She sinks on a couch, seemingly exhausted ; and, as

  Saville *bows reverently to retire, the*

    Drop falls.

ACT THE THIRD

SCENE I. *The platform, as in Act I. Sc. I.*

EDITH. HAMPTON.

Hamp. Only put off, one month — one little month,
  This hated marriage, Edith!
                        Ed. To what good?
  'T will not reprieve thee. I have said, this ring
  Shall sparkle on my finger, till I take
  A plainer one at the altar — not from thee.
Hamp. But 't will at least brief respite be; and that
  Is much to the wretch condemn'd.
                        Ed. So have it then.
  Now, do not kiss my fingers! Hampton, think;
  Thou putt'st us both in peril. Go.
                      Hamp. To-night,
  Thou wilt be here again?
                Ed. No. If I come,
  Thou must not follow. What! my hand again?
  When I forbid thee? There. We shall be seen.
  Go, nor be foolish.
             Hamp. Angel! [*Exit, to left.*
                   Ed. And in time.

Lo, where the cause of respite — my new slave.

Enter, from the right,
MELVILLE *and* SAVILLE.

Mel. Was not that Hampton ?   Which way hath he gone ?
Ed. To the brook, I think.

    Mel. To fish ?

       Ed. He bore no rod.
He talk'd of a stroll to the lake, — would have me go.
Mel. Then thou wilt hardly now make one with us.
 Shall I leave Saville with thee, or wilt thou spare him ?
 I know thou lik'st him ; but he is pledg'd to stay
 Till our marriage, Edith.

    Ed. Which will give more time
Than thou think'st for.   Thou must let the day go by,
For another moon at least.

    Mel. Another moon ?
O Edith !   And thy promise ?

     Ed. It is thine ;
But do not press it, cousin.   'T is unright,
While Athlia is so sad, perhaps even ill,
We should be joyful.

    Mel. But herself so yearns
To see us wedded.

    Ed. Of her own good heart,
For love of both.   Shall we be then less good,
Loving her truly ?   Thou knowest, her poor nerves
Tremble at nothing now.

    Mel. Be it as thou wilt :
 18*

I love thee better.

     Ed. I must now go in
To Athlia. You will hold me, both, excus'd.

         [*Exit above.*

Mel. Thou seest, she is good as beautiful.

       Sav. How else?

She owes so much to that sister, in herself
So worthy of all affection.   •

      Mel. Truly so.

Had she but Edith's beauty, in the world
Who would be like her?

      Sav. Who is like her now?

Wouldst thou have Nature shower all her gifts
On one small head? How barren were the world,
Dotted with mere perfection here and there,
And ugliness, or vices unredeem'd,
In the vast interspaces! Unto me
Athlia's soul-beauty, beaming from her eyes
And mutely eloquent on her mournful lips,
Leaves nothing to be long'd for. Shall I say,
I wonder often that a man like thee
Had not there fix'd.

      Mel. Ay? See this castle gray.

In its bold outlines and its massive spread
Is much to admire; but that is solemn all.
The flowerless ivy, that wraps half its sides
And strains to hug its towers, gives no relief,
Not even when autumn's brief suns and chill nights
Have fleck'd the green with purple and with red:

While evening, with her shadows making black
The many angles, drapes the whole with awe.
So I turn my back to its grandeur and gaze here,
Where beauty glows in the sunshine, and the stars
Have not their light obstructed. Thou must own
Edith is beautiful.

   Sav. Very; with a smile,
When her lips, parting slowly, show her teeth,
Perfect in place and whiteness, worth a day
Of travel to behold it. And her eyes,
When they fix on you with that thoughtful gaze
Their large blue orbs, half-curtain'd by the fringe
Of the full lids, a perilous thing to face.

Mel. Brave! And thou wonderest I should be ensnar'd!
She shall know this praise.

    Sav. No, I beseech thee not!

Mel. Nay, 't is a fair return. She admires thee,
And vows thou art the handsomest, best-built man
She has long beheld.

   Sav. I would her pensive sister
Saw with such partial eyes.

    Mel. Why, man, she doth.
I have heard her laud thee without stint, both mind
And body. 'T is thyself art dull of sight,
Or over-modest.

   Sav. Neither. For I see,
And please myself with thinking, Athlia's heart
Beats kindly toward me. But no amorous heat
Quickens its pulses. In that soul's large house

Is something treasur'd which fills all the rooms,
Or something which perforce bars every door,
That love can not steal in.   Be it this, or that,
'T is sure my image hath no dwelling there.
Mel. It is her illness.

        Sav. No.

             Mel. Know'st thou no cause?

Sav. I seem to see one darkly, or by glimpses,
Like light in a tangled forest, where my way
Threads a thick underwood I scarce can pierce.
Canst thou not guess? [*looking at Mel. intently.*

        Well, thou wilt learn in time.

             [*moving up.*

Mel. What! thou too going in?

        Sav. I seek the home
That is barr'd for me forever, — Athlia's still,
But to me pleasant, though close-shutter'd heart.

        [*Exit into the Castle.*

Mel. I must to the lake alone then. —   Hampton seems
To have taken to musing lately.   Very like
He will refuse to be of the chase to-morrow.
Is he in love then?   And does Saville mean
That Athlia favors him?   That cannot be :
She likes him not — unless her mien be worn
To cover liking.   But that were not she.
And why dissemble?   It is Saville's self
That Athlia loves, if any, and he is blind,
Or knows not to detect, at the fringe of the mask,
What the upper and fix'd part of it conceals.

I hope it is so.   Two such noble souls
Were made for each other.   I must watch their play.

                                        [*Exit to left.*

——— ———

SCENE II.

As in Act I. Scene II.

ATHLIA, *in a melancholy attitude, on a couch.*

Enter SAVILLE.

Ath. Saville. [*to herself.*

          Ah friend, thou comest to my wish,
Though to a painful purpose.

                    Sav. If for me
Alone the pain, it is welcome for thy sake,
Dearest and best of ladies.

                    Ath. Thou goest wide
Of my meaning, cousin (so thou shalt be call'd
That art so good to me.) —   Happily for my view,
We meet alone.

          Sav. I thought to find thy sister
Already here : she went before.

                    Ath. Alas,

We need not fear her coming in such haste.
Of her I would speak and ——

                      Thou hast not forgotten,
Some brief time since I hinted at strange peril
Lurking for Melville, and claim'd thy aid to come,
For his sake.   Thou shalt see now in what trust
I hold thee, avowing what were else not fit
Save for a brother's ear.

               Sav. Let me but earn
That honor as I feel it, and thou wilt be
Well-serv'd indeed.   Deign thou to make me then
Thy brother, — Athlia.

                Ath. Is it then so hard
To name me, that thou pausest ?   I would be
Truly thy sister, since I cannot be
Thy wife. —

      With a sad smile, as he raises reverently to his lips the
hand she extends to him.] 'T is not so fair as 't once was deem'd,
But 't is a frank hand.

              Sav. And the loveliest truly
I have e'er beheld.

             Ath. No, it is thin and wan.
It will be more so, soon.

             Sav. Do not despond :
Thou wilt regain yet health and spirits.

               Ath. Never.
No, Saville, — no, my brother, no; my heart
Is breaking hourly.   Do not look amaz'd.
Listen.   'T is time, — although, alas! not here,

Sister, or aunt, or cousin, will come in
To break our parle.

                Thou hast heard how I have striven
To win for Melville Edith.

            Sav. Lady, yes,
I know thy sacrifice.

         Ath. Ah! Know it? No!
Thou canst not know it. Heaven alone can know
What ——

    Edith haply did not take so well -
To Melville as did I, who have held him dear
From childhood; and thou know'st our uncle will'd
That he and I should —— Let me rest awhile. —
Thou wilt have patience with me. These faint turns
Come ever and anon. 'T is over now. —
So, I would say, I fear that Edith's heart
Is not so firmly bound to his some strain,
Or artful effort, may not loose the tie,
To Melville's sorrow, who — loves her more than life.
Edith is vain, and Hampton long has been
Her ardent wooer, and presses still his suit,
Though it is lawless.

         Sav. Can that be?

             Ath. To doubt
Had sav'd this story and appeal to thee,
Which is some shame to Edith. I am too sure.
Now, as my cousin's best friend, as my own,
I look to thee for counsel, and such aid
As thou canst give by any fitting act.

Sav. Hast thou appeal'd to Edith ?

                        Ath. Canst thou ask ?
She treats it as a trifle, and makes jest
Of Hampton's courtship, — though it is plain to me,
And thou mayst see, if thou wilt use thine eyes,
Thus caution'd, it is passion, and must end.
In death to Melville's peace, if not foul wrong.

Sav. It would not do to appeal to Hampton's self ?

Ath. No, in no wise.   There would be certain strife,
And Melville come to know what from his mind
I would keep ever.

                   Sav. Think'st thou Edith's heart
Inclines to Hampton ?

                    Ath. No, no, not her heart.
She is not unvirtuous ; she but loves the pride
Of conquest.   Did another bow the knee
To her beauty, Hampton's homage were forgot.

Sav. So let it be then.   'T is the surer mode.

Ath. But who will light the newer fire should stay
The ravage of the other ?   There is none.
Thou wouldst not, cousin ?

                     Sav. Not, if 't might be else.
For Melville's sake alone, I should not toy
With Melville's hopes.   It were a difficult task
To escape detection, and, the plot reveal'd,
What would keep whole our friendship ?   Yet for him,
And for thy sake, sweet cousin, I will essay
What Edith's manner, in sooth, alas to tell,
Makes simple yielding.   Why art thou now dumb,

Seeming perplex'd ?

    Ath. I ponder with distrust
A means that is deception, and feel loath
To give assent.

    Sav. 'T is rightly spoken and judg'd.
But what remains, if this course be disdain'd?
Shall we, in terror of well-meant deceit,
Give scope to evil-doing or to fraud?
Or even to levity, which unstopp'd may end,
If not in ruin, yet the wreck of all
Thou hast builded at such cost. For Melville's sake,
If not thy sister's —

    Ath. Yes, for Melville's sake:
Yes, yes, for his sake.

    Sav. — Thou must one thing more, —
Part with the whiteness of thy spotless truth
For a brief while, as I too, dare I add,
Must do with mine, who have kept it still with pride
And made my first of virtues: could I else
So reverence thee ?

    Ath. O generous friend! O brother!
The sacrifice thou mak'st, thyself, the risks
Thou wilt encounter, make more hard my strife
With the unyielding conscience. But the need
Is pressing, and the peril grows each day
More absolute. For dear Melville's honor then,
Do all thou canst with safety, and receive
All I have left to give thee. But beware!
Thou turnest all the peril on thyself,

And Edith's eyes may snare thee.　And what then?
Sav. Speak'st thou this seriously?

　　　　　　　　　Ath. And sadly, cousin.
Men fall as easily as women.　Eve
Listen'd to crafty suasion; but the man
Heard but his partner, looking, may we deem,
In her soft eyes, and yielded, to the thrill
Of the charm'd senses, what no reason's force
Had haply won from conscience.

　　　　　　　　　Sav. I will think
On thee, my sister; and thy matchless love
For Melville, and my faith to him, shall be,
Thus doubly-arm'd, a safeguard, for the nonce,
Sure as the Greek's against the Sirens' wiles.
But how thou lovest Melville!

　　　　　　　　　Ath. Love him!　Yes. —
Thanks for thy goodness, cousin.　I am not well
To be at meals to-day.　But thou wilt come
To see me here to-morrow.

　　　　　　　　　Sav. With what heart!
Ath. Farewell.　God bless thee, cousin!

　　　　　　　　　Sav. And thee too,
O Athlia, sister! [*Exit.*

　　　　　　　　　Ath. Love him?　Melville?　Love?
My God, Thou knowest with what passion! when all
My being, both thought and sense, by day and night,
Is his, his only, for whose sake I have given
My being to death, as I would give 't again,
To a thousand deaths, might that be, dying daily,

As I am hasting, day by day, to death.
Thou hast heard of my sacrifice, thou sayst, poor Saville,
Unselfish, noble friend, whose love and worth
I cannot recompense as thou wouldst have:
Little thou think'st what I have tearful laid
On Love's hot altar!   Fortune thou didst mean.
But what is fortune, what were life itself,
Though it were pour'd by drops upon the flame
That dries up blood and marrow, nor will sink
Till my veins cease to feed it and my brain, —
What is it all to that I there have laid,
My heart itself, with trembling hand indeed,
Yet without flinching?   And the world looks on,
Melville looks on, with sadness too, nor dreams
It is all for him.   So be it till my death.
So be it after: it might give him pain.
Sometimes I think I should be better-pleas'd
If he knew my passion, saw my body thrill
At his mere approach, his lightest touch, his voice,
And knew my fainting came alone of thoughts
I could not stifle, but which were all of him:
But that is selfish, and it lasts not long,
As it should not.   I have liv'd for him alone,
Since my youth's bud, so wither'd now, first open'd
Close by his own and bent its stem to his,
Delighted that the sunshine and the rain,
Which shower'd and beam'd on his and made it grow
And send forth perfume, should at the same time
Glance on and sprinkle mine.   Our stems are twain;

The full flower of his manhood turns its hues
And scent to my sister.   Shall I wish it else,
Who help'd to bend it thither ?   Let mine droop,
And fall to the dust, nor may he know, O God,
He broke it from the stalk and trod it there !

[*Sinks fainting on the couch, and the*

Drop falls.

ACT THE FOURTH

SCENE I. *The Platform, as in Act I. Sc. I.*

EDITH.

Ed. 'T is done. I did not think the hawk so soon
Would stoop to the lure. My sister's chance is slim,
If she wants one, — which I think not. But 't was wise
To close all doors to hazard, which is shut out,
Now, absolutely; and Aunt Bertha's fears
May sleep with the secret which she bad me take
To my last bed with me. It is something too,
To have caught the handsome Saville. This the bait,
Thrown to the vanity of his manly charms,
Hath render'd easy. For so large a trout
He struggles little, and the rod scarce bends
In my facile hand. I have him yet to land.
But O these men! they are not more true to each other
Than we of the more impulsive sex, who love
Variety in charming, and intrigue
Hold dear as life, which we risk for it, now and then.
The ring counts nothing, bridal or troth pledge,
On either side of the compact. Melville's friend
In love with the wife of his bosom that shall be!
That is rare frolic. But to make it sure,

I 'll use the arms the vanquish'd one himself
Prescrib'd, who prais'd their temper even before
He had felt their edge. *My smile — the parted lips,*
With the fine teeth, a journey's worth to see.
Good. [*Takes a small mirror from her pocket and looks on it.*
    And the large blue eyes, with thoughtful gaze,
Fix'd steadily — thus — half-curtain'd with the fringe
Of the full lids, a perilous thing to face.
So shalt thou find it, poet for the nonce.

                    [*Puts back the mirror.*

That easy Melville, thus to go between us
With mutual compliment!

                 Here the rivals come.
How to keep both in hand? though one alone

        Enter HAMPTON *and* SAVILLE.

Is worth the holding, which is not the last. —
Good even to both. Have ye come this way to taste
The sweet air ere the sun go down?

                Sav. 'T is full
Of life as well as sweetness.

               Hamp. And the sky
Blue as the finest pair of eyes I know.
Ed. Whose be those, pray? I do not think blue eyes
The loveliest orbs for women, not at least
The most effective, dost thou, Master Saville?

         [*looking at him in the manner described.*
Sav. I do at this moment, both.

             Ed. Is that reply

A compliment? There, take thou in return,
Who pay'st them rarely, this half-open'd rose.
Thou seest, its vein'd leaves wear a lovelier hue,
As warmer, than my eyes, and like the red
That now o'erspreads thy cheeks, or yonder clouds
That wait to attend the star-king of the day
To his night chamber. O, thou awkward man!
Thou hast prick'd thy finger. Didst thou then forget
The rose has thorns? [*Takes the tips of his fingers with her own, and affects to wrap them in her handkerchief.*
      Nay, I must bind it up:
It was my fault.
    Sav. My fingers well might bleed,
To be so handled. Fy! a simple thorn!
Hamp. Saville forgets, if not a rose has thorns,
  Yet a small puncture sometimes gives more pain
  Than open wounds, and that the conscience' prick
  Avenges oft the short-liv'd flower of bliss,
  Pluck'd heedlessly by hands that had no right
  To rummage in the garden where it grew.
Sav. What is the moral?
     Hamp. That the eyes he loves
  Are green-gray, but his friend's love's eyes are blue.
Sav. Now hear my fable. Hidden in the bush,
  A wolf gorg'd honey, stolen from a tree
  Where the wild bees had hiv'd it. Led by chance
  And not design, another beast drew near,
  Snuff'd with delight, and ey'd, without a thought
  Of making it his own, the store, when, blind

By jealous rage, the wolf forsook his lair,
Rushing upon him, and, assail'd in turn
By the vindictive insects, lost at once
The hope of his malice and his plunder'd prize.

Hamp. And what thy moral?

      Sav. He who seeks may find.

Hamp. I will go muse upon it in the glade
Of the oak-wood, not doubting there in time
To see its point and match it with my own. [*Going.*

Ed. No, Master Hampton, thou shalt not go thus.
What do ye both mean, scowling each at other
As if I was a damsel unbetroth'd
Whom ye might tilt for?   Can I not then give
A red rose to my husband's special friend,
But my own friend must thereupon look grim,
As if it was the sole flower in my gift,
Or the sole worth the taking?   See thou then, —
Here is a white rose taken from my breast.
It has no thorn to it; yet if thou shouldst hurt
Thy hand, I 'd take the kerchief from my neck
To wrap it in, and Saville would feel shame,
I know he would, to take the act amiss,
As thou, old favorite.   But, in sooth, thou 'rt spoil'd
By being made much of.

    Hamp. O, I crave thy grace,
Fair Mistress Edith.   Seest thou that I pout?
'T was but a match of wits, and Saville won.
I am brooding on the game.   So, let me go.

      [*Exit to the left.*

Ed. Thou art too courtly, thou, to leave me thus.

   [*Puts both hands on Sav.'s, looking at him wistfully.*

Thou wilt not follow him, Saville, to the wood.

Promise me. Ye are both too angry now

To meet alone. Indeed thou shalt not go:

I 'll hold thee by thy finger. Dost thou think,

Thou naughty man, what peril might ensue

To my fair fame, me, maiden and betroth'd,

If ye should fight about a paltry rose

Given to one and grudg'd him by the other ?

Why, on my troth, 't is I should be incens'd,

That either of ye should dare to make my gift

Matter of jealous contest ? Am I then

Free to make rivals ? Wind it round the stem —

   [*taking the handkerchief which Sav. has restored to*
    her, and putting it about the stalk of the rose.

So — for the thorns. And keep it. Thou wilt see,

I am not afraid thou wilt mistake my gift,

Like that vain Hampton.

   Sav. Who would not be vain,

However low-like, that could boast of grace

From such as thou, O lady of mien unmatch'd

And beauty peerless !

   Ed. Truly, Master Saville,

Thou hast taken bold Hampton's flattery to thy own,

And art doubly dangerous. He will not be miss'd.

There must be something amorous in the air

Making both false-tong'd. Let us go in-doors.

Sav. Lady, thou wilt excuse me. I must walk ——

  VOL. II.—19

Ed. Not to the wood-lawn ? to seek Hampton ? no !
 Ye shall not quarrel !   Think, sir, where you are.
 No, Saville, no, — my friend, my husband's friend !
 Thou wilt not be so cruel, not so wrong
 Melville, Aunt Bertha, Athlia —

       Sav. Ah !

         Ed. And me.
 Stay then but for one hour ! until this heat
 In the blood be over.

      Sav. What hast thou to fear,
 O lady gentle ?   'T was nothing but the jar
 Of wordy bickering, where no harm was done.
 Let me now leave : I am flurried, and too hot
 For further converse.   In an hour or so.

        [*Exit hastily to the left.*

    EDITH *clasps her hands, lifting them*
      as in fright and despair.

Ed. He is gone to fight !   What shall I do ?   Wo 's me,
 The web I have spun is twisted to a cord
 To choke me.   I will go. [*makes a step to left, but pauses.*

       No, that were death
 To my good name.   I will alarm the house.

       [*Moves up, but pauses.*
 No, no, I dare not : it would give them time ;
 And Hampton —— I will after, come what will.
 O devilish Saville !   O accursed wile !

       [*Exit hastily to left.*

Scene II.

A glade in a forest.
HAMPTON, *walking to and fro.*

After a minute or two,
Enter hurriedly, SAVILLE.

Hamp. Ah ! — What has kept thee, who art not snail-pac'd,
The gray eyes or the blue ?
            Sav. I see the thorn
Still rankles. Hast thou oall'd me hither
To pluck it out ?
            Hamp. No, for thou hast it with thee ;
And the blue-eyes, in pity of thy pain,
Hath given her handkerchief against the rest,
That they may not the finger pierce that thrill'd
So lately, touch'd by hers.
            Sav. Was 't then for this,
The pang-whelp'd cavil of a lustful boy
Cross'd in his first blood-passion, thou hast dar'd
Provoke me hither ?
    Hamp. [*fiercely.*] No ! 'Fore God in Heaven,
Thou art here to answer me. What didst thou mean
By thy beast-fable of the plunder'd bees ?

Sav. Whatever suits thee.

            Hamp. Thou dost well to spare
The answer thou must blush to give with truth,
Thou being thyself in love with Melville's bride
Who art his friend, which I am not.

                 Sav. Thou art
Not less his guest, and dost to sinister purpose
Abuse thy privilege here.   But not for this
Word-bandying are we met in the forest.   Draw,
Lest we be interrupted. [*Throws down between them the
           rose.*] On my sword
Hang Melville's honor, and his wife's to be.

Hamp. Stain'd and polluted.   Thus I cleanse it off.

         After several passes, HAMPTON
      *makes a feint, and laying himself open is run
            through the body, just as
              Enter* EDITH.

Ed. Stop, passionate men !
To Hamp. who leans on his sword.] Thou art not wounded ?

                 Hamp. Ay,
To death I think. [*Falls.*

            Ed. No, let me stanch the wound. [*Shaking
       the rose from the handkerchief, which she uses.*
Thou shalt have help.

            Hamp. 'T will come too late.   Look, quickly,
A last look in my eyes, with those dear eyes
I have lov'd too well.   I cannot see their blue

Now for their tears.   They are dropping very warm —
On my cheeks alone.   I would — I would thou 'dst let
My lips receive them, Edith.

       Ed. **Thus, then, thus.** [*kissing him*
             on the mouth.

Hamp. O joy! I die contented.   'T is not thou,
 Saville — not thou — she —— Pardon, God! [*Dies.*

Ed. Thou art not dead?   Speak, Hampton!   Yet one word!
I have lov'd but thee alone; yes, only thee.
O, he is gone!   Why dost thou stand, bad man,
And lend'st no help?   Thou hast slain him, and by craft.

    Enter MELVILLE, *unobserved.*

Thou shalt answer it.   O Hampton, O my love,
      [*throwing herself on the body.*
For my sake thou hast perish'd!   Would my lips
Could give that blood its life-warmth!

        Mel. It is well
For thee and honor it shall flow no more.
Woman, for shame; rise up; if not for me,
Then for thy sister.   Dost thou hear me?   Go!
This is no place for thee.

    Ed. [*half-rising.*] Here I will stay
Till they bear off that body.   Go *thou*, fool,
Who art not worth a woman's love; go back
To Athlia, who thou hast not heart to see
Is dying for thee daily; take to her
The effeminate face for which she has given all,

Even life perhaps; and take with thee thy friend,
False and a murderer, (but he shall not 'scape!)
I will lie here 'neath heaven, and with a m in.

As she throws herself beside the body, embracing it,

the Drop falls.

AOT THE FIFTH

SCENE. *As in Act I. Scene 2.*

ATHLIA, *on the couch; beside her,*
seated, BERTHA; *at the head, two Women, standing.*

Ath. No, aunt, it may not be. Five times since noon
I have swoon'd away. The sixth, it may be more
Than mimic death.
            Ber. The leech will soon arrive.
Ath. I hope not. I would rather die unvex'd,
With none around me here but thee alone
And Melville, Edith, Saville too.
                  Ber. Alas!
How I have wrong'd thee, child! But 't is not yet
Too late to make atonement.
             Ath. Wrong'd me, aunt?
Think'st thou I have murmur'd ever, that thy love
Was less to me than Edith? Melville too
Has lov'd her best. [*sighing.*
          Ber. Thou wring'st me to the soul.
Stand back, my maidens. [*Women go up.*
              I will whisper now
My shame. Remorse has kept me half the night
Awake with thought of thee. Live, only live! —

By a later act, which for thy sister's sake
I have kept conceal'd, thy uncle's large bequest
Is left to thee untrammel'd.   Thou art free
To marry Saville now and make him lord
Of all thy wealth.   Forgive, forgive my fraud !

Ath. Aunt, I am sorry only for thy sake;
And, with another sorrow, sorry too
For Melville.   But 't will be all one, and all
Will still be his, as I have wish'd.

       Ber. And Saville ?
I thought thou lov'dst him, daughter.

        Ath. As a friend,
Truly, and Melville's friend, — as I must love
All that are dear to Melville, and shall love
Till death, and haply after.

      Ber. O blind eyes,
That have help'd me to dishonor ! —   What is now ?
Thy cheeks gain color ; and wilt thou rise indeed ?

Ath. [*half-risen.*] It is his step !   He comes — to see me die.
            [*Falls back.*

   Enter MELVILLE.

Mel. [*kneeling by the couch.*
 O Athlia !   O my cousin !   Can it be ?

Ath. [*again half-rising.*] That I am dying, Melville ?

       Mel. No, not that.
It is not that I mean ; though that, though that,
Cannot be either, Athlia, nor shall be.
Thou art t o good to die, so young, scarce worn

By sickness, saving of the heart perhaps ——

Ath. And that, though lingering, is sure. — But what
    Hast thou come in to say ? What cannot be ?

Mel. How can I say it ? With those eager eyes
    Fix'd on me thus, thou mak'st me think indeed
    It may be true. O miserable me !
    Who know it but too late, that might have been
    All I should be, all thou wouldst have me be ——
    Bring water ! O Heaven ! Help !

                      Ber. It hath been so
    Often since noontide. She will come back soon. —
    The pillow higher. More lightly, Alice, now ;
    Or, give the fan to me. — I fear, my son,
    She has lov'd thee over —— Where is Edith then ?

Mel. Name her not, aunt !

Enter SAVILLE,
slowly, with head depressed.

    Ath. And Saville too ?
               Giving her hand.] My friend !

Sav. Alas ! I have not deserv'd the name ; I have been
    More weak than I thought to be — have been ensnar'd,
    As thou didst warn me.

          Mel. Saville has told all.
    O cousin, what I owe thee !

              Ath. No, thy friend.
    Seest thou, his danger forms thy best defence :
    The eyes of Edith kill where'er they strike.
      19*

Mel. Kill?   Ah, most truly ; and thy words are sooth
More than thou know'st.

> *Ath.* What mean'st thou, cousin ?

> > *Mel.* [*aside, and low, to Sav.*] Hush ! —

When thou art better ——

> *Ath.* Better ?   But think thou

Less hardly of poor Edith.

> > *Mel.* Hardly ?   Ah !

Ath. What means that noise ?

> *Mel.* [*aside to Sav.*] They are bringing in the corpse.
Let her not know.   'T would kill her in this state.
Aunt —— [*draws Ber. apart.*

  Ath. Why this mystery ?   There is in thy looks,
And Saville's, something fearful.   What is wrong ?
I am strong enough to bear it.   Tell me !

> *Enter* EDITH, *impetuously.*

> > > *Ed.* I

Will tell thee.   It is murder.   Saville there
Has murder'd Hampton.

> *Here* ATHLIA *rises to her feet, and is supported
> by* BERTHA, *assisted by the Women.*

> > *Mel.* Woman, it is false !

False as the tongue that speaks it.   Wouldst thou slay·
Outright thy sister, as thy damn'd deceit
Has sapp'd her life already ?   Get thee hence
Hence to thy paramour, of whose just death
Thou, under God, wast cause.

> > *Ed.* Not so: my right

Is here the same as thine. 'T is thou alone,
Dolt that thou wast, hast trifled with the life
Thou affect'st to reck for. See ; she stands it well.
Now thou art free to claim her, she will do
As our uncle will'd, but as his wife will'd not.

Ber. Peace, thou dishonor'd girl. Go, — lest thou work
A second murder.

    Ed. And reveal, thou fear'st,
Thy own vile fraud. But first — without there, ho !
Arrest that murderer !

    Mel. No, no man shall enter.

Sav. Nor needs there ; I shall not avoid arrest.
I am here where I should be, and here will stay,
Till Athlia is quiet.

    Ber. 'T will be soon,
One way or other. She is speechless now
With grief and horror.

    Ed. Say, with sudden joy,
That, by the death of my true lover, hers,
Who was false to her, is recover'd. There, thou boy,
Take back thy ring, and give 't to her who hath earn'd it.
Scorn'd now, as never valu'd, it hath to me
Its stone blood-spatter'd. *[Throws it to the floor.*

  Here ATHLIA, *sinking in her aunt's arms, is laid*
   again upon the couch ; and EDITH *stands as*
    if struck with remorse and dread.

    Mel. [*falling at Athlia's feet.*
     O Athlia ! best

As dearest of women.   Do not droop!   Live now,
Live and forgive me.   All will yet be well.

Ath. Where, Melville, where ?   Alas, it is too late,
Here on the earth.   I thought to make thee happy :
But the Heart's Sacrifice hath been in vain.

Mel. No, not in vain, dear Athlia, if my life,
My love, as I know it will be, shall henceforth
Redeem it.

   Ath. Think'st thou truly thus, O cousin ?
Or is it but the tenderness of grief,
Haply and pity, move thee ?

      Mel. No, more, more !
I always lov'd thee as an angel, Athlia,
Lov'd thee for thy great heart and faultless mood ;
And, but that I was mad, had lov'd thee else.
But, now the fever is over and the brain
No more bewilder'd, heart and sense come back
To their old places, and I feel I love
With all my boyhood's love, when thou as yet
Wast all in all to me, and in the world
Was none beside.   So Heaven do by me,
As I vow henceforth with a passionate heart
To love thee only, and, I feel, do now !

Ath. Kiss me then — quickly.   [*Puts up her lips, and when he
   has pressed them passionately with his own, falls back.*
   Mel. [*in terror.*] Athlia !
      Ber. She is dead.

MELVILLE, *after one long look, sinks*
with his face on Athlia's.
SAVILLE, *who has stood, with clasped hands, gazing on*
her, now hides in them his face, turning aside.
EDITH, *her expression changing, makes one*
step toward the body. BERTHA,
weeping, appears to be about to bind up the head,
and the Women ready to assist.

The Curtain falls.

NOTE

TO

THE HEART'S SACRIFICE

1.—P. 409. *Here comes the best*, etc.] For the Stage perhaps, as directly indicating the party entering:

Ah ! Hampton. — Why is Melville not as he !

THE MONK

MDCCCLXIX

CHARACTERS, ETC.

BELTRAN' DE SANTOS-SANDOVAL, *Duke De la Villaquema'da.*
IGNA'CIO, *formerly a Dominican friar, — his Confessor.*
MARCO BRULO'TE, *the Duke's Secretary.*
PABLO DESHACEDOR', *his Steward.*
A SERVANT.

ADE'LA, *the Duke's wife.*
SARA, *her fostermother.*

——

SCENE. *A castle of the Duke's, in the Guadarrama mountains, in Spain.*
TIME. *That occupied by the action.*
EPOCH. *The reign of Philip II.*

THE MONK

ACT THE FIRST

SCENE I. *A room in the Castle.*

BELTRAN. ADELA.

Bel. Five years this day, Ade'la, have roll'd by,
    Since, in the secret night, one smoky torch
    To light the chapel, the redoubling peal
    Of thunder for our organ, and the hiss
    And roar of the flooding and wind-driven rain
    For nuptial chorus, and one trembling maid
    For our sole witness, thou didst put thy hand
    Forever into mine.
                    Ade. Since when, Beltran',
    What sunshine hath been ours! what joy of life
    Since our sweet boy was born!
                    Bel. With but one cloud,

The consciousness of that untold deceit
Practis'd upon my sire.   But his gloom
And sternness made me fear.

               Ade. O say not so.
Since the bless'd day when 'neath his horse's hoofs
I fell in the dust, a child scarce seven years old,
Was lifted up, and, though without a wound,
Borne in his arms to the castle, and here kept,
Lov'd, nourish'd, and adopted for his own,
Till his death-hour, the good Duke unto me
Never look'd less than gentle, though oft sad.

Bel. 'T is spoken with grateful reason, O my love.
    But think'st thou, if surmis'd the secret step
    To which my passion led thee, his swart brows
    Had lain for thee unwrinkled ?   See, Adela,
    How we are warp'd by liking or dislike !
    In the good monk that shrives us thou wilt see
    Nothing that is not murky, not one flash
    Over his thoughtful visage that to thee
    Is light of the heart.

               Ade. But many that appear
Like the sharp glare of lightning from a cloud
Heavy with gather'd thunder.   O my lord,
This is not prejudice ; the lurid cloud
Has not discharg'd its terrors, and the flash
More frequent grows and vivid day by day.
Thou mark'st it not, because 't is but alone
When thou look'st elsewhere, that those gloomy brows
Are knit together and the deep-set eyes

Dart out their quick short fire.   There is, be sure,
Hatred, or envious rancor, in the scowl
Which makes that man's fine visage lower to me
Like that of Satan.

   Bel. Yet at times, his smile
Might seem an angel's, for it wreathes his lips
Momently to a shape most like thy own,
Whom he not unresembles.

    Ade. O Beltran!

Bel. 'T is true, and helps me love him.   Why ascribe
 His gloom to sinister impulse, when thou look'st
 Complaisant on my sire's remember'd mood?
 Is it indeed, that memory robs this last
 Of its right harshness, blurring all the lines
 With the dim distance of five years' remove?

Ade. No; but the monk's has scarce a summer's date,
 Is stormy and inconstant.   When first chosen
 To be thy con'fessor, a twelvemonth since,
 The sky of his visage was serene, if dull,
 As at our bridal.   As I see thy sire
 In my heart's mirror, his face and mien were aye
 Reflected from a nature constant-sad:
 A quality of the blood, where is no cause
 To say why 't should or should not be; alone
 We know that it is, and is without a cure.

Bel. Thou err'st from partial knowledge.   Not from God
 My father's visitation.   Till that day
 Of horror, when the crime, if crime it was,
 That robb'd my uncle and his wife of life

And lost their hapless children at one stroke,
Had brought on him, a guiltless man, suspect,
He was not harsh or moody.   From that day
Men shunn'd him as if plague-mark'd, and, devour'd
By a forever-gnawing sense of wrong
Endur'd on a charge where could be no disproof,
Into himself he shrank, as if blotch'd o'er
By a moral leprosy, until thou cam'st
A seraph, at whose touch the soul resum'd
From time to time a color more its own,
And still while thou wast by.   As he had cause,
Why not Ignacio ?

        Ade. He, a priest ! whose age
Is little more than mine !

        Bel. Brulote said
He was bred a soldier.   Haply some disgust
Has taken him for a life that suits him not.
Youngest of con'fessors, a man whose looks
Show in-born pride and blood but little tam'd,
Why should it not be ?

        Ade. But so sudden then ?
It should have shown itself, if such the sign,
In his darken'd mien before.   Not discontent,
But some bad passion, stirs him.

        Bel. Him, the good !
Remember his reluctance, long-maintain'd,
To join our hands in secret, and his words
Of firm dissuasion, spoken, not as priest,
But honest man.   My heart and reason both

Took lesson then, albeit they practis'd not,
And made his place at my soul's ear light to have,
Without Brulote's council.
     Ade. Yet at last
 ' He yielded.
    Bel. That was weakness and not crime.
Recall thou too the father's daily acts
Of alms-grace, done in person and with pain.
Ade. With means that come of thy bounty.
       Bel. Could they else ?
He has nothing of his own. Be not unjust.
Ade. I would not be, Beltran. But thou rise up,
Ere the night fall on thee.
     Bel. I will. And if ——
Lo, where he comes.
     Ade. And in his blackest mood.

     Enter, from the left,
      IGNACIO.

Ign. Hail, daughter; and thou, son. The day looks fair.
Bel. To us, O father, fairer than to most.
 It brings around the year's date of that night
 When thou wrought'st us such service. Thanks again
 ' To thee who, under God, didst shed forever
 Sunshine upon our life-path. [*Extends a hand to Ign.,*
   which the latter touches not, as if not seeing it.
     Ign. Art thou sure
 It was forever ? Joy unchang'd, my son,

Is not for man, no more than is the sun
Without a cloud or daylight without darkness.

Bel. Each hath its service. They who have the most
Of what is best in either may be deem'd
Happy in this life, where the soft, small rain,
The driving shower, and the numbing frost,
Are not without their blessings and give warmth
And light more relish.

     Ign. But when comes the night
Untimely, as when suns are mask'd, or storms
Beat down the harvest, or the earthquake's shock
Tears into fragments cities, then is man
Awe-struck or suffering, and in despair
Blesses his life no longer.

     Bel. Such are spots
Or knobs on the shadow'd sun. Why strain the eyes
Through a smok'd glass to see them?

     Ign. Even for this,
That man should in the greatest of God's works
Find still illusion, something that exists
Which is not visible openly, and seen
Puts all his visions of its perfect state
At fault.

  Ade. His reverence's eyes of late
Seem to see all things shadow'd. Why eclipse
The innocent joys that make my lord and me
For the gift of life so grateful, and our hearts
Perpetual altars?

    Ign. Daughter, for that night

Comes sudden to the unwary and Our Lord
Bids us be watchful.   Round those altars' base
I see the seeds of disappointment springing
Whose growth shall clamber to their very top,
Put out their grateful fires and make their place
Dreary and cold indeed.   May they not be void
Of prayer as well !

       Ade. My lord, we will withdraw.
'T is better than the padre's, in this mood,
The prattle of our boy, in whose bright face
We see not yet the shadow.

       Ign. — Which must come.

    Exeunt above, BELTRAN *and* ADELA.
Not of my will, Thou knowest, Almighty God.
I do Thy bidding, or seem to do.   If not,
Cleanse Thou my vision !

       What, if after all
The Duke is innocent ?   Generous he is
And seeming good.   'T were fitter for my state,
Fitter the man Heaven made me be, outright
To charge him with that crime.   I will, at least,
Well sift the evidence.   Marco's boasted faith
And loyalty may speak boldlier than they ought.
He shall on the instant clear them past all doubt.

      [*Exit, hurriedly, to the left.*

Scene II.

A room in the Secretary's Apartment.

Marco.

Mar. It must be done.   The padre's timid mind
   Poisons resolve with doubt.   But I have that
   Will prove sure antidote, and make more strong,
   By stifling pity and warming into life
   Religious horror, heartless as a stone,
   The purpose of revenge.   'T is frightful.   True.
   But shall the twofold crime go unaveng'd ?
   The true lord rest despoil'd of home and name,
   And in his native nest the cuckoo breed ?
   That hath been, is, must be ; but the false brood
   Shall have their necks wrung.   Where the feathers lie
   Already dabb'd with blood, what matters it,
   Nay, seeming right it is, the avenging fingers
   Should scatter too the plumage and the blood
   That come of the robber bird. —   It is his step.
                    [*Opens the door.*

Enter Ignacio.

My dear lord, Don Alonso.   I was full
Of thought of you.

Ign. And, Marco, I of thee.
But drop that style.   It not beseems my place,
And threats our secret — if that still must be.

Mar. My lord commands.   I am servant to him still,
Whether as simple priest or the high duke
He was born to be.   What b'ds your reverence?

                    Ign. This.
Tell me that tale once more.

              Mar. My lord distrusts.

Ign. Ay, God forbid else!   Quickly.

              Mar. On that night
The villa was made dust, the Duke your sire
Was found, with the Duchess, by the flames so sear'd,
Their bodies scarce were known.   Hence, some main-
    tain'd
They had fallen stifled by the smoke, still more
They had both been strangled ere the house was fired,
While most men whisper'd, since appear'd no sign
Of pillage, that the strangler was none else
Than the Duke's brother, father of this lord
Who now usurps your place.

              Ign. Where lies the proof?

Mar. Nowhere save in my knowledge.   I was then
Your uncle's servant, foremost in his trust.
He urg'd me, and with weighty offers brib'd,
To carry you and your sister, infants then
Of one and two years, to some far-off place
And have ye rear'd as peasants.

              Ign. He then will'd

No murder of the children ?

     Mar. No, their death
In rights and lineage only, — will'd them rear'd
Unconscious of their rank, and known to those
Who were paid to take them, as the bastard-brood
Of an unknown noble.

     Ign. Wherefore then suspect
My uncle of the grosser crime ?   He own'd
Nothing thereof to thee ?

     Mar. No, on his knees,
Before the image of the cross-nail'd Christ,
Swore he was innocent.   I judge his guilt
By that he was, like Satan, darkly proud,
Unscrupulous and licentious.

     Ign. 'T is at worst
A merciless conjecture.   But proceed.
Thou didst with the infants —

     Mar. Partly as he bade.
Near these dark towers, which the new duke made
His changeless home, I lodg'd them 'mid the hills,
But in two dales, secluded each from the other,
Where even the fosterparents could not learn
Of one another's trust.

     Ign. Why didst thou that ?
Mar. I thought to wield a rod above his head
In case of need : but most, to guard you both
Against a change of purpose, should his fears
Prompt your destruction, all the while I kept
His secret and my own.

Ign. The girl, thou saidst —

Mar. Died while an infant.   But the brother throve,
How well your reverence needs not here be told,
Nor how I combated, with all the arms
Of reason and prayerful urgence, that sad change
From camp to cloister.

Ign. No, not all the arms.
Hadst thou but bar'd thy secret ——

Mar. Did I dare ?
Even for your own sake, whom I had come to prize,
And love as one loves a secret treasure, whose worth
Is a cause of care and danger as well as joy.
What had it stead ?   As now, whereto would serve
To assert to Cortes or to King your claim,
Where is no proof but mine ?   Who would lend faith,
When lo you have so outgrown your sometime self
That even my lady duchess would not know,
Could the tomb yield her for that great intent,
In your develop'd aspect the soft face
She had press'd so oft to her bosom and the form
That had germ within it.

Ign. To my cousin then
I will turn, as is most fitting.

Mar. Have a care !
Think you the false duke from his high-plac'd seat
Would step at your bidding, conscious that its base
Rests on the cinders of his father's crime,
Blood-soak'd, with human ashes intermix'd,
Cemented and made hard by living fraud ?

Ign.   What makes him conscious?   Thou hast given no proof;
Not in the past.   Give it now.   Smirch not the son
With the dirt of his father's mantle, far less spot
With the blood of his fingers, were these dipt indeed
In human gore.

          Mar. I have that son's full trust,
Accepted by him solely that his sire
Put in me like trust.   Am I so ingrate,
So foolish-wicked and wicked-foolish, then,
To turn like a mad hound on the kindly hand
That feeds and pats me?   In your reverence' right
I see no hope, — not for the cloister's vows;
Your claim once proven, St. Peter's seal at Rome
Gives easily dispensation, — but for this,
That in me lieth no proof, and out of me
None can be gather'd.   What have I to gain
By urging you to a duty, which perform'd,
I am hurl'd from place and honor, haply trod
In the dust and mire, neglected and disgrac'd,
As treason-spotted and perjur'd, with no voice
To plead for the wretch who plotted to o'erthrow
His lord and benefactor?   If I think
His sire a murderer, I have had more cause
Than thousands who so thought; but can I point
To more than the facts I have told you?   That his son
Was conscious of the crime, that part at least
Which earn'd for him its fruits, lies in like thought:
He was in the villa, a boy then twelve years old,
That frightful night, and, when the nurses fled

Fear-madden'd, saw me, as himself took flight
Dragg'd by his devilish sire, seek the room
Where cry'd the orphans.   Why hath he not sought
Ever through me to bring their fate to light?
He lives on its products and sleeps safe and soft,
Nor asks himself if his cousins, if alive,
Are wanderers on the earth, without a name
Or a mat to couch on.   Be, my lord, a man:
Avenge through him the bloody villain who lieth
Under his own carv'd image as if a saint,
Soaking with foul reek of his rotted corpse
Your parents' ashes that are inurn'd beside him.

Ign.   Hast thou no pity?
                        Mar. I have had for you:
I have none for the seed of him, who, 'mid the flames
His hand had kindled, by the blacken'd forms
Of his own brother and his brother's wife,
Your innocent parents, turn'd you and your sister
Over to my compassion, nor would have reck'd
Had I squeez'd your windpipes, as he doubtless did
With his damn'd fingers theirs.
                        Ign. But then, the wife?
Mar. What wife?
                Ign. Beltran's; my cousin's.   Canst thou see
Her happiness and urge a fate whose wreck
Must bury her likewise and their innocent child?
Mar. Is incest happiness? —
                        Ign. Incest?
                        Mar. — Can its fruit,

Though not of its own will gotten and made life,
Be counted innocent?

     Ign. What dost thou mean
By words like those, half-whisper'd, in that tone?
Mar. The Duchess is the misbegotten spawn
 Of Don Beltran's late father.

       Ign. Wretch! and this
Thou hast kept from me? nay, sought thyself my aid
To that impious marriage?

      Mar. Such reproach, my lord,
Befits me not, and ill requites a zeal
You may put to the death-test, if you will. Perhaps,
I am striding that way for your sake ev'n now.
At the time of the girl's adoption, I had left
For reasons good the Castle, was away
When at your cousin's quest I sought your aid
To his marriage, knowing then no natural let.
Ign. Forgive me. But why only now this tale?
Mar. I knew it not till yesterday, though doubts,
Nourish'd too late, came often o'er my mind,
Weighing the known facts with the late Duke's life.
Ign. And this is sooth?

    Mar. My lord!

      Ign. Swear by my cross.
Mar. There is a surer way to attest my faith.
Ign. But swear. I shall distrust thee else.

      Mar. I swear,
I tell, to my best belief, too true a tale.
Ign. O horrible! that my hands, till then unstain'd,

Were made the doers of so curs'd a deed.l

Mar. Nay, call it bless'd. It was the Almighty's will,
Whereby His vengeance for a monstrous crime
Should best be satisfy'd.

     Ign. Man, wouldst thou make
The Eternal, with a mortal's passion blind,
Strike down the innocent for the guilty's sake ?

Mar. It is the fiat thunder'd from the Mount.
I grav'd not there the laws.

     Ign. Rein-in that tongue;
It utters blasphemy.

    Mar. With pardon, hear.
Your servant has no thought, and would be rash,
To be profane. But did not Heaven make hard
The Egyptian's heart? Why were the first-born slain ?
Not they had sinn'd. And was not Christ our Lord
The escape-goat for us all ?

    Ign. Distract me not.
These are too subtle matters for the brain.
Enough, there is sin, and horrible sin, — if such
Thou canst prove it to me, — and to me, alas,
Guilty yet innocent, will fall the task,
The accursed task, to make it known. No more !
Go for thy proof -— thy proof. I go to pray.

    [Exit ; Mar. reverently opening
      the door, as the

   Drop falls.

ACT THE SECOND

SCENE I. *The same as in Act I. Scene I.*

BELTRAN. IGNACIO.

Bel.   Ay, reverend father, this begets surprise.
What glooms thy visage ?   Is there aught there lacks
Thy comfort calls for ?   Find'st thou wanting here
The observance due thy place from one and all
Of our household or ourselves ?

                         Ign. All things be here
Man's art can furnish, and, save one thing, all
That God vouchsafes to the needs of such as I.
Bel.   And that is ?

              Ign. Peace of mind.

                         Bel. That sometimes lies
Beyond the battle of the stoutest life.
But thou, in yet green youth, whose heart betimes
Was shut from the strife and passions of the world,
Shouldst have that peace unconquer'd.

                         Ign. When without
The invasion comes, and deadly moral fight
Is forc'd on the spirit, what avails it then,
The breast is cuiras'd and the head is helm'd

With cowl and amice ?   Through the monk's black robe
Pierces the poison'd arrow, and the wound
Rankles the more, that in his lonely cell
Is no distraction.

       Bel. Hast thou then such war
With the flesh and the Devil ?

          Ign. With the flesh that clogs
The souls of others and the devil evok'd
By their ferocious passions.

       Bel. This of late.
Find'st thou these enemies here ?   For, till of late,
Thy brow wore not the scowl and gloom of strife,
That thundercloud whose flashes shake with fear
Adela.

  Ign. Should the innocent fear ?

         Bel. Ay oft,
Where the bad tremble not.   'T is instinct given
By Heaven for their protection.   But thy cloud
Comes not of her ?

       Ign. I have been pondering late
Much that is doubtful.   Hast thou alway made
Perfect confession ?

       Bel Father, in this breast
Nestles no secret that is hid from thee.
Servant of God, why ask'st thou ?

        Ign. Canst thou bear
Frank question ?

      Bel. Ask what fitteth thee to ask.
Thy heart to me is as a book of God :

Write what thou wilt therein.

Ign. My son, its leaves
Shall be wide-open. Dost thou know what fate
Fell on thy uncle's children ?

Bel. No ! Dost thou ? [*eagerly.*

Ign.   Mad'st thou e'er search for them ?

Bel. How should I ?   I ?
I was but twelve years old.

Ign. Thy sire ?

Bel. Thou heard'st :
I was a child.   How should I know the part
Taken by my father ?   Doubtless, was it all
That right or natural love could prompt.

Ign. Why so ?
'T was not his interest.

Bel. Priest ! dar'st thou malign
The silent dead ?

Ign. My lord duke, in the priest
Dwell the same honor and love of truth as share
The soul's vain-garnish'd temples in the breast
Of earth's most rich and noble, — and should be more,
Since there is less to cramp them in the place
That in the truest of men is all too strait.
If silent are the dead, yet living tongues
May vindicate them.   In my words, what was
I asserted not, but what might be.   Thou hast
No cause for anger.   Did the late duke never
Talk with thee on this mystery ?

Bel. I have said,

I was a child.   When ripe to hear, five years
Had pass'd already, and the theme was dead.
I did not dare revive it with my sire,
So stern he had grown and silent. —
      Ign. Ay.
       Bel. — And men
Had ceas'd to talk thereof.   Is 't half that time
Even horrider topics often float alive,   `
Whirl'd on that sea with whose full tide and ebb
So many events drift in, are carried out,
Or sink in its depths in an instant and forever ?
If thou hast aught to instruct me of those babes,
Speak out.   I had thought they wholly were consum'd
In the flames where sunk their parents.
      Ign. And no trace
Left o their burning ?
     Bel. Infants, could that be ?
But answer: know'st thou aught ?
       Ign. Wouldst thou have joy
To hear they were rescu'd ?
      Bel. Should I ?   Let me hear !
Ign. I have nought to tell, my son. — Whence came thy spouse ?
Bel. Thou know'st as well as I.
     Ign. That she grew up
Child of thy sire's adoption.   But where rock'd
Her cradle ?
    Bel. She had none, being lowly-born,
Among the mountains.
     Ign. Bear with me once more.

Live her true parents ?

Bel. One, the mother, still.

Ign. Thou hast seen her ?

Bel. Often. Often yet, with me,
Adela visits her ; and both hold her dear.

Ign. Strange ! [*abstractedly and low.*

Bel. What is ?

Ign. It doth honor to ye both.
Peace with thee, son. [*Exit abruptly.*

Bel. It comes not with the doubts
Thou hast cast upon my spirit. — Why that tone,
And questioning which might anger ? Live perchance
My cousins ? So be it. I will do them right.
This mystery shall have fathoming, if it can.
There is Brulote, servant to my sire
About that fearful time. But in the lapse
Of four and twenty years, what chance can live
Of any trace —— It had found the light ere this.
But what should mean the father ? Thou wast right,
Adela ; in his cloud-wrapt brow, his eye,
Lowers what threatens storm. And this the day
That dawn'd on us so bright ! Heaven grant its set
Be not in that night I dread, yet know not why.

[*Exit, as the Scene changes.*

Scene II.

As in Act I. Scene II.

Enter, from the door,
Marco, *conducting-in* Pablo,
after whom he shuts it carefully.

Mar. Pablo, thou knowest how much I have done for thee.
Pab. Need'st thou remind me?
                    Mar. Ay; not in reproach,
But for I would have thee silent and return
The kindness, like for like.
                    Pab. Wouldst thou too ——
                              Mar. Forge?
Not I, by Heaven! Nay, be thou not disturb'd:
The occasion speaks, not I am tongue-rude. No,
Nor would I to my use sequester that
Which came to me in trust.
                    Pab. Don Marco! ——
                              Mar. Still,
Have patience. — But I must perforce do that,
To our common lord, which sinks me even with thee
To the flat beneath that open and decent post
Where good men stand and honor'd. In a word,
Wilt thou for me do what I did for thee,

Straining thy conscience and by timely act
Help an iniquity shall stead thee not ?

Pab. If not —— What wouldst thou do ?

        Mar. Why, put myself
In thy power. Thou art in mine. What ! wouldst thou stand
On a trifle ? a petty sin, which shows to thine
As a mote to the house-beam ?

       Pab. Speak.

        Mar. Wilt thou but keep
My secret just three hours ?

      Pab. Is that all ? Well ?

Mar. But thou wilt do it ?

     Pab. I will

      Mar. Remember now,
Secret for secret, crime for crime !

       Pab. Be quick.
Thou mak'st me shake.

     Mar. As men do oft in dreams.
Know'st thou the monk — that was, the father now ?

Pab. Ignacio ?

   Mar. Ay. Thine ear. He is the lord,
True and true-gotten, of what our so-call'd Duke
Usurps unknowingly.

     Pab. Thou sayst ! —

      Mar. These arms
Bore him, so bid, to poverty. The day
Has come to avenge him : to restore his rights
Is no more possible.

Pab. But thou! what then
Hast thou to do with it?

         Mar. I have watch'd and rear'd
And love him.

      Pab. Not the less, not he thy lord,
But Don Beltran. There is other cause.

          Mar. Thou art shrewd.
There is, and common unto both. Like him,
I would be aveng'd of the new duke's sire, who wrong'd
Both him and me. 'T is a heart's pang to tell:
But —— What wouldst *thou*, hadst thou a wife defil'd
Almost before thine eyes, thyself struck down
And brutally harm'd, for doing as a man
Must do, so outrag'd.

     Pab. Stab the villain dead.
Mar. Ay, but the villain was more strong than I.
Curs'd be my coward thews, I lay on the floor
And felt the heel of the wronger, him I had help'd
To wealth and title, three times stamp my breast,
And his vile rheum ejected on my cheeks
Through teeth that gnash'd with fury and contempt.
Pab. But after?

     Mar. After was too late. I knew
He was an usurper, thought (as still I think)
He was a brother-murderer ; but no proof
I had then, nor have now, of his guilt: to slay him
Had given myself to death. I bode my time.
It is come. Thou must aid me. Look not so aghast.
It is not blood I ask of thee. My lord,

That shall ever be, I have spurr'd in vain.   His soul,
Timid and unresolv'd, despite the force
Of natural pride and passion, shrinks from pains
Put on the innocent for the guilty's sake.
In some ill hour, I fear, his upright mind
Will prompt him to disclosure.   Then down fall
My schemes forever.   Hence I call'd to aid
The pitiless force of his religious faith.
I told him that the Duchess was the child
Of the Duke's own sire.

    Pab. Thou didst not! couldst not be ——
Mar. So false ?   I know not that I was.   'T is like,
In every view, she was so misbegot.
But thou must vouch for it.   He calls for proof.
Pab. I cannot give it.

    Mar. 'T is easier than to forge,
More safe than to embezzle.   Be a man.
Repay to me in kind the debt thou ow'st
And wipe it off forever.   Thou mayst swear,
With a good conscience, she was bastard-born
Of some unknown great noble.   What more like
Than of the Duke's bad sire.

    Pab. Why, know I not
My lady's mother ?   Is 't not I that pay
Her month's allowance, and provide all else
Our lord ordains for her comfort ?

    Mar. Thou know'st not
The woman is her mother.   I know well
She is not, but has foster'd her, the child

Of some high lord: why not the villain duke?
Left by himself, or through some other's hand.

Pab. Through whose?

    Mar. What matters? 'T is all one. The child
Was not the peasant Sara's. That I swear.
Wilt thou avouch it that she was the Duke's?

Pab. Thou sayst it?

    Mar. That she was the Duke's? I do.
Thou 'rt ready?

    Pab. For this only. Then, my debt —

Mar. Is cancel'd and replac'd by mine to thee,
Due to thee ever. I go to bring the Monk.

       [*Exit.*

Pab. There is some mystery that double-darks
This villanous plot. Brulote tells not all.
Whose was the hand bore out the unfather'd babe
To be nurs'd of Sara? Haply, 't was his own.
The Duke? What duke? Evasion. Marco thinks
To blind me like himself. 'T is not of love
To his sometime friar this plot is woven: the fact
Stands naked as my hand, long-brooded hate
Has now but clipp'd the shell, and hatch'd to life
Chirps in his heart for food. Behooves me heed.
Suck'd in the vortex where he whirls, himself,
I may go down with the eddy. I will see
And sift this Sara. Some hell-lifted stroke
Of fate may be impending o'er my lord
And his sweet lady. I have done him wrong:
To right him now may prove a good amends,

And to betray Brulote profit more
Than to deceive my master.   Let me see.
            Pauses,
      raising thoughtfully his hand
         to his chin; and the

         Drop falls.

ACT THE THIRD

SCENE I. *Same as the one preceding.*

IGNACIO. MARCO.

Ign. Man, thou art devilish.

     Mar. 'T is a change, my lord —
Or reverence, as you bid me, since the rank
Your father gave appears to irk and chafe
The once proud spirit I have so joy'd to watch
Plume its broad pennons, which the cloister's mew
Has flagging made and dull ——

     Ign. No more of that:
It lies above thee. Step down to thy theme.

Mar. Rebuke me not for love. I would have said, —
If I am devilish, 't is a change that comes
Alone of you, for whom my once soft spirit
Is steel'd to other pity. Is it thus
High Heaven pursues its vengeance? Doth the wail
Of innocent offspring, to the fourth remove
Of those that have trampled on its bidding, stay
Its punishing hand?

     Ign. Set thou, too, that aside.
Is it for man, short-sighted and brief-liv'd,

To imitate the All-seeing and Etern ?
Thou but revolt'st the sense thou seek'st to sway,
By such audacious parallel.

    Mar. Let then
Our great King pattern give, whose pious zeal
Wades heart-deep through the blood of tens on tens
Of thousands, while St. Peter's heir at Rome
Hounds on the massacre.[1]

    Ign. Peace !

      Mar. It is in point.
What have the patient and hard-working Moors
Done to draw down perdition ? They but pray
As their fathers taught them ; and their fathers' sin
And ignorance must be wash'd out in their blood ;
Nor does Christ's Vicar, who owns not, as you,
The personal prompture of a just revenge,
Avert his face in horror, as you, whose wrath
Is twofold duty. (Let me speak, my lord,
To the end.) Your cousin, if unsmirch'd
By part in the crime which set him in your place,
Lives yet in daily incest. Doth it suit,
If not your father's son, yet the pure priest,
To sanction, for a day, an hour, the space
In time of a single heart-beat, this huge sin
Against God and man alike ?

    Ign. But on the verge
Of that horrible abyss down which my hands,
My hands that thither brought them, must plunge both,
Suffer me pause awhile, thou but for whom

I had not seen its chasm. What do I know?
Thy soul is black as Satan's with revenge.
What shall avouch that in its hell-smok'd caves
This foul-got secret lay not waiting birth?

Mar. That should my love, for four and twenty years
Unwavering, shown to you, for whom alone,
If such its hue, my soul is black as HelL
But, by that cross, I swear, and by that robe,
By all that is in Heaven above to hear,
On earth to judge, I knew of not one bar,
Not even by birth against that marriage-rite
Which I deem'd best for all. I have said before,
Till yester sun I dream'd not of this crime.

Ign. Which still thou know'st not certain.

                      Mar. O my lord,
Hath not Don Pablo sworn? He was in place
With your uncle, as with ——

             Ign. Why too in his breast
Slumber'd till now this secret?

                Mar. Until now
It was to himself a secret, — till I put
Such question as made dawn on him the facts
That wrought conviction.

            Ign. O accursed day!

Mar. Not so, my lord. Behold, Heaven in your hand
Couples revenge with duty. Not now blood
Needs wet your parents' ashes; and your rights
Shall fall to you without struggle. Tell the Duke,
Now, on the instant, while your-heart yet heaves

With pious anguish, tell him, and before
His guilt's partaker ——

   Ign. Mother of his child.
O man! O man! to what thy heedless deed,
Thy tardy counsel, and thy boasted love
Have push'd me! Had it pleas'd the Lord my God
To keep me blind to my birthright, or to take,
In the sole battle I have shar'd, my life,
Henceforth accurs'd —

   Mar. Forgive I dare break in.
—— Your father's ghost would wander unappeas'd,
And in his sister's bed the crime-made duke
Wallow unstay'd, engendering unsuspect,
In bowels too cognate, issue bann'd of God.
Would this content Domingo's sometime son,
The anointed priest?.

   Ign. Hush, hush! Thou dost presume
Too much on thy service and my habit's vows.
Beltran shall not of my fault nurse the crime
Whose birth was help'd by me. I accept the load
Heaven wills my soul to bear.

   Mar. And take the rights
Man has establish'd under Heaven's permit.
For, parted from his sin-mate, Don Beltran
Adopts of need the life was thine by choice,
Or in some drearier loneness shrouds his shame.

   Enter SERVANT.

Ser. My lord desires Don Marco.

    Mar. Say, I come
On the instant. [*Exit Ser.*
     'T is his conscience is disturb'd.
I shall not soothe it. — Slave of the Most High,
My true lord, Don Alonso, let your slave
Dare to remind you what He bids and take
Your strangled father's voice to cry *Revenge !*
          [*Exit.*

Ign. Revenge ? Not all the mountain-heaps of men
Slain against right and cruelly, which the grave
Hath gulp'd since branded Cain, could yield a voice
Would make that lawful. Heaven unto Himself
Reserv'd its terrors. Smother, thou my heart,
The passions lighted in thee, and each day
Fuel'd by this man, who — how know I else ?
May have some aim and malice of his own.
Beltran is generous, open ; and his wife ——
Ah, there the fatal error which makes of me
The torturer and avenger ! Should it last,
There would be horrible sin, and mine tenfold
As horrible as theirs. What if the tale
Is false, new-made or molded into shape
To suit the occasion and nerve me —— No, O no !
Brulote would not dare —— The steward too ——
Why was I curs'd to live to this black day !
Or rather, to that night, when, 'mid the roar
Of thunder and the rush of wind and rain ——
They were portents. Why did not, by their voice
And the repelling gloom, Heaven move our hearts

With fear of the act that seem'd e'en then forbid?
But to man's passions what are omens all?
I would the storm would come now, wind and rain,
And the roof-shaking thunder, that in gloom
That hid me and in noise that made my voice
Scarce audible, I might hiss the accursed sounds
In ears it were better should be deaf to all.
O that they had the force to kill outright,
Poisoning like serpent's venom!   I should more bold
Speak out my mission, and thank for mercy God.

He clasps his hands over his brow, and
pausing a moment,
kisses passionately his crucifix, and Exit.

SCENE II.

As in Act I. Scene I.

BELTRAN.   ADELA.

To whom, Enter
MARCO.

Bel. I have sent for thee, Don Marco, to relieve
Certain misgivings.   For thy lady's sake

Still more than mine, be ready in reply.
Whence came the Padre ? what his birth ?

                           Mar. Unknown,
Save that, my lord, he was to his own belief
The child of peasants, living in a vale
Of the Guadarrama not far hence remov'd.
Bel. Lo a coincidence should make him view'd
    With more of favor, Adela. — Thou hast said,
    He was rear'd in camps. That was not long ago,
    If since his youth.

               Mar. With his first manhood's down,
Came to him warlike longings, and the fight
On the Nevada with the rebel Moor
Gave him their sole indulgence. In disgust,
Perhaps of bloodshed, it may be of men
Who were his mates not equals, from the camp
He sought the cloister, — there was friar, then priest.
The rest my lord duke knows.

               Ade. No, not the rest.
When first he came to the Castle, — this thou knowest,
Thyself, Don Marco, who didst urge the Duke
To obtain his ghostly service, — not his mien
Was what it now is. Though not indeed the sky
Of his brow was bright, as shines the clear blue heaven
Of Murcia, but more dull and gray of tone,
As ours, yet never violent storm swept o'er
Its placid surface. Now it lowers,
Black with repeated tempest, as the clouds
That scowl with gather'd thunder and fury of rain

O'er darken'd Aragon.   Whence comes this change ?

Mar. Haply from physical causes.   Not in man
  To say what gathers thunder and the rain.

Bel.   Ay, in some sort it is, and why some climes
  Are fraught with more th'n others. .Yet be it so
  The Monk is rack'd, from time to time, with pangs
  His visage mirrors, how is it his breast
  Heaves with like torture?   'T is but now, with looks
  Full of dark meaning, and distrustful words,
  He put strange question of the untoward fate
  Of my duke uncle's children.   Is there aught
  To make us hope they are living ?

                          Mar. O, my lord !
  After so many years?   You need not fear
  The little bones will rise with manhood's length,
  Take flesh, and, with the re-incased soul,
  Leap to your seat.

                  Bel. I said not fear, but hope.
  Bring back my uncle's heir, or give a clue
  Whereby I may trace him through that maze of years
  To his perfect, if chang'd, self, and from this rank
  I shall step as gladly as imperial Charles,
  Don Philip's father, to a lower place,
  Nor will my spouse once murmur.   Hast thou aught
  That is new, on this point?   'T is with thee the Monk
  Has consort most.

                  Mar. I know no more to-day
  Than yesterday, — a month before, — a year, —
  Or for all the many years that, fold on fold,

Enwrap this mystery.   For the Padre's mind,
'T is dark to me as his habit.   Who shall see
The breast beneath he cares not to unfold ?

Bel. Then go to his reverence, and request he come
  To us here without delay.   'T is time to end
This trouble.   Perhaps, made bare to us, his breast
Will find prompt healing.   But if not —
                          Ade. My lord,
Then let him carry to some fitter place
A mood that wakes my loathing and my fear.
                    [*Excunt Bel. and Ade.*
                              above.

Mar. [*coming down, after closing the door upon them.*
    Made bare ?   Its doorless chambers will not show
Much to assure thee.   By thy own will, now,
False duke, thy uncle's long-defrauded heir
Brings thee to sentence.   Ay, the priest shall come,
Domingo's monk, King Philip's man-at-arms,
The foster-brat of peasants, given to me
Thy father's servant, by my casual love
Train'd to his sire's avengement and my own,
Ay, he shall come.   But to this last, great leap,
The spur must force him.   'T is a generous steed,
Full of brave mettle, but too apt to shy
At shadowy dangers, which his thin-skinn'd nerves
Give bulk and shape to.   Could the words I have heard
Be listen'd by him ! —— But that must not be.
The usurper has no " hope ", believes in none.
Virtue and selfdenial seem too small

To need an effort, to those who, from their height
Of fancy'd surety, look down on the plain
Of human struggle, and wonder that the mass
Will fight for vanities and grasp at mites
Whose pomp and littleness are not their own.   .
Brought to the test, our large-soul'd duke may take
His father's eyes, perhaps that father's hand ——
What, should his smooth-tong'd righteousness be feign'd?
A lure for his cousin ?   Thereto he shall not stoop.
His ears shall be deafen'd and his heart made steel,
Till God's great work, for him and me, is through.

[*Exit.*

Drop falls.

ACT THE FOURTH

SCENE I. *As in Act I. Scene I.*

BELTRAN.   ADELA.
IGNACIO *entering.*

Ign. The Duke has had me call'd.[2]

      Bel. To put at rest,
If it may be, evil doubts. —

      Ign. Or give them shapes
Of absolute terror.   Art thou then prepar'd
To see those hideous phantoms swell to forms
Solid and hell-shap'd, by thy frighten'd sense
No longer to be shunn'd ?

      Bel. What dost thou mean ?

Ign. What were thy doubts ?

      Bel. Those which of late thyself
Hast call'd to being by thy menacing looks,
And now giv'st shape anew by looks and words
Wild as of frenzy.   What disturbs thee ?   Why
Lowers that brow, where once was holy calm,
With the affraying blackness of the storm ?

Ign. Thou hast call'd down the lightning.   Not of me
If its bolts strike thee.   I have ask'd before

Whence came thy spouse?

      Ade. Here suffer me, Beltran :
'T is I will answer.   From the mountain-huts,
Where, we are told, thyself hadst humble lair.
The memory of their meanness has to me
Taught lowly sufferance, thankfulness to God,
And charity for my fellows, as in thee
It hath brought to growth a harsh disdain of kind,
Ill-rooted anger at thy Maker's will,
And poisonous envy of the better rank
Others are born or rais'd to.

      Ign. Lady, no.
Were it my business now, a single word
Would startle thee to sorrow for one charge
Of those thou hast heap'd on me : the rest my soul
Passes unconscious.   Let me as the priest
I have call'd to mind I am, the priest who put
Those hands together, ask, O daughter, of thee,
Art thou assur'd thy mother was indeed
The goatherd's wife who nurs'd thee.

      Ade. Come, Beltran.

Ign. No, yet a moment.   Comes to this thy boast
Of lowliness and patience ?   Thou wouldst read,
Thou and thy lord, the meaning of my gloom.
Answer me truly, as I hold of God
A solemn mission to ask thee, — has thy birth
Been never a theme of doubt ?

      Ade. To me ?   Go ask,
So it concerns thee aught, the dame herself

I cherish still as mother.

     Ign. I have heard
She is but thy fostermother, thou the child
Of a noble of high rank.

      Bel. [*sternly : Ade. speechless, clinging*
     to him.] Thou seëst, priest.

Ign. — Her strength is little.   Were it not best for both,
She should withdraw ?   I would not crush her heart
By a sudden blow of what must not less fall.
O lady and daughter ! though thou lik'st me not,
I have honor and pity, as I never had
.Less than admiring reverence, for thee.
Let me beseech thee, spare me and thyself.

Ade. [*recovering.*] No, if it is thy cruel task indeed
To turn to bitter what was so sweet, and dark
The light of this day thou holp'st thyself create,
Speak out and quickly, Who my father, then ?

Ign. If the words blast thee, not from me the bolt,
Unhappy lady.   Would that Heaven had chosen
Some other hand than mine to draw it down !

Bel. Torture her not.   Who was he ? if indeed
Thou know'st.   Bear up, Adela.

      Ign. 'T was — the Duke.

Bel. What duke? [*To Ade.*] How pale thou art! It may be false.

Ign. Alas, it was sworn upon this cross, re-sworn
By a sure witness.   Send and seek the woman.
'T were better it were put beyond all doubt.

Bel. Why dost thou palter thus ?   I feel and fear
Thou need'st no witness.   Who were they that swore ?
 21*

Ign. Thy steward, and he who with thy sire had place
Of trust like that with thee.

                   Bel. O God !   The Duke? —

Ign. What else but he who adopted his own child ?

Bel. My sire !

        Ign. Look to thy lady ! —   O Heaven, why ou my
           head ——

Ade. [*to Bel.*] Stay me not ! Touch me not ! Farewell, Beltran.

Bel. Adela ! [*Exit Ade.*

    .. *Pauses gloomily, and, coming back:*
    It is better.

            Ign. Wouldst thou dare
That other horror ?   Save her !

               Bel. And for what ?
From what ?   Accursed priest ——

              Ign. Accurs'd of God.
Before thee I am blameless.

             Bel. Get thee hence.

Ign. I go, — to save thy lady.

       Bel. [*detaining him.*] Didst thou hear ?
Wouldst thou to this damn'd being bring her back,
If senseless, or if dead ? —   My sister ?   Oh !
Oh ! oh !   Adela ! [*Sinks in a chair before a table, his face
    in his hands, and seemingly sobbing; Ign. looking
    up to Heaven with anguish.*

          Leave me ! [*suddenly rising and with
             passion.*

          Ign. But with God. [*Exit.*

Bel. My sister ?   'T is the punishment of Heaven.

Had we not wed in secret; had I ask'd
My sire's consent —— Her sire? And our child!
Born of iucestuous commerce! [*Rings handbell violently.*
                                     It shall not ——

Enter Servant.

Bring my boy hither.
                Ser. With his nurse, my lord?
Bel. No. And be quick. [*Exit Ser.*
                       'T is fitting this should end;
The accideut with the crime, and those that were
The unconscious doers. Canst thou see, O God,
This misery of Thy creatures? Or, through me,
Through her — my sister — is 't Thou wreakst Thy wrath
For my sire's sins? for what perhaps was sin —
So men have charg'd — of most atrocious die.
I will not think it. But be it. I shall make —
She too will make — atonement for it all.
        *Goes again to the table and assumes his
              previous attitude.*

SCENE II.

As in Act I Scene II.

IGNACIO. MARCO.

Ign. No more! no more! This horror is enough.
Mar. Will you here stop? Son of a strangled sire,
A strangled mother, will you turn from God,
The God of Abram, and wipe clean your hands
Ere they have done His work?

       Ign. Thou speakest well:
My hands are filthy with the horrible deed
Thou hast driven me to. Be it Heaven's will or not,
I have done it, and need add no other stain
To what pollutes them and makes sick my soul.
The God of Abram? Was not Isaac spar'd?
My innocent victims — where the thicket ram
That is caught by the horns for them? O man! O man!
Mistake not for God's vengeance what is thine.
I have undone the evil that I did. No more.
Let me go hence unknown, and keep for Him
What rests of the heart thou hast not wholly warp'd
To an undeserv'd revenge.

      Mar. My lord, my lord!
Son of the Duke Alonso! in his name,

Wherewith thou wast baptiz'd, I call on you
To do him justice.   Shall his ashes lie,
His and your lady mother's, by his side
Who with his hungry fingers grasp'd their throats,
Nor by their starting eyeballs, or the groans
He sought to smother, was one moment mov'd
To loose his hold ?

     Ign. Have done !

       Mar. Did Heaven not cry
In the ears of his heart like words ?   And did he pause ?
Think you Heaven wills his impious bones should rest
By his encinder'd victims, and his heir
Sit in the place of their children ?   Let it be
That Don Beltran is guiltless ——

     Enter hurriedly
      Servant.

    Ser. Reverend father !
Don Marco !   O my God, my God !

      Ign. What bodes ?

Ser.   My lord and lady are gone mad.   The Duke
Is strangling his own child.

     Ign. Thou know'st, nor staid'st
To stop him ? [*moving to the door.*

    Ser. Could I ?   And I was dismiss'd.
Scar'd by his looks, I watch'd him through the door,
By the hole of the lock, and saw him clutch the neck ——
Come, come !

Ign. Yes, yes.

   Mar. [*detaining Ign.*

    For what ? It is too late.

         [*Noise within.*

What is that cry ?

    Ser. Oh, oh! they have found it true :
'T was said my lady had hung herself.

       Ign. I sent
To save her. Go ; call in thy fellows, all ;
Take from the Duke all weapons. Go ! I come.

         [*Exit Ser.*

To Mar.] Take off thy hand ! Art thou a fiend indeed ?
Mar. If such wreak Heaven's vengeance. Heard you not ?
They have died the death your sire and mother died. -
'T was the Duke's fingers —— Yes, go now, my lord.
Go to complete the solemn work.

      Ign. I go
To save one victim.

    Mar. [*again detaining him.*

     Can aught harm him more ?
Death were a blessing. Go, my lord, reveal
All yet untold. Your rights recover.

      Ign. Never !
Mar. Forgive me, is this duty ? For my sake,
Who have rear'd you (must I say it) by my means,
That you might do —

    Ign. What better had been done
Openly and at once.

    Mar. At risk of life.

Sav'd by my care, will you now shrink from that
Which can alone reward it, and for which
Heaven itself hath spar'd you?   Take the name
Of your sire, if not his rights, and end what else
Were better not begun.   What now from man
Can hurt the false duke more?

                   Ign. Alas! —   Come then.
I need thy witness.   Bid too Pablo come.
Mar. He is gone, I know not whither.   Let us haste.

                          [*Exeunt hurriedly, by the door, as*

             the Drop falls.

ACT THE FIFTH

SCENE. *As in Act I. Scene I.*

BELTRAN, *leaning on the table, as before.*

Enter
IGNACIO. MARCO.

Bel. [*rising gloomily.*⁹] Adela! No. What summons such as ye?
   I sent for my dead wife's body, not for you.
Ign.   Beltran de Santos, know'st thou who I am?
Bel.   Perhaps the Devil. Thou art at least to me
   A loathlier sight than were thy visage grim'd
   With smoke of Hell. Take from my eyes at once
   Thy damned presence.
              Ign. Thou hast ask'd to know
   Of thy uncle's children. One at least is here.
   I am thy cousin, the true heir of him
   Thy father strangled.
              Bel. Liar! whether priest
   Or noble. Wast thou born my uncle's son,
   Thou 'dst shrink to stain his brother's name with crime
   Was never proven.
              Ign. Stands the witness there,

Thy servant and his own.

                   Bel. He will not say it.

Ign. He doth. I reck that not, but leave with God

The secret of a fate He may have will'd,

Not man devis'd. But to Brulote's hand

Thy father gave my sister and myself. —

Bel. [*eagerly.*] Thy sister? Was she sav'd?

                        Ign. I am told she died.

Bel. Alas, I had hope —— 'T would make my sin less black,

But not my fate less frightful, and on thee

Heap horror that would crush thee. Look thou there!

Enter Servants
with the body of Adela.

Lay her down gently. Leave us. But thou, stay. [*to 1st Ser.*

          [*The rest Exeunt, after covering the body.*

It is my — wife. I meant on this, her corpse,

To finish —— But a fitter end is nigh.

Adela! [*kneeling before the body. Then, suddenly starting up.*

       No; I will weep no more. Look thou. [*drawing*

            Ign. to the body and uncovering the face.

Could that not move thee? such a face as that,

Which Heaven would love, and Hell might find too sweet

Not to feel pity for? Yet thou, yet thou,

For a villain's tale, which may be false, hast turn'd

Her hand against herself and made of me

My own child's murderer! Art thou weeping, too?

Leave tears to women. They insult the dead

Falling from thee. —

   Ign. Beltran ——

     Bel. Ah yes, ah yes : *

Thou com'st for thy right. If thou wast not a priest,

And knew'st the sword, I 'd bid thee take one now,

Like a man, and right thyself.

       Ign. Though I am such,

Nor us'd to the sword, I have borne arms and seen

How fencers practise, and with Heaven's aid

Will take thy weapon, nor shall I feel regret

If I should fall.

    Mar. My lord, my lord Alonso !

Ign. Loose me, Don Marco, and ye both stand back.

I know well what I do.

      Bel. And know I now

That thou art my true cousin. Take this blade.

'T is a Toledo and the best I have.

They could not force me yield them, as thou bad'st.

    BELTRAN *and* IGNACIO *engage.*

The former purposely fences ill, and IGNACIO,

who has become heated in the contest, using his weapon

vigorously though awkwardly, passes it

through the Duke's body.

Bel. 'T is as I meant. I have no wish to live.

[*Drags himself to Adela's body, and is supported by 1st Ser.*

   Enter, hurriedly and eagerly,

    PABLO *and* SARA.

Pab. Too late ! too late ! But not perhaps to save

From other misery.   O my lorᴅ the Duke,
How is it with you ?

    Bel. Even as I wish'd.

Didst thou too plot agaiṅst me ?

     Pab. O forgive !

I was bound to that traitor, who knew and kept conceal'd
My frauds in office.   But I sought, my lord,
To unmask his horrible guilt; and it is done.
Behold the dame who nurs'd, my lord, your lady.
She swears she·was brought to her by Marco's self,
The night of that awful fire.   There is no doubt
She was your uncle's daughter ; and there stands,
In the priest's frock, her brother.

      Bel. Is that true ? •

Look on her face. [*to Sara.*

     Sara. O God! she is dead. [*beating her hands*
              together.

        It is
My fosterchild ; and he, Don Marco there,
Brought her to me.

    Bel. Thou hast lifted from my heart ——
My breath grows short.   Alonso, ask that fiend
What urg'd him ——

    Mar. That which urges Hell and Heaven, —
Vengeance for wrong.   I have wreak'd it to the full,
Both for myself, whom your detested sire
Foully abus'd, and for your uncle's heir.
Could I have done it else, I had not drivcn
My lady to that act for which I grieve.

Sara speaks sooth.   The Duchess was the child
Of the dead Duke Alonso.   But the hand
Of God hath stricken her for your father's crime.

Ign.   Impious, speak no more !   Beltran ——— [*taking his hand.*

                          Bel.   Again

Thou weep'st, and scalding tears.   Nay, mind me not.
Keep them ; thou wilt have need ; for — for Adela.
Thou hast now thy rights.   Be thou content therewith.
Forgive my father — as I — pardon thee.   [*Droops over*
                the body of Adela, then falls back, dead.

Ign.   A moment, all.   But see, that crawls not hence
That serpent.

        Servant locks the door, then presently returns,
   •   *when he and* PABLO *put themselves on*
               either side of MARCO.

        Mar.   It needs not.   Were all the doors
Wide open set, I abide here, my lord duke.

Ign. [*hanging over the body of Adela.*

   Known only now, my sister ; and, now known,
To be so parted !   We shall soon re-meet.
'T is my first kiss, Adela.   Let thy soul,
Where it will know me, pity and forgive.

                [*Covers the body and comes down.*

Ye who are here bear witness to these acts.
I have slain my cousin, and innocent have caus'd
My sister's and my nephew's death.   The laws
Would have no punishment for me beguil'd
And driven to these misdeeds ; and in the priest
The atonement would be penance, which my rank

Would make scarce real. It is fit these crimes
Should have their sacrifice, and God himself
Requires it at my hands, last of a house
Too wicked not to fall. In His name then,
I make it: thus. [*raising the sword, grasped by the middle.*
   Mar. [*throwing himself before him.*
    No, no, in Heaven's name,
I, though I am Hell-doom'd, I, implore you, pause!
Ign. Thou? who hast brought me to this pass? Stand back!
 Touch not my robes, which are stainless but for thee.
Mar. Hear me! I have nurs'd for two and twenty years
One love, one hatred. *That* has been deceiv'd:
The last is sated. I shall die content,
Will you but live for that place, wherein to see you
I have forfeited my soul. Forgive, my lord,
Duke Don Alonso, that, in heat of zeal,
I have brought you into error and to wo.
Ign. Ask it of God, misguided wretch. In me
Is sorrow alone for thy mistaken soul.
With devilish malice and remorseless craft,
Thou hast glutted thy own hatred and revenge,
And hugg'd the thought it was of love for me.
Hadst thou done justly and by open ways
Maintain'd my right, there were no bloody deaths
 Upon thy soul, nor could that harmless boy
And his mother, at the judgment-seat of God,
Now blessed angels, cry against thee. Thou,
In the life-prisonment which must be thine,
Wilt find time for remorse, which Heaven send:

For me, there is but one way order'd.   This.

                          [*Stabs himself.*

Mar. O me accursed! [*his head to the floor.*

            Ign. Lay my coffin over

Or between theirs.   To Thy hands, Lord, my spirit ——

                              [*Dies.*

Curtain falls.

NOTES

1.—P. 484. — *whose pious zeal   Wades heart-deep, etc. etc.*] In Grenada and the Alpujarras, 1567–70. The revolt was caused by the enforcement of a barbarous decree (originally of Charles V. but not by him carried into effect,) and, on both sides of the contest, was marked by excessive and often atrocious cruelties. See Rosseeuw de St. Hilaire: *Hist. d'Espagne*, XXVII. i. (Tom. 8. pp. 419–457. Paris 8°. 1839.)

The account of the insurrection and its consequences is given in ample detail by Ferreras: *Hist. Gen. d'Espagne*; Trad. d'Hermilly, (Paris et Amst. 4to. 1751,) t. ix, commencing at p. 563 (but previously, pp. 524 sq.), and t. x. pp. 1–236.

2.—P. 493. *The Duke has had me call'd.*] Otherwise: "My son, thou hast had me call'd." But the reading in the text is preferable. Under the feelings and with the purpose with which he enters, *Ignacio* would have repugnance to assume the usual paternal style of address. Indeed, his position as confessor would be forgotten.

3.—P. 502. Bel. (rising gloomily.] Or, *starting up;* which was the first conception. But I doubt whether he would not be more depressed than excited. His excitement only comes when, his eye resting on *Ignacio*, his grief changes to fury.

4.—P. 504. Ign. *Beltran* —— Bel. *Ah yes, ah yes :*] Otherwise

         Ign. Beltran — my cousin ——
                 Bel. Yes :

Which reading, as clearer, may be preferable for the Stage. But the first, which is the original one, is the best. When *Ignacio* begins addressing *Beltran* by his proper name, the latter is instantly reminded of the former's rights and recalled to his own purpose, implied in the previous words " a fitter end is nigh."

MATILDA OF DENMARK

MDCCCLXIV

CHARACTERS, Etc.

CHRISTIAN VII., *King of Denmark.*

FREDERIC, *his half-brother, — son of Frederic V. by Juliana.*

STRUENSEE, *principal Minister of the King.*

BRANDT, *Chief Master of the Household, and favorite of the King.*

BERNSTORFF, *formerly Minister under Frederic V.*

UHLDAL, *a counsellor.*

MOLTKE, *ex-minister of the preceding reign.*

RANTZOW,
KŒLLAR, } *along with Moltke, of the Queen-dowager's party.*
EICHSTADT,

SIR ROBERT KEITH, *British Ambassador at the Danish Court.*

CAROLINE-MATILDA, *spouse of Christian, and sister of George III. of England.*

JULIANA-MARIA, *Queen Dowager.*

AMA'LIE, Countess Svider, *Chief Lady of the Queen's Household.*

A LADY *in waiting.* PAGES. *An* USHER. *Struensee's* CHAMBERLAIN.

SCENE. *For the most part in the Royal Palace at Copenhagen, but finally in the Fortress of Cronenburg.*

MATILDA OF DENMARK

SCENE I. *A room in the Palace of the Queen-Dowager.*

JULIANA. FREDERIC.

Fred. Madam and mother, no. It follows not,
    That being ambitious I must crouch to climb.
Jul. No, but who climb use not their grasp alone,
    Nor is their motion decorous, or what shows
    The body to advantage. By fair ways,
    I mean by open and direct approach,
    Thou never wilt achieve the royal heart:
    That citadel surrenders but to craft.
Fred. And to assail in front, with flag and trump,
    Summons the foe, and gives him odds against us
    For that, I have no better will than thou.
    But thou wouldst have me march by devious ways,

Tangled and dark, and, be it said with leave,
Not over-clean.

    Jul. What is thy better path ?
Thou wouldst destroy the favorite, tear to shreds
His fine-wove schemes of dissolute reform,
But leave the Queen her influence.

        Fred. No, not that,
-Only her character; which to take away
May suit a woman's strategy, not mine.

Jul. These are proud words, and sharp. Their point, my son,
 Could not be meant for me. We take away,
 Not what is gone, but is; and Struensee
 Is known to usurp the functions of the King,
 Not merely in his throne. 'T is current talk.

Fred. Not with those near the Queen. Our warmest friends,
 And Struensee's sworn foes, assert it not.

Jul. But think it none the less. What! 't is the King
 Whose honor is involv'd, and thou thyself
 Art half his brother on the better side :
 Would loyal men, or prudent, or well-bred,
 Insinuate unto thee, even if they durst —
 Knowing the law of treason, what on this point
 I may discourse at will ? But, be thou sure,
 Their eyes, though reverent, see; they think, if silent.

Fred. I too have thoughts and eyesight, and I mark,
 Often what is unseemly in the Queen,
 But nothing that gives token of a crime,
 In act or even intention. Undue warmth,
 And levity, and a too familiar tie

Between them, all of this is seen ; and this
We owe unto ourselves, whose futile acts
Instead of weakening either, made them join
For mutual support and strengthen'd both.
But all of this is all. Even Rantzow's self,
Who hates the upstart German as I do,
Conceives no more : and think'st thou honest Brandt
Would lend his friendship, conscious of such crime ? ;

Jul. I do. But thou — when didst thou learn to see
In Christian's minion aught but one block more
Of stumbling in thy way ?

                Fred. When I essay'd
To scan the obstacle, before I leapt it
Or try'd to heave it bodily from my path.
Thou art my mother : am I therefore blind
To see that lust of power now eggs thee on ?
Because the Queen, and Struensee, and Brandt,
Threaten my progress or obstruct it now,
Must I find her adulterous, and them fools
Or profligates ? 'T is not by scurril words
We shall unseat the favorites, nor the Queen
Bring to disgrace by charges hard to prove.
Try kinglier craft, or, if we must, let force
Sever these wires which give the puppet king
His semblance of life-motion. I am prompt
For either ; and what time so fit as now
When every class, invaded in its rights,
Is furious, or disgusted, or alarm'd ?

Jul. My son, thou wilt not trust me, or thou seest

Not half so far as I. Thou lov'st not women :
Why car'st thou for the Queen ? Destroy her lover —
As I maintain him, — yet, if she be spar'd,
To exert her influence on the facile king,
How are we better ?

    Fred. She will not be spar'd.
Let us not quarrel. Keep thou to thy plan,
And leave me mine. The two may be combin'd.
The ascent to power is not the spiral road,
Broad and continuous, where a king might drive,
Up Brahè's tower[1], but has broken steps
Of various height, with spots to land between
Where one may rest forever — and often does.
Whether your steps are lighter to ascend,
Or mine, my mother, matters little ; all
Lead to one top and make one common stairs.
Time presses ; and our friends, thou know'st, will soon
Meet here in council. Suffer me to leave.

      [*Exit.*

Jul. Thou play'st it well. Or, be thy scruples fair,
Thou gott'st them from thy soft-soul'd drunken sire ;
Yet thou art not his likeness, but ap'st me.
Thou 'dst kill thy enemy ; but in one way ;
Compass thy ends by craft ; but not by such
As women use, such as befits a man !
What should that be ? Nay, bless the word, a king !
I know no such distinction, and despise
These subterfuges of the o'er-dainty mind
That startles at a name, yet dares a deed

Whose bloodiness or meanness is so hid
Under a cloak of pretext, or so lisps
Its purpose through the fringe-piece of a mask,
That shape and sound are travesty'd.   Yet when need
Demands it, and the world its million eyes
Hath turn'd upon us, I too can dissemble,
Flaunt scruples and be haught of mind as thou.
This may attest, who knows it to her cost,
The shallow-brain'd Matilda, whose full brood
Of royal bastards, hatch'd and to be hatch'd,
Stops from our natural rights both thee and me.
It may not always.   I will make the germs
Of this prolificness know never more
The fecundating power, come whence that may.
She may be innocent (yet I doubt it much,)
Innocent of the act wherein alone,
In the world's eyes, consists the sexual guilt,
But not in thought, not in the lecherous will.
Give time and nice occasion, and this will
May ripen to fruition ; and for that,
I am the goddess-mother which shall send
The Dido and Æneas to one cave,
Though not in storm and darkness.   But, before,
There may be caverns of another kind
Which shall receive them separate, whence to come
Will not be into sunshine.   Take then heed,
Thou royal wanton ! who art yet too weak
To hide thy dalliance ; even this festive night,
A hundred foes shall watch thee in the dance,
     22*

See with my eyes, and judge thee for my ends.

[*Exit.*

Scene II.

Struensee's Apartment in the Royal Palace.

Struensee. Brandt.

Br. How canst thou doubt me, Struensee?   My fate
Is bound up with thy own.   As unto thee
I owe the royal favor, so thy fall
Carries me with it.   Thus, were I of men
The most ungrateful even, my sad voice
Could have no meaning in it but thy good.
Stru. I doubt thee not.   I never had a doubt.
How couldst thou think it?   But I lend no faith
To popular rumor.   That the nobles hate me,
I well may credit; that the Norway troops,
Whom I disbanded, gladly would revolt,
We late had proof, and how I put them down;
But the poor people whom I cherish love me,
And the King favors still.
Br. As he doth me.
Seëst thou what he is, in whose weak soul

There is no strength for steadiness, and deem'st
Thy throne a rock?   Alas! the sand is firmer.
And for the people, credulous and dull,
Servile, suspicious, living for the hour,
Prone, like the goats, to follow any head,
Yet at the first fright scattering like sheep,
What canst thou hope from them?   Thou art not so
    planted —
Forgive me! in the general regard
As to make front against the blasts of fortune:
Not like the elymus, whose spreading roots
Bind fast our sands and broad leaves break the winds.
The first storm will upheave thee, and the drift
Bury thy growth forever.   O, be warn'd!

Stru. I am, but flinch not.   I can not be brave
Like Rantzow's foresire, nor may know throughout
His constant fortune, but I can, and will,
Like him, be faithful.[2]

                Br. It was to his king.
Thou thy allegiance vowest to the mass,
And the broad arms of thy far-reaching duty
Embrace the nation, and would fold with love
All its entangled interests to thy breast.
'T is for a god, an angel, — not for man;
Not in one lifetime; not in Denmark.   [3] Here,
Bethink'st thou? since the monarchy was fix'd,
Bound by no law, yet making laws for all,
All things must needs go backward, or stand still,
Or fall, confus'd, corrupted, and decay'd,

Into a mass inextricable, vile,
Which poisons, or by mere inertia baffles
The would-be disentangler.

                 Stru. Thou hast heard
Of Justesen, of Hitteroe, in Trondhjem.'
' A simple peasant, a hireling: yet this man,
Untutor'd, and uncounsel'd, guided solely
By his clear sense and judgment, and sustain'd
By his strong — let me call it lofty, heart, —
For such as he are nobles of the earth,
Earth-born and not created, and endow'd
With all the virgin vigor of the soil, —
This peasant-lord made even nature bend
To his behest.   He took a little farm,
Free for two years from rent.   The rocks, the waters,
The soil itself oppos'd him; but he made
All yield to him.   He turn'd the water-courses,
Hew'd him strait passages in the solid stone,
Fill'd up the marshes, made a barren patch
Between the rocks and sea bloom like the rose,
Nor even when old gave o'er.   Shall I do less?
Men laugh at me.   'T is nothing: they mock'd him.
Men hate me.   It is something: he had none,
In his low state, to hate and envy him.
I have thus one impulse more; for I shall toil
To conquer hatred and make envy die
Of very shame.

               Br. If the rocks crush thee not,
The waters not submerge, and, worse than all,

The soil be not what cannot be reclaim'd.

Stru. That were impossible.   There is no soil
May not be made to yield, if not of itself,
By means prescrib'd of science.   There are no rocks
May not be split in twain: Amil'car's son
Would not be baffled by the pil'd-up Alps.
There are no waters, even the ocean's own,
But may be turn'd aside, at least shut out.
Shall the slow-plodding Dutch do more than I,
Whose brain is fire and whose exhaustless nerves
Have Heaven's own electricity ?

       Br. But will
Success make envy of less life than now ?
• Did not then Thygè Brahè, name renown'd
Wherever man aspires to read the stars,
Did he not fall by envy, and the prais'd
Of all men in one reign become the oppress'd
Of the succeeding, and, forbid to use
The science which to the remotest time
Has made him, and his country with him, fam'd,
Forsake the ungrateful Danes to die in Prague ?

Stru. But not inglorious ; he was honor'd there,
As erst, ere malice ruin'd him, at home.
And hast thou not o'erlook'd his dying phrase,
When his prefigur'd glory rose before him
In his delirium, and he cry'd and cry'd,
"I have not liv'd in vain !" ?

       Br. Alas, my friend,
Thou hast forgotten, thou ; for Brahè died

The martyr of an idle scruple. Thus,
He liv'd, it might be said, as lives the sage,
But died as fits a fool.⁷ And do not men
Contrive, who praise him, to remember too
His foibles ?

      Stru. But his better points outlive them,
Even as his system's faults can not obscure
His true discoveries. The world does not
Indeed stand still; but neither does his name.

Br. Hug to thy breast that solace; for thou soon
Mayst need it all. Euvy dies not of shame,
And knows not dread. Could fear disarm the envious,
Heinesen had escap'd.⁸ But neither valor,
Nor virtue, nor long services avail'd him.
He died as he had liv'd, without a fear,
But died upon the scaffold.

            Stru. But his doom
Was presently revers'd.

            Br. Ay, o'er his grave.
Did it call back the spark of mortal life
To his cold ashes ? Could it reunite
The head and trunk that fell so ignominiously ?

Stru. Not ignominiously I The blade touch'd not
His honor, and the scaffold has no shame
Save for the guilty.

      Br. Be it even so.
But what avail'd his sentence thus revers'd ?

Stru. It joy'd his heirs; and history learns to honor
Whom envy could not keep disgrac'd.

Br. Amen,

If that contents thee.   And I dare not laugh.

The poets struggle for as poor a meed.

But like that kind of men, whose dreamy souls

Live in the future, while their senses sleep

To famine and neglect, so mayst thou yield

The quiet and the joy of present good,

And have no future, even for thy tomb.

Does history never lie ?

    Stru. Do men that think

Take upon trust its records?   Let it lie:

There are, and will be ever, men whose eyes

See for themselves; and such as these shall judge.

Perhaps from out my bloody grave some hand,

Even of that class thou mak'st to dream as I,

Shall disinhume — no ashes, but my name ;

And Struensee, once more on earth, the stage

Of life shall tread, more honor'd than of old,

And not a secret buried with his corse

But shall find breath again to do him right.

Br. [*after a pause, in which he regards Stru. with melancholy*
   interest.

 Thou sleepest on thy ruin.

     Stru. Amen, if 't be

The bed of honor.   Wake me not.

      Br. It is

The bed of death.   Thou shalt not sleep,

If my alarm can wake thee.   Listen now ;

I have not told thee all.   I did not dare it

There 's treason in the whisper.

                Stru. Yet 't was bruited :

For thou didst bring but popular report.

Speak boldly.

          Br. 'T is a single word : The Queen.

Stru. Count Brandt !

            Br. Nay, be not angry : I am still

Thy friend, thy loving friend, who owe thee all.

I could not be such, though I owe thee all,

Did I believe thee guilty.

              Str. And of what ?

O this exceeds in malice all the rest !

O thou hadst cause, couldst thou believe me guilty !

Who could contrive this wickedness, who spread

The damn'd detraction through the pôpular mind ?

Br. Who but thy chiefest enemies, who but those

Who hate thee and the Queen alike, — the Prince

And his ambitious mother ?   Shall I speak

With plainness ?

          Stru. Without fear.   I trust thee all.

Br. Why wilt thou lend a color to their lie ?

The Queen, 't is plain, admires thee, holds thee dear.

'T is natural, that, neglected by the King,

Young and fair-favor'd, she should over-rate

The zeal of thy attentions ; that —

            Stru. I vow ——

Br. Do I not know thee ?   — That she should conceive

Thou hast, thyself, forgotten, what, well I know,

Thou never wilt forget, the many ties

That bind thee to thy king, and make even thought
Of an infringement more than common crime.
Stru. O spare me!

    Br. Yet a little.   There is fear —
Stru. Never! of my so falling.

      Br. There is fear,
Not that thou mayst mislead, but be misled.
Be not impatient.   Thou hast learn'd to read
The hearts of men and women, and know'st the force
Of habit in all nature.   Thou 'rt a man,
In form and mind, such as a queen might choose,
Had she election, and, being such, hast gain'd
Knowledge of women.   Need I say to thee,
How step by step the best of them come on
To venture farther than perhaps they thought?
One innocent indulgence, as they deem it,
Leads to another less so — not at once,
But after iteration of the old —
Leads to another less so, till the soul,
Startled no longer, craves for, pines for, seeks,
Seeks without shame, but not without remorse,
Which yet grows less and less, the envenom'd food
Which habit hath made needful as the air.
Stru. 'T is true.   But it shall not apply to her.
 Br. Not to the *Queen.*   Remember! there is guilt
That looks like innocence, and unsmirch'd innocence
May through self-confidence so dark itself
As to put on the attributes of guilt.
One spot of this swart color may suffice,

Under an absolute king, to blot out life.
Think of Kay Lykkè.[9]   For a braggart phrase,
That sham'd no woman really, and deserv'd
Contempt not chastisement, stripp'd at once of rank,
Of name, of fortune, everything but life,
And that sav'd but by flight.   Thou treadest, then,
Upon a Hekla, which at any moment
May burn or bury thee.   Even now meseems
I hear its bellowings under us.   Step back,
Before it be too late.   But hush! no more:
For lo where comes her Majesty's Chief Lady,
Thy dark-brow'd widow with her endless suit.
Ponder, and pardon. [*Exit.*

     Str. Nay, I love thee more.

   Enter AMALIE.

This, Countess, is a pleasure unexpected.
Ama. Your tone would say, vexation.

      Stru. For my tone,
It takes its color from what was, not is:
My friend was with me, and has made me think.
I am sorry that your cause should move so slow ;
But the law's course is to a proverb such —
And the Queen —— [*becomes abstracted.*

    Ama. [*after observing him awhile.*

     Queen !   What does she with my cause ?
I could myself have urg'd her ; but I thought
The King alone ——

Stru. Pray pardon.   Where was I?

Ama. Should I reply exactly, With the Queen,

Stru. Madam!

  Ama. Pray pardon me in turn.

      Stru. Your cause
Has neither been neglected nor deferr'd.
But steps in law I need not say are tedious,
And many disappointments balk our aim.

Ama. Many indeed!

 Stru. [*abstractedly.* Ah many!   So is well.
'T were better were there more.   It is in life
Often the saving grace. [*Lapses into silence.*

    Ama. Is that for me?

Stru. What? — No, no; pardon me again; my thoughts
Wander despite myself to anxious themes
Which Brandt suggested.   But it matters none.
I could not be of service to you now,
Even were my mind at ease.

    Ama. I do believe you.
When next I call to press my tedious claim,
Your Excellency will be more at home. [*Going.*

Stru. Depart not angry.

    Ama. Have I then no cause?

Stru. None in your disappointment.

    Ama. O no! none;
None in my disappointment.

    Stru. What means that?
Why speak you thus? why look thus?   And those tears?

Ama. Tears, say you?   Yes.   They are shed, not for my cause.

[10] That to defer has been a pleasure, till —
Till you grew languid in it.

     Stru. Is not this
Unjust, ill-tim'd? Have you then never thought
That I must be at moments overwhelm'd,
Weary with headwork, and may well appear
Languid, unsympathetic?

     Ama. Were that all!
Am I a child, to weep for that? except
It were to weep for your sake. But your tone,
So cold; your absent and chang'd looks; your speech,
Suddenly interrupted by strange words,
And follow'd by a silence that were rude
But that you seem'd lost to yourself and me;
And — and —— I am a fool, I know, — a child,
I feel; forget what you have seen — these tears,
As I shall — all the past. [*going.*

     Stru. And what is that?
Have I been so misconstru'd? Has my zeal
To aid a lady with my power in court,
To press even with the King her righteous claim
For a dead husband's service, has this pains,
So gladly taken to help her ——

     Ama. Say no more,
Or you will make me lose my sex's pride,
As you forgot your manhood to offend it.
Had you been always what I see you now,
You had been spar'd that pains; I should have scorn'd
To be so burden'd. O that these tell-tale eyes

Had been sear'd up with fire before they wept!
That I should thus! —— "But no! you are not of those
Who angle for a woman's heart for pastime,
Feeding their vanity by brief amorous tokens
Forc'd from the weakness of her own : there 's more in 't ;
I have not been cajol'd ; I am supplanted.
From your heart's fullness, ere that dreamy pause,
Your lips reveal'd it, — "And the Queen."

      Stru. For Heaven's! ——

Ama. They were the words. Your face has color now ;
 You are no longer weary and o'erwhelm'd.
Stru. O be appeas'd! This is all madness — all
 Mistake, and the distorted forms of things
 Seen through excited feelings. Do sit down !
 We will talk over —
    Ama. Nothing in this spot.
 Forget, if you are noble and a man,
 The tears you have wrung from me, the incautious words ;
 I shall remember what I owe — *the Queen.*

        [*Exit.*

Stru. Ah, most untoward! — Little thought'st thou, Brandt,
 The trouble thou wouldst cause me — and (alas !
 I cannot shut it from me) the delight.
 O, I am madder than the mad! This is
 An angling in a pool of dangerous depth,
 Not that where swim such vanities as thine,
 Thou proud and froward countess. O my God,
 Thou knowest mine is not meditated guilt ;
 Keep my weak soul from yielding ; [12] let the thrill

That is such fascination be resisted,
Forgotten, and avoided, lest I sink
Where is no bottom, dragging down with me
One whom I dare not name ! — But does she then
So estimate my attentions ? holds she me
Indeed so dear ? Would thy well-meaning words,
Too candid friend, had flatter'd less ! Till then
I was more innocent. But now — oh now,
What shall disperse the dangerous-wicked thoughts
That rise before me, ingrate to my king,
False to my office, to my trusts, and false,
Wickedly false — for it is all a lie,
Fraud and delusion, this too intimate bond
That is between us; 't is the Devil's own snare,
And must be broken, or 't will strangle both, —
False, cruelly false to her. Let me go forth ;
I am not fit to be alone — not now ;
My blood is all on fire, a dreamy joy,
Vague but yet certain, real though undefin'd,
Pervades my brain, and makes me wish to rest
Alone in self-communion, while my pulse
And nerves make quiet hopeless. Let me forth,
Mix with the careless crowd and try to seem
If not be tranquil. Thus to be alone
Is not to bring composure, not to breed
Thoughts that are wholesome. Haply never more
I shall know such ; for though I were so wise
To take that step back from the hidden fire
Which threatens to consume us, how shall I

Dare to prescribe like caution unto her ?
This night, when, in the mazes of the dance
And the blood heats with motion, again we meet,
(It thrills me, the mere thought ! but not with fear,)
Save Heaven shall help us, she will tempt me still,
As woman's nature prompts, and both are lost.

> [*Exit, pensively, in a direction opposite to
> what Amalie has taken.*

.

Scene III.

An antechamber in the Royal Palace.

AMALIE *and* KŒLLAR
in the act of passing each other.

Kœl. [*saluting.*] Happily met, fair countess. — Pardon me !
I did not see you were absorb'd, or ill.

> [*Bowing again profoundly.*
> AMALIE *passes, while he remains standing,
> and looking after her.*

Ama. [*suddenly turning, while he eagerly approaches.*
I was ungrateful to your known regard.
You will ascribe it, not to my disdain,

But to my trouble.

     Kœl. Were it greater slight
Than I at times have borne, I well were paid
By this unusual kindness. But indeed,
I rather would it were such, the caprice
Of your imperial beauty, than to hear
That plea of suffering, and to mark its signs.
What is your trouble? Dare I ask?

       Ama. A friend,
Devoted as I deem you, has a right
To ask and to be answer'd. Come this way.

    They come forward.
You have profess'd to love me, and have sought
Return of your affection. Is your love
So vital you could make my cause your own,
Espouse my quarrels, and resent my wrongs
Even to the death?

    Kœl. With that look in those eyes,
Even to a thousand deaths. What shall I do?

Ama. I have been this moment outrag'd in a point
The tenderest known to woman. Who shall avenge me,
May name his own reward.

     Kœl. And this by whom?

Ama. By the King's Minister, Count Struensee.

      Kœl. I thought
You were the best of friends! What durst he do?

Ama. Seek not to know: that is not in the bond,
Nor ever shall be. Dare, and do; then ask
Thy recompense, and take it. I will love,

O with a love impassion'd as my soul,
Him who avenges me.   Wilt thou ?
        Kœl. I will,
And instantly.   Shall I defy and slay him ?
Ama. No, ruin him ; and with him —
      Kœl. Whom ?
        Ama. Why, no one :
Stone walls have ears, and — " curse not thou the —
  Queen."
Kœl. " Even in thy thought: a bird o' the air shall carry it,
And what hath wings shall noise abroad the matter."
Ama. Thou art well-read.   Be silent and discreet ;
And if thou serve me —— Live in hope.   There 's earnest.
     [*Extending him her hand to kiss.*
   Exeunt, different ways.   And, during the
     movement, the

      Drop falls.

Vol. II.—23

A C T   T H E   S E C O N D

SCENE I. *An antechamber of the King's apartments.*

MATILDA. STRUENSEE.

Matil. These are my joys, this is my wedded life,
  Such is the queenly state which thousands envy!
  The meanest housewife in my brother's realm,
  If wedded to the husband of her choice,
  And he considerate, and fond, and kind,
  Is in her poverty happier than I
  The consort of a king. — It irks you, this.
Stru. Your majesty will pardon: I must needs,
 [13] Being favor'd of my sovereign, and so trusted,
  Feel that this confidence, though it honors me,
  Is yet not fit for me.   But, that it irks —•—
  O honor'd and liege lady! whom I owe
  At once a servant's duty and the zeal
  (So you will have it) of an humble friend ——
Matil. What would you say?   Having truly said so much,
  What should embarrass you?   Are you not indeed
  Sole being in all this Court in whose good faith
  And singleness of heart I put firm trust?
  What can you say that will not be receiv'd
  •

As it should be from you, who are my friend,
My counsel, my sure solace?

              Stru. In that praise —
Which may I live to merit! I find the excuse
Was needed for my freedom.   O royal lady!
Am I your counsel, am I your true friend,
As most devoted servant, heed my words.
Let not the King's faults dwell upon your mind,
But rather strive to heighten in yourself,
And make more active for your people's good,
Your own particular virtues; so your light
Shall qualify his darkness, your redundance
Make up for his deficiency.   The queens
Of history have often thus supply'd
The marital want of merit; and this land
May boast exemplars equal to the best.
At your command, I furnish'd, some time since,
Their records, which Your Majesty might read
For Denmark's profit and your own renown.

Matil. I did so.   'T was in vain.   The an'tique voice
Woke not an echo in my English heart,
Which is no heroine's.

              Stru. Not perhaps for war.
But there be other fields.   Your wrongs, O Queen,
Are they not Philippina's? [14]   Eric's dross
Could not debase the metal of her soul,
Who was more truly King than Eric was.

Matil. Ay, I remember.   She was guerdon'd well!
Fortune took sides against her, and her spouse

       ˙Punish'd her loss of victory at Stralsund,
       They say, upon her person.   What remain'd ?
       A cloister, and the long dull death of grief.
Stru. All men are not like Eric.   Were they worse,
       The wife has still her duties, and her love
       Is often their sole honor.   Uhlfeld's spouse,
       True daughter of a truly royal king,
       Cherish'd her traitor lord for all the woes
       His profligate ambition wrought them both.
[15] Exile nor prison, nothing could affray her, .
       Whose woman's-breast throbb'd often, for his sake,
       Under man's raiment, and who pleaded for him
       As he durst not, and sav'd him, once at least,
       The penalty of his too manifest guilt.
Matil. And what was *her* reward ?   A score of years
       And more in prison.[16]

                  Stru. No, her trial, that.
       Her recompense was in her soul, the sense
       Of duty well perform'd, unshaken faith,
       And conjugal devotion well-approv'd.
       O that my Queen would add another wreath
       To these the fadeless garlands of her sex,
       And be its pattern not alone in grace
       And negative virtue !   [17] Haply then her lord
       Might turn to nobler fancies, and his soul,
       New-plum'd by her, aspire with stronger wing
       The upper heaven of worldly royal fame.
       Was 't not thus Harald Haarfager, from king
       Of part of Norway, over which he reign'd

With one and thirty others like himself,
Became its monarch? Gida nerv'd his soul,
Who made her hand the guerdon of his deed.[19]
Through all her history Denmark boasts her queens ——
I am presumptuous, and I tire.

    Matil. Not so.
If bootless, yet the lesson gives delight.
Let me hear more.

    Stru. Not bootless, O my Queen,
If heard with even interest. — No realm
Is richer in the wealth of female worth,
Gather'd through centuries, and treasur'd still
For emulous admiration. Thus we read
Of Dannebod, of Dagmar, more than all
Of Margaret, whom Denmark styles the Great
And other lands unite to name the North's
Semiramis. True daughter of her sire,

[19] Of Valdemar Atterdag, the Third so call'd,
Firm as was he, as fearless, and as shrewd, .
She knew to join three kingdoms into one,
And for three lustres rul'd them all, and dy'd,
Even as she had liv'd, the mother of the State.

[20] She was a woman, yet all things went well.
The man who follow'd her could not hold up
The sceptre that was in her nervous grasp
Light as a shuttle; sway'd it to and fro,
As doth a bauble in a baby's hand,
Till it was taken from him. Does the tale
Convey the moral I presume to teach?

Matil. So far as this; that not the sex decides
  The qualities which make a monarch great,
  But prudence, foresight, firmness.
       Stru. And the will
  To make the meanest subject's cause his own,
  Even as a sire his son's.   Who might not then,
  By balancing the present with the past,
  Foretell some future princess born to rule
  Likewise a three-fold land, but with a sceptre
  Stretching o'er mightier realms than Rome e'er saw,
  And, without effort, through the State's wise laws
  And by her people's love, rule all in peace?
Matil. Her triple crown it needs no seer to name.
Stru. Nor her high blood, which is your royal sire's.
  Yes, Queen of Denmark, England may, one day,
  Place on the forehead of a tender girl
  A grander diadem than adorn'd the brow
  Of the first Christian emperor, and brighter
  Than wise Elizabeth ever dream'd to see;
  Yet the head shall not tremble; for wise laws
  Justly administer'd bear off the weight,
  By making the people careful to sustain it,
  On whom its rays shine everywhere alike,
  And over whom the sceptre, everywhere,
  Extends a like protection.   O my Queen,
  Be in your consort's weakness doubly strong,
  And strive to gather round you those true hearts
  That bolster-up a throne; for this believe,
  That mutual interest is the surest base

Of mutual liking, often its sole cause ——

Enter,
at the side opposite Struensee and behind Matilda,
AMALIE. STRUENSEE *observes her and stops, and* AMALIE
begins to retire softly backward, in the direction
whence she came. MATILDA, *observing*
Struensee's look, turns just before
AMALIE *makes her Exit.*

Matil. What disconcerts thee ? Ah, I see ! What brings
The Countess Svider hither ? She is gone.
Is it that, made you suddenly be still
And grow so pale ? Why cast you down your eyes
And answer not ?
    Stru. I dare not.
      Matil. Dare not ? Then,
There is betwixt you ? —
     Stru. Anger on her part,
And dread on mine.
    Matil. Dread ? And for what ? Why then
Should she be angry ?
    Stru. Ask me not, O Queen,
Most honor'd and dear lady !
     Matil. Struensee,
Thou hast no liking for her ?
     Stru. No, dislike;
Dislike and dread. But not for me. Forgive ! ——
Matil. Forgive thee what ? Thou hast said nought amiss.

Is then Matilda, for she is a queen,
Therefore the less a woman? See I not,
What thou dar'st name not, 't is thy dread for me,
Out of that woman's malice and this scene,
Which yet has been, what but a schoolhouse-lesson,
And thou the teacher, unto one unapt?
Unapt to learn, but not unapt, oh no!
To gratitude, to friendship, to the best
And warmest feeling I dare entertain
For thee who art, shall I need say again?
My surest if not only friend and guide
In all this labyrinth of courtly guile,
Envy and hatred, malice and revenge.
Dread not for me; or, let me dread for thee,
And leave thee now. [*extending her hand.*

      But 't is to meet again.

       [*Stru. presses it warmly to his lips.*

  At this moment, unseen by either,
     Enter,
 from the quarter where Amalie had appeared,
  KŒLLAR, *and instantly retires. —*
MATILDA *withdraws her hand in confusion, but without*
   displeasure, and Exit.

Stru. 'T is done. I would 't were undone! Wo is us,
The first of those successive steps is taken
Which Brandt forewarn'd me of. Here shall they end.
How shall I meet the King? He looks for me.
Unhappy chance, that stopp'd me on my way!

And yet, it is not loss that I deplore.
How shall I meet the King — with that mad touch
Still burning on my lips! My guilt will show
In my unsteady eyes and faltering tongue.
O luckless act! Would it might be undone!

Enter MATILDA.

Matil. Why dost thou linger? Hasten to the King.
How discompos'd thou look'st! Thou hast no cause;
I am not angry. Stay not to reply.

[Exit Struensee.

I am not angry? Ah, thou saw'st that well!
Unhappy! yet too happy, knew'st thou all
Which that rash pressure of thy lips reveal'd
Then only to myself. O fatal act!
Will it not lead to others? See I not
In his unsteady mien, his tremulous voice,
His cheek's hue and the brightness of his eye,
All that this brief half-hour has made too plain
In my own soul? And he will read the signs;
He must have read them in my act and speech.
What brought me back to him? Ah hapless impulse!
He will have mark'd my trouble and my joy,
My hurried and yet soften'd tones; alas,
All that my pulse, in pain that is delight,
Makes conscious to my guilty heart. Give aid,
O Thou, who knowest my unintended sin,
Give aid to both! for him still more than me!
I seem to halt before a chasm, where down,

23*

In the vague blackness of the terrible depth,
Demons stand waiting.   On the opposite verge,
Laughing, half-hidden, crouch my many foes,
Watching to see me plunge.   That shall not be.
Let me think who I am, and what I am,
Shun such occasions, be no more alone.
A queen, a wife, a mother!   O my God,
I am already sunken.   Bear me up,
Nor let me touch that bottom of my sin!

                 [*Exit — the Scene closing
                     as she retires.*

Scene II.

A chamber in the King's Apartments.

CHRISTIAN.   BRANDT.

Christian in the act of laying down a battledore.

Chris. There, that will do.   Now Struensee is come —
    Though I had rather play with thee than talk;
    For I can beat thee, but he bandies words
    With more effect than I, and tires me out

With saws political, — thou mayst begone.

Enter STRUENSEE.

See if the preparations for the ball
Are toward, then come thou back and let me know.
                              [*Exit Brandt.*
                STRUENSEE *comes forward.*
Well, our grave Minister. And grave indeed
Thou look'st now ! What has fallen ? Have thy plans
For popular good been frustrate as were mine ?
I came from England back with generous hopes
To make our farm-folk prosperous as there :
Thou know'st how I was thwarted.
                              Stru. Know I well,
The principle of evil, gracious King,
Rises up everywhere to frustrate good —
Chris. How sad thou look'st now, yet how flush'd !
                              Stru. But good
Will finally prevail, if men be strong
And struggle with the dragon.
                     Chris. Now thine eyes
Flash with their wonted fire, and thy tone
Is all it should be. 'T is a happy spirit,
Thine, Struensee. I would thou couldst impart it.
Stru. I would I might. But to hope on through all
Is in the being, a quality of the brain,
Not to be taught, acquir'd, or even lost,
Though bodily weakness, or depressing passion
May, as with other faculties, awhile

Suspend its exercise.   But th's observe :
They who strive zealously the place to fill
Which God assigns them, need not for their task
The stimulus of hope.   If then the King —
Chris. If then the Queen. —   Thou weariest mé ; give her
The lesson.

      Stru. Sire, I have.

          Chris. And found her
Dull and refractory.

         Stru. Pardon, the reverse ;
Docile and apt.

        Chris. What couldst thou teach ?   I thought,
Seeing the cloud of thy " depressing passion,"
Which thickens now, come o'er thee, thou hadst found
That queens were, even less than kings, dispos'd
To lectures from their subjects.   What thy theme ?
Stru. I ventur'd to remind my sovereign's spouse
Of Denmark's glory in her ancient queens,
And urge her, as an humble subject might,
To emulate them.

       Chris. That was venturing much.
What pity, that, for her sake as thy own,
Luther has dispossess'd the Pope ! thou mightst
Be con'fessor and beadsman to the Queen.
Already thou art Minister for more
Than the King's cabinet.   Fy, now ! turn not red,
And pale again ; we did but jest, and are
Aught but displeas'd, enjoying in thee so much
That is gratuitous : and a gift for all —

Finance, the courts, war and affairs extern,
With preaching added — is a genius rare
Few kings find in their statesmen.   Prais'd be God,
Who gave it thee !   But gravely, since my jest
Has made thee grave, what bond is there between
Thy moral wisdom and the affairs of State ?
Can Denmark's annals furnish types for us
As well as for our Queen ?   Come, let me hear
The words that made her apt : I will at least
Be patient, if not docile.

Stru. O my King !

Who have a generous nature and are prone
To what is good and just, why ? —   Shall I have
Your royal grace for what I now may utter ;
Truth is not music to the ears of kings ?

Chris. No more than to their subjects.   Were thy words
Not simple flattery, what hast thou to fear ?
The generous and just-minded cannot blame
Reproof that is well-meant.

[21] Stru. Why let the gifts

And graces Heaven bestow'd on you, be shorn
Of power and lustre by a fatal want
Of strength of purpose ?   That I dare thus far
Is not more owing to your royal word,
Than to that gentleness and yielding spirit
Which, while they make men love you, make them cease
To fear you, as, for their own sakes, they should,
And make you often subject to the frauds
Of the designing.   This is what unites

The utterance of the views it has pleas'd my lord
To mock as his poor servant's moral lore
With my true duty and my present task.
Will the King listen? There is discontent
With the new measures everywhere.

      Chris. Suspend them.

Stru. And give up the grand thoughts, the generous hopes,
The plans so near completion that should make
Your realm like England's and your hapless people,
Down-trodden by the mutinous nobles, free,
And in their freedom prosperous as hers?

Chris. What wouldst thou? Thou complain'st that discontent
Broods everywhere.

     Stru. Stirr'd-up by the designing
And treasonably ambitious, the King's foes and mine.

Chris. Granted it be so, shall we stand forever
Listening the uproar on this boisterous sea?
Its flood may overwhelm us.

      Stru. If our bark
Sailless and rudderless drift before the waves.
It should ride o'er them, breast them, and, stem on,
Cut its way through the opposing billows that dash
To froth against it, wet, but not submerge.

Chris. All which sounds well: but, in thy sea-phrase still,
Thou hast not carried easy sail, but drivest
Under full canvas, and thou wilt wreck us both.
In plainer words, thou, count, hast had a power
Unlimited and hast mov'd too fast.

      Stru. Man's life

From manhood to old age is all too brief
To suffer him be languid.   Could we, like
The gods of Iceland, taste Iduna's apples,
And thus renew our youth [22], it might be well
To move more slowly ; but my life is vow'd
Unto the glory of my sovereign's reign.
I would have all completed ere I die,
Leaving no window in his house of fame
For others to build up.   My King has ask'd,
In mockery, could I furnish types for him.
I would remind him, with his gracious leave,
Of Norway's monarch, Sverrè Sigurdsen,
Who kept the encroaching bishops in their bounds,
As fits a king, and bid the Pope defy,
As being the lord of his own realm by soul
As well as right.   What matter'd it to Sverrè,
His nobles rose against him, who was king
Of poor as well as rich, nor had two kinds
Of justice, for his right hand and his left ?
[23] He crush'd all opposition, and with the valor
Not of the warrior only but the sage ;
For he, who wrote the Mirror of the King,
Was skilful in the closet as the field
And chang'd at will the sceptre for the pen.
Chris. 'T is a good tale, but told of Norway's kings
Before the three crowns glitter'd in our shield.
Stru. But Denmark's annals proper have as good.
Witness, in your ancestral House, the Third
Of your own name, whose resolute will put down,

Never to rise again on Danish soil,
The giant form of papal power. His son,
Rich in the old-time spirit of the Dane,
Wore, like the sire, his crown upon a casque.
A loftier hero and a greater man
Then rose, in his son's son, who check'd the Swede
And forc'd the foolishly divided Duchies
To own their rightful liege. ²⁴ Unwearied, strong
Of purpose, self-reliant, scheming, bold,
His hand as active as his brain; the King
Was everywhere, nor let another do
What to work out befitted best himself,
Ruler at once and guardian of his realm
As well as king. Their reigns, which stretch beyond
A century in duration, shine afar,
Bright with —

       Chris. — The lurid blaze of war, and rich
In human sacrifice, and waste, and ruin,
And wives' and orphans' suffering and tears;
· Results which may be glory in Valhalla
And joy to Odin, but are none to me.

Stru. But peace, Your Majesty, has her triumphs too;
Triumphs which not impoverish, but make rich,
Whose spoils are blessings, and whose car is drawn
By ease, not suffering, and 'mid smiles, not tears.
Christian the Fourth is hero even here.

Chris. At what a cost! To do, he must undo.
Forever in excitement, with a pulse
Which age could not make languid, headstrong, vain,

Fierce in his passions, selfish in his pride,
Is this the standard thou sett'st up for me?
25 *Stru.* Not in all things. Even were it to be wish'd,
The fiery temper, the strong vital force,
The love of combat, and the restless spirit
That must expend its nervous power somewhere
And agitates the brain, even while in sleep
The body acts not, are not to be gain'd
By longing or by imitative love:
They are gifts of God, the accidents of birth,
.The nerve and blood and fibre of the man.
But would my lord aspire ——

　　　　　　　　Chris. And of such clay
Are built the models that amus'd our Queen?
Set in the air of truth, they shrink distort,
And crumble at a touch. Look on your type,
Your dauntless warrior, your unshaken sage!
Could all his efforts stay the invading Swede?
He toil'd like any drudge, yet from his works
Left nothing that was safe, but might have look'd
Back on the world to see his crown'd heir stripp'd
Almost of all his kingdom, everywhere
His enemies victorious, and alone
Discord triumphant. *I* care not to toil
For nothing.

　　　　Stru. Pardon, dear my liege; is name
Then nothing?

　　　　　　Chris. No, for thou art Count, who wast
Simply the Doctor, and by this time knowest

A name is something, for thou art the same
And yet another, and that other only
By reason of that name.

     Stru. My gracious King,
That you have made me noble, is your gift,
For which I am ever bounden. But, being made
Thus noble, it were not grateful but to be
The mere physician you were pleas'd to raise.
Rank has its obligations. To receive it
Is to owe service to the sovereign giver;
And I were recreant, did I not so do.

Chris. [*impatiently.*

  And unto whom, sage counselor that thou art,
Am I then bounden?

   Stru. [*solemnly.*] Unto God.

     Enter an Usher.

     Ush. The Count
Of Rantzow craves admittance of the King.

Chris. Let him come in.

     Stru. Have I your gracious leave?
       [*bowing, as to retire.*

Chris. No, thou shalt learn like Pallas from the swine.

     Enter RANTZOW.

Thou com'st in time, good Rantzow. See this sage.
He was a leech — physician, I should say;
He is a count: wouldst thou believe, he still
Aspires to more?

Rant. O readily, my liege,
Knowing your Majesty's generous nature well.
The open hand makes an importunate mouth.
Chris. For a fool, Rantzy, that was not ill said.
But Struensee does not accept; he takes —
Or would, I mean — Canst guess at it?

             Rant. [*maliciously.*] Your sceptre?
It often passes by another name —
Yet passes still.

        Chris. How wise thou art to-day !
And yet how dull ! My sceptre is a toy;
But this bold Struensee would catch and keep
What is still more a toy. Dolt, 't was my conscience :
He would be priest, as well as doctor, this
Lord Count and Counselor. But, thank our sires,
We are but protestant and have no need
Of a director. [*Signs to Stru. who Exit, while*

        Enter BRANDT.

Now for gayer talk.
Well, my ambassador, what of the ball?

        Drop falls.

ACT THE THIRD

SCENE I. *As in Act I. Scene* 1.

JULIANA. FREDERIC. MOLTKE. RANTZOW.
KŒLLAR.

Fred. Thus much then is decided.   Ere the sun
Lights a new day, these men must both be seiz'd ;
The King shall sign the order of arrest —
But will he sign it ?
                       Rant. That admits no doubt,
Save as to Brandt.   For Struensee himself,
His super-meddling seems to have lost him favor.
The King made merry with his mushroom-growth,
And bid me note the muck-heap whence it sprung,
Even in the fungus' presence, whose High-Dutch stalk
To-morrow we uproot.
                       Molt. With pardon, count,
Let an old man correct you.   The great oak,
Whose trunk for centuries has spread out branches,
Should be too large and lofty to despise
The little plant, whose growth is wondrous more
For that it is so sudden.   Had Brahe's birth
Been less illustrious, would your great foresire,
The wise, the generous Henry of your house,

Have lov'd or help'd him less?   He who arrang'd
The Royal Law, the Count of Griffenfeld,
Was simple Peter Schumacher by birth,
Son of a mere wine-merchant in this town,
And had applied himself to physic first,
Like your new mushroom.[26]

    Rant. No offence was meant;
Most surely, none to you.   I spoke the hate
I, as a noble, feel toward this new man,
Who wars against our order. —   If the King
Refuse, after all, to have the pair arrested,
What does your Highness then propose?

     Fred. To arrest
The pair without him.   Do not look aghast.
To fail is to be ruin'd; but, our foes
Once in our power, it were an easy task
To appease the King, who finds no fault with change,
Save as it gives him trouble.   But my friend,
Count Moltke, shakes the head.

     Molt. 'T is not alone
At the rare boldness of your Highness' plan.
That will not come to trial.   The King will sign,
If properly urg'd, the order for the arrest.
Teach him his personal safety is at stake,
His crown, his sceptre, and his favorites fall
More easily than they rose.   'T is in the urgence
Lies the great peril which awakes my doubt.
The Royal Law pronounces whosoever,
Of whatsoever rank, in any wise,

Though in the smallest degree, shall cause the King
To contravene his absolute power and right
As monarch, or grant what derogates therefrom,
Shall of high-treason be accounted guilty
And undergo its penalties, and the act
Or grace obtain'd shall be accounted void.
What shall close-up for us our master's ear
To the Queen's instance brought against us?

                            Jul. That
Which shall close-up thy master's ear against
His Queen herself. Thou look'st astounded. What!
Has my wise counsel and old friend forgotten
His ancient craft? 'T were engineering rare,
To dam the narrower sluices of our wo,
And leave the main gate free!

                            Molt. But in the attempt
To shut the vast tide in, the outrushing flood
May whelm us all. Your Majesty must see
This is no common peril.

                            Jul. 'T is to dare
Largely, I grant; but think, with what great aim!
Its issue, if successful, makes us all,
Stops in mid flow that sea of wild reform,
Which, than our real inundations worse,
Threatens all Denmark, and secures the state,
Safe in its old embankments, from the fears
Of now perplexing change.

                            Molt. But if it prove
Disastrous?

Jul. Can that be ?   The Queen,
As implicated in the traitorous plot
To rob the King of power, — it being indeed
For her behoof, — can scarcely hope for mercy
More than her creatures.   Is the royal heart
Yet flexible, we have what to the core
Will make it hard as steel.   Speak, gallant sir.

Kœl. 'T is with regret. —   It was my lot to see,
This very hour, the Queen and Struensee,
In the King's antechamber.   Struensee,
Holding her Majesty's fingers in his own,
Kiss'd passionately her hand.   I saw no more,
Retreating at the act; but on his cheek
The hue was deepen'd, and the red on hers
Was not of anger.

    Jul. Does my son believe ?
Or must he put his fingers in the wounds,
To make faith certain ?

     Fred. 'T is enough.   This night
Let us have action.

     Jul. What dost thou propose ?

Fred. To arrest the counts, and it may be the Queen,
Before the ball.

    Jul. No, after.   At the ball,
The royal wanton will confirm this tale
Of her dishonor, if there needs more proof.
Then, in the still, dark hours of the morn,
When all ears are benumb'd with sleep, the arrest
Will be more easy and excite less tumult.

Fred. 'T is sagely reason'd. But our prudent Moltke
Is not yet satisfied.

    Molt. Not of the safety
Of this precipitate act. Perchance my age
May make me timorous, and it oft befalls
That in the affairs of state; as in the field,
A bold and seeming-reckless stroke wins all.
Still, let me venture to advise my Prince
Not to allow delay. The mandate sign'd,
The arrest should follow instantly. The King
Might else repent. And if 't is to be done
This act, which I dissuade from, as most rash,
Ill-weigh'd, and fraught with peril, it were well
To do it by surprise. Rous'd from his sleep,
Confus'd, excited, it may be alarm'd,
The King may hastily sign what else by day
He might take time to ponder and refuse.
But who of us shall dare for this invade
The King's bedchamber?

    Jul. I.

     Fred. And I. The rest
Will need your act, brave Kœllar, and your arm,
My fiery Rantzow.

    Rant. No, by Heaven! not mine.
I will not play Ulysses for my part,
But dare, like Magnus Erlingsen,[27] by day,
Nor murder even my enemies asleep.

Fred. Who talks of murdering? Death indeed may come,
But not by us. What gallant Kœllar here,

And Eichstadt, who has promis'd his support,
Scruple not doing, why shouldst thou refuse ? —
Whose regiment provides the guard to-night ? [*to Kœl.*
Kœl. Mine, please your Highness.
                              Jul. 'T is the will of God !
Fred. Good fortune at the least, and augurs well.
Our course thus smooth'd, thou wilt not, Rantzow, sure,
Withhold thy valiant spirit and strong arm
From this brave venture.   Erling's son himself
Would not have scrupled where surprise alone
Averted ruin and made victory sure.
To entrust the enterprise to meaner hands
Were to invite betrayal; with us few
The plot is safer and success ensur'd.
'T is a man's part, fear not ; Count Brandt, who struck
The King himself at Hirschholm [26], will not yield
Without a struggle.   I depend on thee.
I see I may.   We shall·not be ungrateful.
Return with Kœllar hither in an hour.
Eichstadt will then be here, and all our parts
In their detail made perfect.   Moltke's pen
Meanwhile will write the order, which, when sigu'd,
Hurls from his borrow'd and misguided car
This would-be god who drives too near the sun. —
Rant. — Gives to us nobles our ancestral lands
Free of the taxman's gatherings.
                              Jul. — And to me
The joy to see that shame of royal wives,
English Matilda, thron'd where she deserves.
              [*Exeunt Rant. and Kœl. —   Scene closes.*

SOENE II.

As in Act I. Scene II.

STRUENSEE,
standing by a table.   A Servant holding open a door.

Enter BERNSTORFF.
·*Stru. steps forward to him, courteously, but with some reserve.*

Bern. Your Excellency hardly would expect
    To see me here.
               Stru. And wherefore not?   I know
The Count of Bernstorff just, and great of soul.
And seeing and knowing, that 't was not I displac'd him,
He could not, being just, hold me in fault,
Nor, being great of soul, could feel it.
                      Bern. I have drawn
This praise unwittingly.   But let that pass.
Know you why I have come?   Can you believe
It is in friendliness?
             Stru. I can, and do.
How can I serve you?
            Bern. Briefly, save yourself.
Your liberty, nay life, is now in peril.
Stru. This is Brandt's warning!   Whence should danger come?
    I have sought to do all justice, and have liv'd,

During my ministry, with no thought but this,
To save, to increase, to strengthen, to defend,
Make Denmark prosperous and her commons blest.

Bern. 'T was against reason.

                      Stru. Says Count Bernstorff so ?
He who disdain'd to profit by the poor,
And freed his new possessions from their chains,
Making the serfs be masters.

                      Bern. And 't is hence,
That I have so befriended, if you will,
The poor and the oppress'd, that your vast schemes
I censure, while I own your motives right.
I follow'd in the footsteps of my queen : [29]
But who has trod in mine ?   It was my loss,
And concern'd no one that I freed my serfs.
That gave me not the right to urge the like
On others ; how much less to try to enforce
Like action, as you do.   Your vast reforms,
That cover all the kingdom and insert
Their hundred hands in every part, must fail
Because they rouse all factions and all ranks
In common cause against you, and your works
Will not be honor'd even by the oppress'd,
For none will understand you.

                      Stru. Be it so.
I may reply as Tavsen, Ribè's bishop,
" My honesty shall plead for me hereafter." [30]

Bern. That is the noble thought of noble minds,
Ere age and disappointment have benumb'd

Enthusiasm.   Well indeed, if such
Take not their first great lesson from the grave !
Perhaps I should say, ill ; for violent death
Stops short the heart-beat while the soul throbs warm
With its best impulses.

     Stru. Should fear of death
Deter then from well-doing ?

      Bern. Such a thought
Count Struensee will not impute to me.
I come to warn him, not for that his life,
Or liberty, is in peril, but that life
And liberty are peril'd both in vain.
You will not ask me whence I have the tale ;
But it is whisper'd, even so soon, the King
Grows restless with your discipline.   In sooth —
Let me be candid — what can you avail,
Though you toil hourly in the generous task ?
Can nature be remodel'd ? can you crush
The force of habit ? or by reasoning make
The selfishness of self-indulgence yield
A moment's pause to ponder and step back,
When thought and retrogression both give pain ?
Cease to hope this.

     Stru. Why should I not prevail ?
Did not Sterkodder [21], in the ancient time,
Turn from his baseness, after long ado,
His royal master's son, from her vile bonds,
The bonds of shame, relieve bad Ingild's sister,
And sweep his dissolute minions from the court ?

He labor'd long, I grant; but 't is the end
Makes the reward, and labor is forgotten
When the fruit ripens and requites his toil
But for whose care the worms, the very sun,
Had eaten its heart out or dry'd up its sap.

Bern. But if the end come not, the ripen'd fruit,
Before the gardener's senses all are seal'd
To its perfection ? What, thou generous soul,
(Let me requite thy courteous praise in kind,
And not less honestly,) — what should to thee
Be the King's reformation, which may come
Too late, or never ? Wast thou sure indeed,
Then, to resign thy liberty, or life,
Would be heroic, and thy steadfast faith
Would, as with martyrs, make thy sufferings light,
And death seem triumph.

     Stru. If it be at all
A hero's part, is 't less so, that the fight
Is all but hopeless ? or does Bernstorff's lord,
Who has avow'd his goodness brought him loss,
Gauge duty by its profits ?

     Bern. Said I so ?
It was my loss. But, did I damage those
Whom I would favor, should I persevere ?
There is our difference. With o'erheated zeal,
And giant grasp that clutches all at once,
Thou crushest much and lett'st the rest escape
Through thy clos'd fingers. Wilt thou now give heed ?
There is, Count Struensee, a dangerous plot,

Wherein your enemies most near the Court ——
But we are interrupted.

Enter Servant.

Ser. From the Queen. [*Exit.*

Enter Page.

Page. Her Majesty awaits His Excellency
In the King's antechamber.
            Stru. Say, I come — [*Confused ;*
                Bern. regarding him with surprise.
I will attend Her Majesty. [*Exit Page.*
            Bern. We part.
I had nearly said too much.   You will give heed,
And profit by my hint ? and pardon it,
Like my intrusion ?
            Stru. Pardon ?   While I live,
Happen what will, I am your debtor ever.
                        [*Exit Bern.*
    STRUENSEE *appears to collect himself a moment,*
    then snatches eagerly his hat, and follows.

Scene III.

The King's antechamber.   As in Act II. Scene I.

Matilda.   *The* Page.

Matil. Was he alone?
                    Page. Your Majesty, the Count
Of Bernstorff parley'd with him.
                                   Matil. Ah!   That was
Unfortunate.   I mean — that I am griev'd
To have broken-up their parle.   Thou mayst retire.
                                        [*Exit Page.*
The Count of Bernstorff?   What should he do there?
What must he think, that I should send?   But why
Should I not send?   It is my conscience puts
This color on an act which in itself
Is nothing wrong, nor misbecomes my state,
Albeit unusual.   Yet, if Struensee,
Thus call'd, betray'd confusion ——   It is he!

Enter Struensee.

Stru. Your Majesty was pleas'd to send ——
                            Matil. Yes, yes.
I sent ——   What did the Count of Bernstorff want?
Stru. He came to warn me of some unknown danger

To liberty — to life itself, he said.
'T was generous in him.

     Matil. In him — Bernstorff — Yes.
He came to warn you — O God, Struensee!
He had good cause. For this it was I sent.
Heed thou the warning. Wilt thou, wilt thou then?
Stru. What is it that for my unworthy sake
Alarms Your Majesty?

     Matil. O stand not now
On ceremony. 'T is a peril more,
That I have sent for you, to meet you here, —
Though better here than elsewhere. Listen now,
And haste to thwart the plotters. A good maid
Who serves me overheard, some moments since,
A colonel of the guards in secret talk
With Countess Svider. That malignant woman
Seem'd to have made a compact with the man
For your destruction, which, he said, was sure
And close at hand. The listener thought that I
Was mingled as a victim in the plot,
But could hear nothing certain; for the man,
Reminding, as he said, of her own words,
His vile accomplice, that "stone walls have ears,"
Drew her far from the door and talk'd more low.
When done, the countess kiss'd him on the mouth.
Remember how that woman lately here
Espied our meeting: think —— Why art thou dumb?
What did the count advise thee?

     Stru. Bernstorff? Nought.

He had but time to warn me.

        Matil. As have I.

Go, Struensee!

      Stru. And whither?

          Matil. From the Court,

From Denmark; only go, without delay.

Stru. And does Your Majesty command me this?

Matil. Implore you — with my whole heart. 'T is for life,

Bethink you. 'T is perhaps for more — for me.

Why do you stand so silent, seeming lost?

Must I say more?

      Stru. O no, no; all is said

In bidding me to go. How can I go?

Since here ——

    Matil. Since here? — What is 't —— I cannot stop

To ask your meaning. Nay, this is no time

For womanly reserve or queenly pride:

I know it well. It is a reason more

Why you should fly from Denmark. Go at once.

Stay not for preparation, nor for means.

Fly to my own free England: once there safe,

All will be sent you that your rank, your tastes,

Your habits need. See, Struensee, 't is not

The Queen exacts, it is the woman urges

Her friend, whose liberty, whose life perhaps,

She knows in peril, to save it for her sake.

'T is, Struensee, Matilda on the knees

Of her heart's anguish prays thee, for that heart,

To save thyself and her.

    24*

Stru. Yes, for those words,
Which wake I dare not say what feeling in me,
Of mingled joy, and terror, and remorse,
Reminding me my duty 't were to flee
Though nothing threaten'd, — for those precious words,
I will do all your bidding; but one grace
Suffer me still to supplicate, the last
Perhaps, alas, you ever will accord.
Command me not to go until the dawn.
This night, the ball — it is the last, last time
The honor you have done me in the dance
May, through like grace, be mine.

      Matil. Imprudent man !
Is such a pleasure to be weigh'd with life ?
Is this your duty ? is it mine ?   Go now ;
For my sake, go.

    Stru. It is the last, last time.
I will be prudent; I will bear in mind
The debt I owe to Denmark, to its Queen,
And, wo is me, its King.   But this one night !
Matil. 'T is madness.   It is worse than weak to yield.
But, since for this night only, — be it so.

     Enter, hurriedly,
     BRANDT.

Br. Madam, the King.
    Matil. Help, Heaven !   [*Exit.*
      Br. [*low and reproachfully,*
      to Stru.] Was this well ?

Rouse thee.   For *her* sake, then !   [*in same low tone, but
                                            earnestly.*

                              The King is here.

Enter, with hat on,

CHRISTIAN,

preceded by an Usher, and followed by BERNSTORFF
and RANTZOW, *all uncovered.*
They cross slowly the scene, the King speaking as he walks.

Chris. [*To Br.*

Ah! thou art here ; and with thee our right hand,
Playing the mope again.   Thou naughty Brandt!
Hast thou been lecturing him, as he has us ?
Be not abash'd, our Minister ; rest sure
We like thee none the worse ; but keep henceforth
Thy lessons for our Queen, who loves thy talk.
Here, at our side ; we need thee.   Follow, Brandt.

STEUENSEE *ranges himself at the left hand of the King, a
little behind him, but in advance of* BERNSTORFF *and*
RANTZOW.   BRANDT *follows last.   Exeunt, —
the Drop falling ere they
disappear.*

Act the Fourth

Scene I.   *A room in the sleeping-apartment of the King.*

Juliana.   Frederic.

Fred. [*facing the side scene, and speaking as to one within.*
    You have done your best, sir, and need have no fear
You we shall hold exonerated.

Enter, through a door above,
Christian,
in his dressing-robe.

                    Chris. So.
But who will thee?   What means this outrage here,
Here in my chamber, at this hour of night?
Where be my guards?
                    Fred. My royal brother and King,
Pardon!   That this is not an outrage meant,
Though violent intrusion for your sake,
Whose throne at least is threaten'd, witness here
My mother, our departed father's spouse,
Here, for this only, with me.
                    Jul. — But to thwart
Your traitor minister, Struensee, whose scheme

To set aside Your Majesty, and make
  Your consort Regent, only now discover'd ——
Chris. Think'st thou I am mad, or Struensee a fool?
  What could it stead him, were the Queen in place?
  This is invention !
             Jul. Must I then respond?
  The Queen herself aspires to sovereign power;
  And Struensee is recogniz'd her slave
  At once and master.
             Chris. This is all too much !
  Are we the King in Denmark, and must hear
  This calumny? be summon'd from our couch
  To welcome insult?
             Jul. Patience, royal son —
  Let me so call thee : in my dead lord's name
  Who was thy sire, I pray thee hear.   What cause
  Could keep me and thy brother from our beds
  And make us summon thee, our king, from thine,
  But danger imminent to thee or us?
  That it is not to us, its source will show.
  Has not this Struensee contriv'd to usurp,
  Little by little, all functions of the state,
  So that he may be said to guide the sceptre
  Your Majesty does but hold?
             Chris. So Rantzow said,
  Or so implied.   This must be look'd to.   Well?
Jul. If the thick-witted Rantzow saw so much,
  What must observers of more brain than he?
Chris. Well, well?

Jul. Wherever danc'd the Queen to-night,
There mov'd Count Struensee.   Your Majesty
Had the first honor; afterward her hand
Was his, and his throughout.

                       Chris. And may again
Be, as 't has been before.   And for this prate,
Mere woman's gossip and a widow's grudge,
You have dar'd to rouse me in the depth of night,
Thrusting my page aside, and by the noise
Of your forc'd entrance breaking my first sleep.
'T was kindly and most reverently done.
Will you now both withdraw ?

                         Fred. May it please Your Grace
It is not woman's gossip, royal brother,
What a brave colonel of the palace guard
Relates, who saw himself this day the Queen ——
Chris. Beware, sir !

            Jul. If Your Majesty averts
Your face from common frailty, it is vain
To offer more.   To-morrow when the plot
Bursts o'er your head, which then will be discrown'd,
Do us the justice to acknowledge ——

                       Chris. Stop.
What is this plot ?   I will not listen aught
That dares impeach Matilda as a wife ;
But, is there threat of treason, let me know it,
And prove it.   Speak thou, Frederic, and be brief.
Fred. To prove it would be long.   Enough that now
We have it certain that to-morrow's sun

Will shine upon a crownless king, whose power,
Given to the Queen as Regent ——

     Chris. Is this true
That seems so little truth-like ?   Dost thou swear ?
Fred. Why am I in your chamber at this hour ?
Why is my mother here ?   O royal brother,
Who art my king, let me, not less the first
In loyalty than rank of all your subjects,
Adjure you, thus upon my bended knee,
Have mercy on your people as yourself
And give heed to our warning.
     Chris. What to do ?
Rise, brother.   Hast thou come prepar'd to save
As well as warn ?
     Fred. What else ?   It is that now
Is the fit time for action, we are here.
Your faithless Minister, your favorite Brandt ——
Chris. Not he, not Brandt!   My Minister at times
Grows wearisome and makes me yawn.   I have thought
I would displace him and call Bernstorff in.
But Brandt is genial, loves me, and makes sport.
Fred. He renders service, not unto his king
In the first place, but to the man through whom
Comes the King's favor.   All the immediate friends
Of Struensee must share his fate.   The arrest
Should be immediate. ——
     Chris. No, to-morrow be it.
To-morrow I will play the king.   To-night
I am a tired mortal ; let me sleep.

Fred. To-morrow is their hour, to-night is yours.
    This moment, when the palace and the town
    Are hush'd in darkness and the death of sleep,
    Is most propitious. Thus, without the risk
    Of popular excitement, or defeat
    In any movement of our needful plans,
    All may be finish'd almost when begun.
    Your Majesty must pardon me — the Queen,
    As chief in the conspiracy ——
               Chris. No, no;
    I never will believe it. Take the rest:
    Let her be spar'd.
             Fred. Alas, knows not the King
    The power of women? We shall harm her not.
    No longer reach'd by those who warp'd her mind
    Unto this treason, in a little time
    The Queen will be once more your faithful spouse
    And loyal consort. But, until that hour,
    'T is needful that she be, like them, constrain'd.
    This is the order. [*unfolding and extending a paper.*
         Chris. You have come prepar'd.
Fred. Have we not said, there is no time to spare?
    Will it please Your Grace to sign?
               Chris. Well, give it me
    I wish, like Gersdorf,[32] that I could not write.
    But since it must be, hand me quick the pen,
    And let me back again unto my sleep;
    'T is nearly four o'clock; I am getting chill'd.
       CHRISTIAN *stoops to sign the paper,* —

*JULIANA and FREDERIC exchanging over his shoulder
looks of exultation; and Scene closes.*

<hr>

SCENE II.

A room in Struensee's Apartment.

STRUENSEE *and* BRANDT
*seated at a table.   The former's dress-sword,
unbuckled, lies on the table.*

Br. Let us not argue further.   'T is enough
     Thou hast recogniz'd thy danger, and the Queen
     Exacts thy going.   Would that thou hadst gone
     Before she had need to exact it for herself!
Stru. Be not so cruel, Brandt.
                     Br. I am not cruel.
     Thou know'st I am not.   But this fatal love,
     Even now so heinous guilt, and, if indulg'd ——
     Let us dismiss the theme.   Art thou prepar'd
     To start, as thou didst promise, with the dawn?
Stru. How could I be? the ball is scarcely over:
     I am weary, and will snatch a brief hour's rest,
     Then give my orders.
                Br. No, that must not be.

What Bernstorff, what the Queen, what I have thought
Is imminent danger, wilt thou thus despise?
Lose not a moment. There is none to lose.
Better before the dawn than after. Sleep,
If sleep thou canst, beyond the city walls,
While in ' thy carriage. Here thou art not safe,
Not in the Palace, not perhaps an hour.
What is that noise?

> *Rant.* [*within.*

> In the King's name. Stand back!

Br. They are on thee now! [*springing up.*

Enter

RANTZOW, KŒLLAR *and* EICHSTADT,
with drawn swords. Struensee's CHAMBERLAIN *following
anxiously.*

> *Stru.* [*rising.*] What means this, sirs?

> > *Rant.* Arrest,

By the King's order.

> *Stru.* I submit.

> > *Br.* Thou wilt?

That will not I. [*drawing.*] Does the King have such work
Done by such hands as these? If thou 'rt a man,
Draw upon these assassins. That for thee,
Degenerate Rantzow. [*crossing his blade on Rantzow's.*

> > > *They fight.*

> > *Kœl.* [*seizing Stru. by the throat, at the
> > same time snatching up his sword.*

> *Thou* shalt have no chance.

Eich. [*going behind Br. and disarming him.*
　　Neither shall he.

　　　　　　Br. O cowards that ye are,
As well as cutthroats !　[*To Stru.*] Hadst thou drawn in
　　time,
We might have put down three such dastard knaves.
I am enough for two, come both in front.
That thou mayst guess [*to Rant.*] thou ruffian Count, who
　　hast
A man to help thee.
　　Rant. [*furiously.*] Give him back his sword.
Give it, I say !　I 'll let his insolent blood
Out at his heart !
　　　　　　Kœl. With pardon, noble sir,
This is the King's affair, no private brawl.
Stru. The King's !　What is the charge ?　What has he
　　done ?
Though your plot aim at me, as I was warn'd,
Count Brandt can have no enemies.　Let him go ;
I will submit me patiently.
　　　　　　Br. 'T is waste
Of gentle language on such rascal kind.
They know me for thy friend ;. that is enough.
Rant. [*to Br.*] When thou art loos'd, thou 'lt answer unto
　　me.
Kœl. Pardon, Count Rantzow ; 't is a waste of time
As well as words. —　Call in the guard, thou there.
　　　　　　[*To the Chamberlain.　He stands sullen
　　　　　　and motionless.*

Art thou so faithful to thy fallen lord?
'T is well. Get hence. I 'll summon them myself.
    [*Kœl., moves toward the door, following Chamberlain
      and Scene closes.*

SCENE III.

*A room in the Queen's sleeping-apartment.
A door, leading to an inner chamber above, partially open.*

JULIANA. FREDERIC.
standing expectingly, looking at the door.

*Enter
from the inner chamber, followed by one of her ladies,*
MATILDA.

Matil. I had not come, but that I fear'd to see
· My sleeping-room invaded.
                Jul. 'T would not be
The first time it was enter'd, not invaded,
By feet that had no business to be there,
Or you are much malign'd.
    MATILDA, *as if disdaining reply, turns her eyes
      slowly on Frederic.*

Fred. [*To Jul.*] Permit me speak. —
We have an unpleasant duty to perform
Against Your Majesty, which compels us break
The privacy of your chamber and the night.
We might to meaner hands have given the task,
But come ourselves, my mother for my sake,
To give more seemliness to an act, itself
Not decorous though needful, I for yours,
In reverence to your own rank and the throne
Which you have grac'd. —

      Jul. Disgrac'd; but shall no longer.

Matil. Peace ! I am mistress here. I know you well,
 Princess of Wolfenbuettel ", whom my lord
 Receiv'd as stepmother and gave to me
 As stepmother and mother-in-law combin'd.
 But little more than children as we were,
 You easily gain'd our confidence, and us'd it
 To sow dissension 'twixt us; but we grew
 Too old for dupes. My lord, whom nature form'd
 Gentle and princely, you have made debauch'd,
 Ruin'd in mind and body : and now, me ——
 What want you now with me ?

      Fred. I answer that:
To arrest you, by the order of the King.

Matil. Arrest ? The King ? He has been tamper'd with !
 What is the charge ?

      Jul. You 'll find it in the law
Of Moses, Seventh of the sacred Ten.
The upstart Count who help'd you break that law

Already is arrested and borne forth.

Matil. What is this horror ?   Speak thou, Prince, who art
    At least less insolent.

            Fred. Even what you have heard ;
Count Struensee is arrested. —

                 Matil. Struensee ?

Ah, this is infamy ! —

          Jul. Why, so we think.

Matil. — A plot to murder him.   Where is the King ?
    I 'll seek him on the instant.   You shall see ! —

Fred. [*Stepping between her and the side door.*
    Nothing to aid Your Majesty, or him :
    The traitor has confess'd.

            Matil. Confess'd to what ?

If Struensee you mean.   He can confess
To nothing that is not like his own soul,
Noble and stainless.

           Jul. Have we this avow'd ?

Why dost thou dally, Frederic ?   Seize the wanton !

Matil. [*stepping back.*] It is a falsehood, black as your own soul
    If you imply, as seem you by those words,
    That any criminal act has taken place
    'Twixt him and me, or any thought of such. ·
    It shames me even to think of such a thought,
    Which you have dar'd to express in insolent words
    Before this lady.   Struensee confess'd ?
    What could the man confess ?   What, being a man,
    Would he, even if he could confess, to wrong
    A lady and a queen ?

Jul. What in itself
Involves high-treason: in directer words,
Adultery with the Queen of Denmark, thee,
Whose bastard daughter all the world may note
Is his true image.

      Matil. Woman! whom mischance
Made Queen as Princess, — for a peasant's wife
Would blush, if chaste, to use such scurril words, —
I tell thee, in thy own talk, 't is a lie,
And that thou know'st it such: and from this hour,
Happen what may, I vow to never more
Hold speech with thee again.

      Jul. And thou ——

           Fred. No more.
Let me complete this act. — Your Majesty
Protests then solemnly, what the Count avers
As solemnly is false.

      Matil. Is false? That tale?
That infamous fiction of a most vile plot
Of disappointed placemen, led by foes
Of kindred spirit and still loftier aim?
It does not need protesting. But the Count,
The unhappy victim, never did aver
Or even admit such horror. He could not do it,
And would not, in his senses, if he could,
For his own sake would not.   •

      Fred. In personal fear
Men lose their senses, and betray their hearts.
The threat of torture shook his coward nerves

At the first hint ——

   Matil. He is like me belied.

If just arrested, where was found the time

To make the threat or listen the avowal?

Fred. Your Majesty may stoop to asperse my truth,

  As in your excitement you forgot your state

  To vilify my mother. It nor helps,

  Nor harms you. Briefly, — you deny the facts

  Confess'd by Struensee?

      Matil. The facts? the fables.

The infamous slanders, whether count or queen

Invents them or repeats them, all or part,

That breathe an imputation on my fame

As wife or woman, are the shapeless work

Of envy, hatred, and vile lust of place.

Fred. Enough. Your Majesty has preordain'd

  The Minister's condemnation. To asperse

  The honor of the Queen well merits death:

  And such will be his sentence by the law.

Matil. Not death? not his? not Struensee's? O Heaven!

  Have mercy on him!

     Fred. 'T is not I condemn him.

Your Majesty's own lips forbid him hope.

Matil. What can I do?

    Fred. Revoke what you have said;

Sign an admission he has not malign'd you.

'T is but a minute's work, — and all is done.

Matil. And if I were to avow myself so base ——

  But no! I see your motive; and were there none,

I should do wrong to seek to save a life
At the expense of what makes life of value.
Let Struensee in terror of the rack
Asperse my fame, I will not libel his,
Not even to save him.

     Jul. [*to Fred. in lower tone.*
     I admir'd your art.

It was too soon.
     Fred. [*without regarding Jul.*
     Remains to obey the King.
Prepare for your departure.
     Matil. At this hour?
And whither?
     Fred. To the walls of Cronenburg.
Without delay.
     Matil. I will not!
     Fred. Think again.
'T were better to the palace-gate with us,
Than with a guard, and dragg'd, if it must be.
Matil. O Heaven! I see it all now; ruin — ruin!
Ruin for all! Poor Struensee! — My child?
May it go with me?
     Jul. The adulterous brood?
. By all means.
     Fred. Mother! — Take the child. Take too
This lady, if you will, and she desire. But quick.
Matil. Let first my lord's stepmother quit this room.
I go with you alone: while she is here,
I will not stir one step, except by force.
 VOL. II.—25

Fred. Be it so.   Madam ! — [*to Jul.*

                 Jul. Who would wish to stay

Where is pollution, where adulterous feet

Have made the very carpet vile to tread ?

For thee, thou·'lt see me once again, and there

Where I have joy'd to think thou soon wouldst be,

Thou shame of English dames and royal wives.

         [*Exit, — Fred., after seeing her out*

     replacing himself at the side-scene.

MATILDA

throws herself, weeping, into the arms of her

attending lady, and the

Drop falls.

ACT THE FIFTH

Scene I. *Before the Palace at Copenhagen.*

Bernstorff, *intercepting* Uhldal.

Bern. Uhldal! So fast? I might suppose you shunn'd me,
As anxiously as I sought you. What presses?
Uhl. Sickness of heart. I am hasting home to bed, —
To hide in darkness: I abhor the light.
Ugh! 't is scarce two hours since; and I was there;
And had you seen! — You know where I then was.
Bern. I may conjecture. You are very pale.
Uhl. Yet I still feel as if I was bedropp'd
With human gore and breath'd its sickening steam.
I tried to lose it, wandering here and there,
And mixing with this group and that, and sought
Relief in study; but the blood was there,
Stain'd each law-page, and the two headless trunks
Rose up before me, spirting out their streams
Of purple gore in the blithe noontide-air.
It was the damn'dest ending of a farce,
A travesty of justice, that the world
Or Satan ever look'd on. I could weep
To think that I am human.
       Bern. Not so loud.

Come with me to my house; you will be heard,
And give offence.

    Uhl. There was a time, a man
Might speak before this Palace what he pleas'd,
Nor give offence in Denmark. I am not
Afraid to utter my opinion here
More than before the bench, when those two men
Were sentenc'd to be murder'd. It was so;
Murder'd — nought else; for evidence was none
Sufficient to condemn them; and their blood
Will spot the mantle of our law forever.

Bern. But on the skirt your name will shine in gold,
Who hurl'd your voice in thunder for the right.

Uhl. How could I else? I was not of the crew
The Dowager had brib'd to do her work.
The Court were all her minions.

     Bern. True. But speak
Lower for my sake. Let your lightning flash,
But without resonance.

    Uhl. The bolt has now
Nothing to shiver. O that fatal want
Of nerve in Struensee! Had he but defied .
The unprincipled Commission, both were now
Haply alive.

   Bern. I see not that.

     Uhl. The law,
Retaining that curs'd relic of the past,
The Question, limits, well you know, its use
To criminals condemn'd, and only then

(The case first ponder'd by the King in Council)
After a special warrant duly issu'd,
Sign'd by the sovereign's hand.   They had not dar'd
To apply it otherwise, or had so applied it
At their own peril.   But the unhappy Count,
Shown privately the instruments of torture,
Forgot his rights, and own'd there had been love
Between him and the Queen, when not an act
More overt than the kissing of her hand,
Which any lord might have when specially grac'd,
Could be adduc'd against him !   All the rest,
The charge of peculation, and misuse
Of royal favor, or abuse of power,
Were baseless imputations, or a count
Of errors of imprudence, lapses else
Of ministerial wisdom, which no court
But such a one could twist into a crime
Of capital treason.   O that fatal lack
Of self-possession !

       Bern. 'T is to be deplor'd ;
But for the Queen's sake only.   For himself,
I cannot think it had avail'd.   The Court,
Determin'd to condemn him, would have found
Some pretext for his murder.   Look at Brandt,
Charg'd with a blow struck at the King, whereof
The King had no remembrance, or had long
Forgiven it !   And this indeed was so.
No actual blow was given.   So tells me one
Who stood in Hirschholm when the affair transpir'd.

The King, at play, became enrag'd with Brandt,
And challeng'd him to combat. Brandt declin'd.
His Majesty, more furious, thrust his hand
Into Brandt's open mouth and grasp'd his tongue.
Struggling, in pain, in danger to be chok'd,
Perhaps indignant too, the sufferer did
What any man of mettle would have done,
Push'd his assailant back with all his force
Till he had freed himself. Even on the spot,
The King, who wants not nobleness, declar'd
He never would remember the affront
To Brandt's discredit; and he kept his word.

Uhl. As well he might. It was for him, by Heaven!
To ask Brandt's pardon, not for Brandt to ask his.
Had he been truly noble, as you claim,
He would have done so.

              Bern. Hush! we cannot take
The part of History here; we live but in
The present, and, where kings have absolute power,
Must keep our lips shut, though we use our eyes.
Did Struensee — I almost fear to ask —
Show nerve?

            Uhl. No, no. But he was sorely try'd.
Brandt suffer'd like a hero; but his friend,
Excitable by nature, of a kind
Of men whose courage is not the nerve of beasts
But wholly of the mind, had had beside
To wait beneath the scaffold, where he heard
The dull sound of the thick blade 'falling twice

On hand and neck, and saw the warm blood dropping,
Drop after drop, between the ill-jointed planks.

Bern. It was enough, even had he lov'd him less.
We know he had manhood not to plain his fate,
But only mourn'd his friend's.

                    Uhl. — Who died for nought
But that he was his friend. The moral man
Was brave enough. But listen now the rest.
'T is the harsh epilogue to this sad drama,
Yet points not at the dead, but only us
Who live in Denmark. You will think, perhaps,
The murder'd men sleep in their graves? They bound
The yet warm bodies each upon a wheel,
Set the head on it and nail'd fast the hand,
And left them there, for crows to do the rest.[34]

Bern. This in a Christian country! at this day!
May Heaven forgive us Danes!

                    Uhl. Why yes, amen!
For History, where each nation graves in brass
All vices but its own, will not. Farewell!

                [*Exit abruptly; Bern. slowly following.*

SCENE II.

A room in the Castle of Cronenburg.

MATILDA, *seated.*
SIR ROBERT KEITH. A LADY IN WAITING

Enter
JULIANA, *followed*
by KŒLLAR *and* AMALIE.

Jul. I have come to make that final call I promis'd
Your *Royal Highness*. Nay, look not amaz'd;
Being now disjoin'd, in bond as well as bed,
From Christian, I address you here in prison
As fits your royal birth.
             Matil. You see, Sir Robert,
What I must yet endure.
             Sir R. The royal child
Of England is above such poor affronts.
Your *Majesty* is mistress to withdraw
And leave the offender. Shall I dare to offer
The service of my arm ?
             Matil. No, here is best.
We can outsit the malice of our foes.

But ask her, with what purpose she is here.

Jul. To wish Your Highness joy — since Struensee

Was nothing to you, as he claim'd to be —

That your calumniator is no more.

Matil. Ah ! [*covering her face with her hands.*

Sir R. Madam ! — [*sternly, to Jul.*

        Matil. Mind me not, Sir Robert. I needs

Must weep for one who perish'd through my fault.

It was foul murder !

        Jul. By the grace of God,

Through whom this odious treason came to light,

That could not be. No, he was fairly kill'd,

Though somewhat mangled. That was his own fault;

Why could he not keep steadier on the block ?

Braver were wiser. If Your Highness faints,

We must suspend the tale. That were a pity.

Give her your salts, Ama'lie.

        Matil. Not from her !

Sir R. Your Majesty must permit me ——

        Matil. No, Sir Robert ;

Let her proceed. I have nerve enough to bear

The worst that she can offer. Have I not

Been Queen as well as she ? and am I not,

What she can never be — whence all this hate, —

The mother of a King that is to be

Despite her arts ?

        Jul. Your Highness wrongs yourself

As well as me. The Crown-prince was begotten

Before there were two fathers in the bed.

    25*

Sir R. This to a queen, the sister of my king !

                            [*Matil. rises, as in act to leave*

Your Majesty does well.   I would you had chosen
This part before.

                Jul. 'T is not too late to avoid
The hearing of a tale she cannot bear.
I thought so from the first.

                     Ama. She sits again. [*to Kœl.*

Sir R. Your Majesty will not be so imprudent —
Pardon my boldness, — will not so forget
Your presence should command respect even here ?

Matil. I 'll sit it out, Sir Robert.   She shall not boast,
The fear of what her scurrilous tongue might utter
Could drive us conscience-stricken from our seat.

Jul. That will be seen.   Paint, Colonel, — thou wast there, —
The ultimate scene.   'T is justice, in this point,
To gratify her Highness.

                  Sir R. I protest ! ——

Matil. Give her free course.   She cannot harm me now,
Nor yet the dead.

                  Kœl. Count Brandt ascended first,
Steady and bold.   His sentence read, his arms
Torn by the headsman, on the boards he knelt
And pray'd, then spoke a few words to the crowd
Simply and well.   Rejecting then with pride
The executioner's aid, who would disrobe him,
He threw off his pelisse, then firmly laid
His right hand on the block, and, at a blow,
The hand was sever'd.   In a moment after,

His head lay in the dust.

> *Matil.* O God!

>> *Lady.* The Queen

Is drooping!

> *Sir R.* Stop, sir! [*Matil., one hand covering her face,*
>> *waves the other to Sir R. dissuadingly.*

>> *Jul.* What remains to tell

Will probably revive her.   Pray, continue.

Kœl. [*exchanges looks with Ama.*

> Poor Struensee, who stands below the scaffold,
> Sees and hears all, growing white as any shroud.
> Trembling and faint, he stumbles, as if blind,
> On the rude steps.   They have to help him up.
> His eyes fix on the block, all soak'd and wet
> With his friend's blood.   He shrinks, he cowers.   Three
>> times
> He strives to keep his hand down, but three times
> Draws it back, taking on the fingers' joints
> The terrible stroke, and, when at last it falls,
> 'T is mangled horridly.   So they have by force
> To hold him down.   And now the headsman lifts ——

Ama. The Queen has fainted! [*stepping hurriedly towards Ma-*
>> *tilda, as if to help her.   But, seeming to recollect her-*
>> *self, she stops half-way, and stands fixed and*
>> *haughty.*

>> *Jul.* And our part is play'd.

There speaks the moral of the Seventh Commandment.

>> [*Looking on Sir R., and pointing to Matilda.*

Your Excellency sav'd her life, but not

Put back, you see, the judgment. Let her lie :
To wake her is to waken her to shame. [*Turns to go.*
Sir R. Shame is for guilt, and guilt is theirs alone
Who forc'd one victim, in the law's despite
And mercy's, aid them break the *Ninth* Commandment
Whereby, that twofold murder, and this wo.

[*Jul. Exit.*

SIR ROBERT *goes to the chair where*
MATILDA *is still in the hands of the attendant Lady,*
and, as KŒLLAR *and* AMALIE *are about*
to disappear after Juliana,

the Curtain falls.

NOTES

MATILDA OF DENMARK

1.—P. 518. — *Brahe's tower* —] WRAXALL says of this round tower, "built by Christian IV. and designed for an observatory": "There is not a single step in it, though very lofty. You ascend by a spiral road, of near fourteen feet broad, from the bottom to its summit. A professor, who showed me over it, assured me that one of their kings, Christian V., as I recollect, drove in his carriage up and down it; and he even produced a book, as I doubted it, to prove the veracity of his assertion. I must own it may be easily done, though probably at some risk of the driver's neck." *Cursory Remarks made in a Tour through some of the Northern Parts of Europe.* Lond. 8°. 1775. p. 20.

2.—P. 521. *Like Rantzow's foresire*, etc.] John Rantzau, in the 16th century, — whose fidelity to his sovereigns, Frederic I. and Christian III. of Denmark, was so marked as to become proverbial.

3.—P. 521. *Here* —] Omit to the end of the part.

4.—P. 522. *Trondhjem.*] A bailiwick in Norway. — Pron.

Tron'yem. Make the *oe* in "Hitteroe" one syllable, sounding it as *ur* or *a,* or anglicising it to ô. *J* in "Justesen" is sounded as *Y: Yoos'tesen.*

5.—P. 522. *A simple peasant* —] Omit, to "This peasant-lord," seven verses.

6.—P. 523. *Did not then* —] Omit to "Envy dies not of shame," in the 24th verse below.

7.—P. 524. *He liv'd, it might be said, as lives the sage,* etc] The epigrammatic sarcasm imitated in the text, and which was of a later date than that of the Scene, is, as is often the case with such witticisms, more pointed than just. His scruple was one for which I cannot blame him; it but marked his delicacy. Every man possessed of that innate feeling, whose cultivation gives the manner which alone is truly styled well-bred, would have acted similarly. The circumstances of Brahe's life, from the time when the jealousy of his merits, and of their recognition by the royal favor, culminated in the malignant vengeance of the Grand Master Valkendorff, which drove him, stripped of everything but the moderate revenue of his little isle, to the genial friendship and protection of the Emperor Rodolph in 1597, are too well known to need to be repeated. I may however, as descriptive of the errors of his system, presently alluded to, cite the elegant observation of BAILLY (*Hist. de l'Astron.* as given by MALLET: *Hist. de Dann.* liv. ix): "Tycho était assis sur les confins de deux siècles. Il tient aux ténèbres qui l'ont précédé, et à la lumière qui l'a suivi."

This great man was a poet. There is a fine elegy of his, in which, bidding farewell to his country, he fails not to do justice to his king and to his compatriots at large. Mallet (*u. s.*) has afforded us two small specimens. It commences thus:

" Dania, quid merui ? Qui te, mea patria, læsi,
Usque adeo ut rebus minus æqua meis ?
Scilicet *illud erat, tibi quo nocuisse reprendar,*
Quo majus per me nomen in orbe geras."

8.—P. 524. *Heinesen —*] This brave man was of the Feroe
islands and was employed by Frederic II. (in the latter half of the
16th century) to clear that group, as well as Greenland and Iceland,
from the pirates, British and French, which infested them. Every
year the English fishermen would descend upon their defenceless
shores, carry off the people as slaves to help them in their fishery,
and when they were done, would set them down on any the near-
est land. Heinesen accomplished his task. But, in the minority
of Christian IV. (end of 16th c.,) he was falsely accused, and, by
a precipitate judgment, was condemned to death. He refused to
have his eyes handaged, saying, he had seen too many naked sabres,
and bade the executioner not to be afraid. His sentence being re-
vised, he was proved innocent, his accusers were condemned in
3000 crowns of amend to his heirs, and his body was disinterred
and buried with honor in Jutland. Malling: *Traits mém. de l'hist.
de Dann.* &c. (trad. fran. Copenh. 12°. 1794) pp. 174, 5.

9.—P. 528. *Kay Lykkè.*] This nobleman was the first victim
of the absolute power given for the first time to a Danish monarch,
(Fred. III.) He had boasted in a letter, that no woman could
refuse him her favors, not even the Queen. For this he was condemned as for high-treason, and, as he had fled, the execution of the
sentence, which was to fall on his head and hand, was performed
on a wooden effigy ! Not the least striking feature in this odious
act of tyranny was that the King had the benefit of the confiscation
of fourteen out of the fifteen of his estates, the fifteenth only going
to institutions of charity. See Mallet: *Hist. de Dann.* (éd. in 16°.
1788.) t. ix. pp. 114, 115.

10.—P. 530. *That to defer*, etc.] Omit, to "that all" (inclusive),
six verses: then, from "your speech," (3d verse after,) to the
semicolon.

11.—P. 531. *But no !* etc.] From here, omit to "Forget, if you
are noble", — 15th line below.

12.—P. 531. — *let the thrill* —] Omit to "lest I sink." Then,
below, the words between "But" and "holds she me". Then, all
after "That rise before me", to "Let me go forth," in the 6th
verse below it.

13.—P. 536. *Being favor'd*, etc.] Omit this verse.

14.—P. 537. — *Philippina* —] Wife of Eric, King of Pome-
rania, who treated her with indifference and gave his love to other
women. Yet, faithful to him, when he had irritated his people by
issuing base money, she, in his absence, had her plate melted up
and made into proper coin, which she issued as by order of the
King. Eric too deserted his capital of Copenhagen on the approach
of the Vandals, but Philippina remained and repulsed them. The
Vandals then commencing a system of pillage and piracy on Denmark, which Eric seemed not to regard, Philippina, taking advantage of her unworthy husband's absence in Sweden, equipped a
fleet and sent it against them at Stralsund. The result is told in
the text. Malling, *u. s.* 351, 2.

15.—P. 538. Exile nor prison —] Omit, from here to "well-
approved," (both inclusive,) — ten verses.

16.—P. 538. — *in prison.*] *Eleonora Christina*, the accomplished
daughter of Christian IV. by his left-hand marriage with Christina
Munck, furnishes another of the many examples in history of the

pitiless vindictiveness of women. She was three and twenty years in prison, although probably innocent of any complicity in the rash as well as unscrupulous designs of her husband Corfitz Uhlfeld, whose marriage with a daughter of the King, by a legitimate though not recognized marriage, made a traitor of him; and as she was released only on the death of the Queen of Frederic III. in 1685, it may reasonably be supposed that that proud woman resented in Eleonora either her supposed aspirations, or her want of deference in bearing toward herself, or both. Christian V., the grandson of Eleonora's father, in giving her liberty assigned her for life the castle of Mariboe with a proper maintenance, and she died at an advanced age in 1698. See MALLET *Hist. de Dann.* tt. viii & ix, but especially t. ix. pp. 116–125. Her pleading before the royal Swedish commission, appointed to examine her husband, is not mentioned by that historian. I take the trait from Malling's interesting collection, p. 354.

17.—P. 538. *Haply then* —] Omit from here to " queens " (inclusive) — 9th line below.

18.—P. 539. *Gida nerv'd his soul,* etc.] Mallet tells the story in his *Introduction* (Hist. &c. t. i. p. 286.) *Gida* was the daughter of a rich Norwegian lord. Proud and ambitious, she refused her suitor's hand until he should have subjected all of Norway. Harald, who was vain, it would seem, of the long, silky, golden locks which gave him his surname, vowed to neglect them until he should achieve the conquest she desired. Mallet cites *Torfœus.*

19.—P. 539. *Of Valdemar,* etc.] Omit this and the next verse.

20.—P. 539. *She was a woman,* etc.] Omit, to " Does the tale ", in the 5th verse below.

21.—P. 547. Str. *Why let the gifts*, etc.] Omit, of this part, all but the two last verses.

22.—P. 549. — *taste Iduna's apples*, etc.] *Iduna*, in the Icelandic Edda, is the wife of *Braye*, the majestic god of poesy and eloquence. She keeps in a casket certain apples, of which the gods, when they feel the approach of age, taste and renew their youth, which thus will last till the final day of darkness. See, in the translation of parts of the *Edda* given by Mallet, the 14th Fable, (t. ii. p. 141. *Hist.* &c.)

23.—P. 549. *He crush'd*, etc.] Omit, to the end of the part.

24.—P. 550. *Unwearied*, etc.] Omit the entire sentence.

25.—P. 551. Stru. *Not in all things.* Etc] Omit, to "He toil'd " —, fifteen verses.

26.—P. 555. *He who arrang'd*, etc. etc.] See MALLET: *Hist. &c. Liv.* xiii. *ad init.* (t. ix. p. 116 ed. cit.) If the only proof of his ability lay in the digestion of the *Royal Law* of Frederic III., on which however the historian compliments him, I should esteem it difficult to assign for his elevation any cause but the caprice of the monarch, or gratitude for his subservience in compressing, or rather expanding into its forty articles, every provision for absolutism and hereditary right that it seems possible for the human mind to contrive.

27.—P. 558. — *Erlingsen* —] That is, *son of Erling.* He was King of Norway. Having surprised his foe, Sigurd Sigurdsen, (who was endeavoring to get possession of part of Norway,) he had it in his power to do as his soldiers wished him, — to fire his house and burn or butcher him and his adherents. But he made his soldiers lie upon their arms, declaring as in the text, and when day broke attacked and conquered the Count.

28.—P. 559. — *who struck the King himself at Hirschholm* —] The particulars of this strange affair, which I found in Wraxall's *Tour*, and which are said to have furnished the conspirators with their absurd charge against the unfortunate favorite, are recounted later in the play.

29.—P. 561. — *my queen:*] Sophia-Magdalena, who had freed her serfs in the bailiwick of Hirschholm.

30.—P. 561. *I may reply*, etc.] In the course of the Reformation in Denmark, the nobles were permitted to imitate the King in the revocation of the grants of their ancestors to the churches and religious establishments. This naturally led to abuses, many claiming what had never belonged to them. *Tavsen*, zealous Protestaut though he was, acted in these cases like an upright spirit, and opposed with all the ardor of his nature such attempts, pleading even in a certain case, before the King and the Estates at Colding, in behalf of the establishment. This drew on him hatred and the danger of revenge, but, nothing moved, he answered the condolements of his friends, in the noble words assigned him in the text. See Malling *u. s.* 365.

31.—P. 562. *Did not Sterkodder*, etc.] Born in Norway, he served Frode IV. King of Zeland and Scania. Frode being assassinated by Sverting, Duke of Saxony, and Ingild, his son, having no regard for men of merit, Sterkodder took service with the Swede. But still his care was for his master's family. Ingild, far from avenging his father, had married his murderer's daughter, and lived in debauchery with her brothers. His two young sisters he left to themselves; and the younger formed a connection with an ordinary

man of no character. On learning this, Sterkodder came to Denmark, punished the lover, and removed the girl, who, reforming her
conduct, was subsequently married to a son of a king of Norway.
Sterkodder then left Ingild, who neglected him, to his own bad
counsels, and returned to Sweden. But Ingild going on from bad
to worse, the hero returned to Denmark, appealed to the King in
the very midst of his minions, and, showing him the frightful and
daugerous state to which he had brought the country by his vices,
reminded him of his father, and adjured him not to consort with his
murderers. This was the true spirit of freedom of the olden time,
and it moved what yet was sensible in the soul of Ingild, who,
coming to his senses, punished his father's murderers. *Id.* 356,
sqq.

32.—P. 574. — *Gersdorf* —] Marshal of the Court under Frederic III. —   When Charles-Gustavus was before Copenhagen,
Frederic, constrained to offer peace, sent *Gersdorf* as one of the
Danish Commission to the Royal Swede. After great efforts to
avoid the conditions imposed by the conqueror, which exacted the
cession of various important territories, he took the pen, and signed,
remarking, after one of the ancient emperors, " Vellem ne me scire
literas." *Id.* p. 88.

33.—P. 579. — *Wolfenbuettel* —] That is, *Brunswick-Wolfen-
buettel.* For the Stage, the former half of the title may be used;
thus :

Princess of Brunswick, whom my royal lord :

but the designation in the text is better, being used contemptuously
and for the purpose of irritation by Matilda.. The *e* of *ue* is merely
the modifying vowel which is suppressed in the German form *ü*,
and which gives properly to *u* the slender and peculiar half-lisping
sound of the French *u* in *dessus;* but *ü* is rarely sounded by the

Germans themselves otherwise than as the slender *i* with us. Pronounce it therefore either as *u* in *pure*, or as *i* in *wit*.

34.—P. 589. *And left them there, for crows to do the rest.*] Two years after the event, Wraxall, writing from Copenhagen, says: "The skulls and bones of these unhappy men are yet exposed on wheels about a mile and a half out of town. I have viewed them with mingled commiseration and horror."

END OF THE SECOND VOLUME.

List of Mr. Osborn's Plays

Comprised in the present six volumes of the Series.

Now ready,
And to be had separately, Vols. I., II., and IV.: 500–600 pp. each.   Price $2.50.
For sale by the *American News Company.*

117–121 Nassau-st.

www.ingramcontent.com/pod-product-compliance
Lightning Source LLC
Chambersburg PA
CBHW031146120726
47905CB00006B/1837